CW00326696

'What are we doi...

Chloe's question snagged... hoped. He studied her fa... champagne flute to her n... and sipped. His bright blue eyes, focused solely on her, did wonderful things to her senses.

She could still feel the brush of his knuckles through her panties, hear the catch in her breath when he brought her to climax. She could still see the swell behind the fly of his trousers…

His finger began a slow trail up her spine. 'What are we doing as in why are we standing here instead of mingling?'

She shook her head.

'What are we doing as in why didn't we stay in your office where we could be writhing naked by now?'

'Would we be?' She considered him carefully, letting her tongue dip in the bubbles of the wine.

'Look at me like that again and we'll be writhing here where we stand.'

Dear Reader,

What do you want to be when you grow up?

If you read my bio at www.blazeauthors.com, you'll see that I didn't know I wanted to write until I was thirty. And the rest of my family?

My older daughter manages a pizza parlour and intends to focus her studies on marine biology. My younger daughter has decided business is the practical way to go...for now. My son dabbles in music while putting in ten-hour days at a 'real' job. And my husband, a degreed geologist, works as a dot.com graphics specialist.

Life is nothing if not one surprise after another. Interests change. Economics boom, then bust. Any number of reasons can precipitate a change in careers—including capricious whims. (Who, me?)

In *No Strings Attached,* Chloe Zuniga, vice president of gIRL-gEAR's cosmetics and accessories division, is making good use of her degree in fashion design. Or so she thinks...until she makes a devil's bargain with Eric Haydon.

Enjoy! And keep an eye out for the third book of the gIRL-gEAR mini-series (published by Mills & Boon® Blaze™ in February), when I'll tell you about Sydney Ford's first time. And her second time – which was *Bound to Happen*.

Alison Kent

PS To learn more about the girls, the company and the series, visit www.girl-gear.com, where you can always find the latest in fun, games, dating tips and more!

NO STRINGS ATTACHED

by

Alison Kent

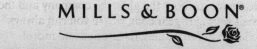

MILLS & BOON®

First published in Great Britain 2003 by Harlequin Mills & Boon Limited, Eton House, 18-24 Paradise Road, Richmond, Surrey TW9 1SR

© Mica Stone 2002

ISBN 0 263 83598 7

14-0103

Printed and bound in Spain by Litografía Rosés S.A., Barcelona

For Hollee, Megan and Casey.
You're good kids. I think I'll keep you.

And for my two career partners.
I can't put into words what you mean to me.
I think I'll keep you, too.

gIRL-gEAR
urban fashions for gIRLS who gET it!

SYDNEY FORD
Chief Executive Officer

MACY WEBB
Content Editor
www.gIRL-gEAR.com

LAUREN HOLLISTER
Design Editor
www.gIRL-gEAR.com

CHLOE ZUNIGA
Vice President

gRAFFITI gIRL   gADGET gIRL
the cosmetics line   the accessories line

MELANIE CRAINE
Vice President

gIZMO gIRL   gOODY gIRL
the technology line   the gifts line

KINSEY GRAY
Vice President

gROWL gIRL   gO gIRL
the party wear   the active wear

1

CHLOE ZUNIGA STEPPED inside the doorway to Haydon's Half Time and flinched at the unholy blast of noise. What was it about team sports that turned a civilized gathering into a loutish milieu, complete with the roars, growls, honks and snorts of a teeming jungle habitat?

The primitive racket ricocheting off the sports bar's walls had her longing for earplugs or cotton balls. Protective headgear, even. And she'd trade two gRAFFITI gEAR luxury spa packs for a can of air freshener right about now.

Fanning at a plume of cigar smoke with one hand, squinting into the gaudy neon glare, Chloe searched the raucous crowd for a pair of shoulders worthy of Tarzan.

If Eric Haydon wasn't here, she was going to kill him.

The man had some nerve, refusing to return her phone calls, forcing her to resort to this ridiculous extreme. It was April, a gorgeous Saturday afternoon. So what if it was—as spelled out on the parking lot marquee—the Houston Astros Season Opener, and Haydon's Half Time was Houston's Richmond Drive's hot spot.

She had better things to do with her time than dodge rabid fans, and certainly better places to put her feet

than a floor littered with spent peanut shells and cork
beer coasters and whatever that sticky stuff was gum-
ming the soles of her shoes to the glossy concrete.

Uncouth. That's what it was. Ill-mannered and
crude. What was wrong with these people?

The fact that their enthusiastic word of mouth had
put Haydon's Half Time on the map, that their pa-
tronage provided Eric's bread and butter, hardly gave
them carte blanche to act like they were raised in a
barn. Team sports. Ugh. Chloe gave an affected shudder and blew out a loud puff of breath.

The very idea of all that sweaty grabbing and paw-
ing, that tackling and blocking and sliding into base!
The silly pants, the silly nicknames, the silly sports
drinks colored like kiddie crayons. What a ridiculous
waste of spirit, not to mention entertainment dollars.

Men. Honestly. They could be such children, she
thought, even as a feminine shriek of excitement cut
through the din.

Okay. So the place was coed.

The women were one thing, standing by their men,
rooting for his team or often their own alma mater.
And, yes. There were women who did the team sports
thing for no other reason than the love of the game.
The women didn't factor into Chloe's aversion for athletic fanaticism.

The women didn't stir memories of being sidelined
for no other reason than being a girl, a girl who in a
heartbeat would've traded her secret baseball card col-
lection for the chance to strap on shin guards and play
a game with the neighborhood boys.

The women didn't bring back memories of petti-
coats and patent leather and the punishing discomfort
of the cold metal bleachers where she'd sat primly at

her father's side—Daddy's little girl, pink-cheeked and petite, come to watch her brothers compete on the field.

The women didn't leave her heart hopelessly hollow, her body crazy-hungry for heat, as did the incredibly clueless males of the species who, in Chloe's wide world of experience, preferred their women to remain on a pedestal, between the sheets, or three paces behind.

The entire concept of love and romance was going to hell in a handbasket.

"Hey, sexy lady. Wanna beer?" The slurred voice interrupted her thoughts.

Chloe sighed and looked to her left. Ex-jock. Muscles gone to fat. Gaze flicking to three grinning buddies at a nearby table. "I think I'll pass," she replied.

"Pass? On a beer? Then how 'bout I give you the best night of your life?"

Puh-leez. "Not interested."

"Aww, c'mon, baby." He leered his way down the front of her new football jersey. "If I could see you naked, I'd die a happy man."

"Yeah, sugar. But if I saw you naked—" she reached out and poked his beer belly "—I'd probably die laughing. Thanks, but no thanks."

Turning her back on the whoops and sympathetic groans, she headed in search of some breathing room away from the cluster of tables.

Men. All so predictable. At the first sight of breasts, they turned into boobs. Keeping an eye out for Eric, she moved away from the common room back toward the entryway, and searched the bar from that vantage point.

It was obvious that what the modern world needed

was another Cary Grant. A real ladies' man. A true romantic.

Chloe might be only twenty-six years old, but she'd spent years devouring the favorite movies of the mother she'd never known, the mother who'd died before her first birthday.

And Chloe was not too young, too jaded or too cynical to envy Ingrid Bergman those heated looks shared in *Indiscreet,* Deborah Kerr the courtship of *An Affair to Remember,* Grace Kelly that spectacular kiss in *To Catch a Thief.*

Chloe couldn't help but wonder if her mother, too, had been compelled by those cinematic glimpses into human nature, intriguing snapshots of what love could be. If she had longed for that broader experience, that deeper well.

Was that why she'd so adored romance classics? Or had she simply been a film buff, watching for no other reason than the love of a good story? How Chloe wished she could ask. And listen.

And learn the truth of the relationship her mother had shared with her father, the man who'd enshrined her memory and held her up as an example of the type of woman Chloe would do well to emulate.

Maybe if she better understood what had made her parents' marriage the heavenly match her father had avowed—a match of the type so often idealized on screen—she wouldn't feel so driven to find a man who filled her own movie bill.

A man who knew how to make a woman feel as if no woman had existed before her, knew how to make her believe that if he didn't have her now—right now, here, this moment—he wouldn't be able to breathe. A man who shared her own intoxication in impatient, restless sex. Sex unplanned and uncontainable, in the moment, on the edge.

Sex Chloe knew about. Sex was easy. Sex was power. It was that crazy little thing called love that she wasn't certain she'd ever recognize.

"Hey, sweet thing. What's your name?"

Chloe turned to face her newest accoster. A squat muscle-bound man stood much too close, his frog-eyed gaze aimed straight at her chest.

"Ice Princess," she said coldly.

The toad only laughed, then moved closer. "So, what do you do for a living? Besides play hard to get, that is."

"I'm a female impersonator." Before he could respond, she brushed by him, leaving the bar's entryway and walking briskly toward the rest rooms.

Men. Duds and bores. Her patience with them had grown Calista Flockhart thin.

Was it so much to ask? To be utterly, completely understood by a man? Had her idea of relationship reality been warped by her movie fantasies as well as by those of her mother? Was it truly impossible to be so attuned to another person that one could finish a sentence the other began?

Because that was what Chloe wanted. That connection, that completion, that bond. That, and the sex.

She paused near the door marked Jocks, shifted direction and entered the door marked Jills. Small, but spotless, she noted with approval, though she wasn't the least bit surprised the room resembled a mini locker room in design.

Nodding at a tanned, short-haired woman washing her hands, Chloe proceeded to do the same at a second sink. What was she doing here? Tonight, in this bar?

What did she hope to accomplish, really? There was no prince waiting out there, ready to fight for her honor, slay her dragons, no questions asked.

What had she been thinking, turning to a man when she had five girlfriends standing by, women who understood her and who she could call on day or night for comfort, career counseling and chocolate?

Men. Who needed 'em, anyway?

"Nice jersey," a startlingly low voice said.

Chloe's gaze jerked to the other woman's, which seemed to be admiring more than the new Houston Texans logo. It was a sad state of affairs when a girl could no longer find refuge in the ladies' room.

Muttering her thanks, Chloe returned to the bar, where a sudden loud burst of applause and an exuberant apelike, fist-driven echo of "Whup, whup, whup!" reiterated beautifully the reason she was here, and renewed her determination.

He might not be a prince riding to her rescue, but, for all his boisterous behavior and cocky top jock attitude, Eric Haydon often conveyed a hint—admittedly, the *barest,* the most *infinitesimal,* the tiniest *microscopic* hint—of suave sophistication, a sort of cultured finesse that kept her Cary Grant hopes up.

And that played nicely into her plans.

Abandoning what she could of the smoke and the noise, Chloe wove her way through the common room and up three short steps onto the glossy hardwood floor of the bar's more intimate pub. The place was softly lit by glowing brass lanterns. The rich wood toppers of the red and green padded booths gave her cover to sneak up and blindside her quarry.

Fortunately for Eric and his well-being, Chloe knew she'd find him here. The black Ford Mustang GT

she'd seen in the bar's back lot was his; the person-
alized plates that read HALF TIME were hard to miss.
It was a hotshot car, an extension of his male ego. A
show-stopping, attention-grabbing, top-of-the-line boy
toy that had accomplished its objective.

Her attention had been grabbed.

With proof of his whereabouts, and a firm resolve,
she was not about to let him blow her off in person
the way he'd blown off her phone calls. Just let him
try and hide out in the kitchen, or ignore her while
working behind the bar.

She would not be deterred from her mission. Like
it or not, she needed a man.

And even if he was a living, breathing, sleeping,
eating, twenty-four–seven sports nut, Eric Haydon was
the man she wanted. She would deal with his obses-
sive nature. She'd done it before, while partnered with
him for the month-long scavenger hunt designed by
Chloe's business partner, gIRL-gEAR editor Macy
Webb, for her monthly gIRL gAMES column.

Reaching the far end of the pub, Chloe sidestepped
the waitress wearing old-fashioned baseball flannels,
and looked up in time to catch sight of her victim
behind the bar. A brief glimpse only, as Eric moved
quickly out of range.

A smile touched Chloe's mouth, and it was hard to
deny the rush of a schoolgirl thrill tumbling through
her empty belly, hungry as she was for food and his
company.

During the month they'd spent on the scavenger
hunt, they'd shared dinners, drinks and dirty jokes, not
to mention one incredibly intense deep-throated kiss.
She'd been banking on that making them friends.

And friends didn't let friends drive their careers into the ground.

Chloe took a deep breath and headed for the bar. Eric turned then, walking toward her as she approached. The gray jersey T-shirt he wore snugged tightly over his shoulders and pecs, hung loosely to his hips.

The man's body was a piece of work, hard and fit and deserving of a calendar spread. Chloe boosted herself onto a padded red stool, propped her elbows on the shiny black bar and settled her chin into the cup of her palms.

He really was drool-worthy with those shoulders and that butt and the wide white smile that dimpled both of his cheeks. He'd cut his dark blond hair recently, so it was shorter than usual, barely long enough to need a brush. And then there were his blue eyes, and his…

…oh, so loud mouth!

Chloe grimaced as Eric shouted and whistled at whatever sports thing was going on across the room on the big screen TV. Macy had been right when she'd called him a Tarzan. Chloe could just see him, muscles bunching, swinging from a vine, beating on his chest, wearing nothing but a skimpy loincloth….

"Well, if it isn't Chloe Zuniga, Miss Pretty in Pink in the flesh." Eric slapped both palms on the bar, jarring Chloe's elbows.

At his reference to her wardrobe's usual color scheme, Chloe smiled sweetly while trying to recall her well-rehearsed, extremely witty opening.

Having forgotten everything now that she was here and he was so close and so incredibly—and annoyingly—cute, she held both arms out to the side and swiveled back and forth on the bar stool. "Not a speck of pink, visible or otherwise."

Eric stepped onto the bar's low storage ledge and leaned forward, peering as far as he could over the counter. Chloe helped him out by lifting a foot to show off her socks, her cross-trainers and her long denim shorts.

Looking impressed, Eric stepped down and then grinned. "I feel like it's St. Patrick's Day and I'm searching for any speck of green I can find."

"Nope. Not on this girl. No green and no pink." Chloe wanted to stomp a foot in frustration. He hadn't said a word about her cross-trainers.

Or about her Texans jersey, which was the hottest thing going, according to the teenage salesclerk who'd watched, tongue lolling, while Chloe had shimmied the jersey down over the midthigh hem of her skirt when she'd tried it on in the middle of the store.

Eric studied her face closely, snapped his fingers. "Your eye shadow. Definitely pink."

"Definitely not. This is gRAFFITI gIRL's Mosh Pit Bruise." She closed her eyes and ran a fingertip over the lighter color just beneath her brow. "And this is Strobe Light White."

Eric frowned in earnest this time, as if seeing something that didn't quite click. And then both brows lifted in disbelief as it hit him.

"Chloe. Don't look now, but you're wearing a football jersey. And I think I saw athletic shoes on your feet. If I didn't know better, I'd think you were up to no good."

Chloe pressed her lips together, waiting for him to put the two of her phone calls he'd avoided together with her laughably out of character ensemble. It didn't take him long to do the math.

He backed a short step away, yanked the green towel printed with a red Haydon 'H' from his shoulder and wiped both of his hands. "The answer is no."

She'd never thought this was going to be easy. She just hadn't counted on coming up on a dead end so soon. "Now, sugar. How can you tell me no when you don't even know the question?"

"I've got news for you, princess." His head continued to shake from side to side. "You're in enemy territory. You start trying to bust my chops and the uproar's liable to bring down the roof on your head."

Chloe did her best to look demure and damaged. "I'm crushed to know that's what you think of me. Enemy indeed."

His attempt to remain firm dissolved into a chuckle under his breath. "I spent a month as your scavenger hunt partner. Don't think that poor pitiful me act is going to cut any of my mustard. Now, I have customers to see to."

Just like that? He was blowing her off just like that? "Excuse me, but I *am* sitting at your bar and I have yet to see any service."

The towel went back to Eric's shoulder. His hands went to his hips. His expression went from bemused to businesslike. "What can I get you then?"

This wasn't going at all like she'd planned, and she had only herself to blame. Had she really thought dressing like a car pool mom would fool Eric into thinking she was anyone other than who she was?

He'd spent a month in her company, and no pair of shoes or sports jersey would make him forget her tendency to be a bit aggressive at times, assertive at others—a personality blip that held top honors on her list of self-improvements to make.

Her potty mouth was another issue.

Right beneath her bad girl reputation.

Which she needed Eric to save.

She couldn't afford not to play this his way. She pulled a glossy menu card from the stack pushed against the wall at the end of the bar. ''What's good here?''

He shoved a basket of peanuts in her direction, then a basket of pretzels. ''Take a look at the menu. I have twenty-five beers on tap. Or one of the bartenders can mix up whatever tickles your fancy.''

She pretended to pout. ''I think my feelings are hurt. We spent an inseparable month and you have to ask?''

''A hazard of the job. Jason,'' Eric called over his shoulder, his eyes never leaving Chloe's. ''Bring the princess here a cosmopolitan.''

Eric knew it was too early in the afternoon for Chloe's favorite party drink. But she wasn't about to call him on it because she knew that's what he was waiting for. For her to tell him he'd gotten it wrong, that he knew better, that he should use his head and stop acting like a brain-dead jock. But not one of those comebacks crossed her mind as a serious option.

Her days of busting his chops had to come to an end, or she would never get him to agree to her proactive, career-saving strategy. And since Eric played a major role in her plan, she took a small sip of the bright pink drink when it arrived, and smiled as a peace offering.

Eric had been standing back, watching her. And when she actually went to sip more of a drink he knew she didn't want, he pulled the glass from her hand.

"What are you up to, Chloe? The answer is still no, but I'm curious what you're doing here."

She picked up a pretzel, snapped it in half. Eric was cute when he was so…discombobulated. "I'm not sure I want to tell you. Not when you think such ugly things about me."

"I knew it. You are up to something." Eric whipped the towel over the bar, which was already clean as a whistle.

"Well, yes. I *am* female."

"Exactly." He jabbed a finger toward her. "Which means that whatever you're up to, whatever you want, is going to benefit you and leave me out in the cold."

She fingered the stem of the glass she'd retrieved. "That's not necessarily true. I seem to remember sharing a tequila kiss that warmed you up plenty."

"We were both just this side of drunk—" he held his thumb and forefinger a millimeter apart "—and you know it."

"Just think what might have happened if we'd been rip-roaring." A thought that had often crossed her mind.

Eric, obviously, didn't share her curiosity. "Think what might've happened if we hadn't been drinking at all."

"You tell me." And she truly wanted to know.

For all their mutual flirtation, there were times when she felt he was only humoring her. And, perversely, she wanted to explore that feeling further. She had no desire to be any man's comic relief.

"Give me a break." Eric was back to rearranging the bar, moving the pretzels this way, the peanuts the other. "I'm not your type and we both know it. At least we know it when we're sober."

She pushed the cosmopolitan away and thought about leaving. Surely she had no face left to lose. "Could you have Jason bring me a diet soda?"

Hands shoulder-width apart on the bar, Eric hung his head. "Ah, Chloe. Don't do this to me."

"Don't do what, sugar?" She really did want to hear his reservations, his doubts, his reasons why joining forces was out of the question. She needed to know the dimensions of the wall she'd be butting her head against.

"Don't pretend you want something from me that you can't get from any other man." His head came up sharply then, and he gestured beyond her, toward the common room and the pub. "In fact, I'll prove it to you. Ask a favor of any man here and I'll guarantee you a resounding yes."

Chloe raised a brow. "As opposed to your no."

"You got it."

"Eric, sugar. I've been here twenty minutes and there hasn't been another man who's said a word to me." White lies had their uses.

"Only because I've been monopolizing your time."

"You've also been giving me your undivided attention and ignoring the other customers sitting at the bar. And neither one of us is the least bit tipsy." As if to punctuate her statement, Jason arrived with her glass of ice and diet soda. Chloe thanked him and stared at Eric while she sipped.

All he could do was shake his head. "You know, Chloe, I enjoy you too much for my own good. And you know me too well for mine."

"I suppose you can blame it on Macy. Her scavenger hunt ended up having repercussions I don't think she ever imagined."

"Yeah." He lifted a hand in greeting as a patron took a seat farther down the bar. "I heard about Anton splitting from Lauren."

"You mean Lauren splitting from Anton."

"Go ahead. Believe your bogus female facts." Eric turned back to face her, his expression cocky, smug, totally male. "I'll stick to the real man's telling of the story."

Chloe looked at him for a long, intimidating minute. The noise of the bar continued to burst like balloons over their heads. Glasses clinked and televisions blared and the doors to the kitchen swung inward and out. She toyed with the straw in her diet soda, ran her finger around the rim of the glass, dunked a persistent ice cube each time it resurfaced.

She'd grown up the only female in a household of five males. Eric Haydon could do his best to stare her down, but there wasn't a question in her mind that she would win the battle of wills. He'd admitted to his curiosity already. All she had to do was keep from revealing too much too soon.

She knew that about men. When they wanted something, wanted it badly enough and had to wait for a woman to decide whether or not they were worthy, men were putty in a female's hands.

And because that idea was so entertaining, she drove the final nail into his coffin. She looked up, over his head, at the television mounted above the bar. "Who's winning?"

"Huh?"

"The Astros' game. Without looking. Who's winning?"

Eric blinked, then blinked again, as if working to

jar loose the subliminally recorded score. "Okay, I admit it. You've distracted me. Happy now?"

"I'd be happy with an unqualified admission of your curiosity about what I'm doing here and what I want."

"I said I was curious."

"You qualified it by saying the answer is no."

"C'mon, princess. You can't expect me to give you an unqualified yes. For all I know, your request involves torture or public humiliation."

Chloe glanced beyond his shoulder toward two men at the bar. They were cheering on a third, who was working to down a draft beer without stopping to take a breath. The drink dribbled out both corners of his mouth and down his chin, soaking a line down the center of his T-shirt to the crotch of his jeans.

"I don't think you need me to provide public humiliation." Shuddering, she tipped her head toward the threesome as proof.

"What do I need you for, Chloe?"

Chloe pretended to consider Eric's question while inwardly, her mind raced. She really hated the thought of having to turn on her helpless-female bullshit meter.

But over the years she'd honed her shtick to a true science. And this situation, more than any other one she'd been in, merited experimenting with her skills.

She continued to toy with her straw, but now she averted her gaze from Eric's, keeping her lashes lowered, her pout humble and subdued.

"You're probably right," she cooed, and sighed. "I don't have anything that you need. But you have something that would really help me out a lot."

"A favor? That's it? You need a favor?" Wearily, he rubbed a hand down his face. "I thought you were going to want me to jump through seven kinds of hoops or something.''

She wouldn't yet rule out hoops or tricks. Not until she'd convinced him that he'd be doing this favor of his own free will. Maybe if she played her cards right, she'd even convince him the entire idea, from conception to completion, had been his own.

''Where should I start?''

He peeked at her from between spread fingers. ''The beginning is always a good place.''

The beginning was one place to which she preferred not to return. Look at the trouble she was in now because of where she'd begun. ''I'm not sure my, uh, situation has a beginning as much as a sudden realization by others that it exists.''

''English, Chloe. Plain English.''

''It's about work and my reputation for savoring a good expletive.''

Eric let out a loud whoop. ''I knew it was bound to happen. You've been called on the carpet for your potty mouth, haven't you?''

''And that's another thing,'' she responded, rising to the debate. ''Why is it a potty mouth for a woman and straight business vernacular for a man? Another totally unfair double standard.'' It was one of her pet peeves.

Eric was scarcely able to keep a straight face. ''I'd think it would be hard to be one of the guys when you work for a company called gIRL-gEAR.''

''It's perfectly acceptable for me to be one of the guys when it's a partners-only situation. When we have late night meetings or when we do our thing at Macy's loft. Make that Lauren's loft, since Macy is in the throes of cozy domestic bliss with Leo.'' Chloe went back to toying with her straw, dunking her ice cube. "It's when I...forget myself at the office that Sydney tends to get bent out of shape."

"It's hard to imagine Sydney Ford getting bent out of shape over anything."

"She takes the business seriously. And that includes how each of the partners' actions and reputations reflect back on gIRL-gEAR."

"So, you've been busted."

"In a manner of speaking, yes."

"Sounds like it *was* your manner of speaking."

This was where she needed to tread carefully—and where she most needed his help. She held up her own thumb and index finger. "There's a little bit more."

"More?" Eric braced both forearms on the bar edge and leaned into her space, as if he couldn't stand not knowing what other trouble she'd gotten herself into.

Funny how she wanted his interest on the one hand, but hated that he showed it on the other. She wished she was here for any other reason.

Now that the time had arrived, she hated that she'd had to come here at all. That she couldn't get herself out of this ridiculous mess on her own.

She drew long and hard on her straw, swallowed and, before she could think twice, blurted out, "It's my dating habits."

"You mean, the men you go through like diet soda?" he asked, spinning her now empty glass on the bar. "The first sip satisfies, but then the ice melts and the fizz is gone?"

She narrowed her eyes. "That's not one hundred percent accurate."

"What is accurate, Chloe? Because no matter how hard I try, I can't find enough fingers and toes to count the number of men I've seen you with this year. And it's only April.''

Was it really over twenty? She'd obviously lost count. "I like men. I like dating. But it doesn't take a rocket scientist to figure out immediate incompatibility.''

"Wait a minute. Let me get this straight." Eric shook his head, signaled a time-out. "Every time you go out with a new guy, you give him a compatibility test? You don't try for friendship first? Or for just plain fun?''

"Fun and friendship also require compatibility, sugar.''

All girls had their expectations and fantasies, didn't they? So what if hers were nonnegotiable. She knew she'd heard at least one song about a woman bemoaning the absence of her own John Wayne.

Chloe's preference just happened to be Cary Grant.

"And you and me?" Eric asked. "You think we're compatible?''

They had fun together. She counted him as a friend. It was a start, wasn't it? "We spent a month digging through one another's baggage and I'm still here, aren't I?''

Eric seemed momentarily at a loss for words. But his thought processes seemed equally stunned, judging from the sudden blank look on his face. But then he caught her off guard, retorting, "Didn't we just determine that you're here because you need a favor? Not because of any compatibility issue.''

"I do need a favor. I need an escort." She stated it flat out, hoping the shock value would knock him off balance and into capitulation.

"You want me to take a poll? See which of my

customers meet your criteria?'' Eric cast a sweeping glance around the bar, then narrowed his gaze on her. ''Or you want I should call in a favor from a buddy you haven't met yet? Press one of the high-profile athletes I know into service?''

As if! ''No. I want you.''

He frowned, backed a safe step away and crossed his arms. ''What do you mean, you want me?''

She placed both hands, palm side up, on the bar. ''I want you to be my escort.''

''So you can bust my chops all the way to next Tuesday?''

The first uncomfortable twinges of failure stung the backs of her eyes. ''You're jumping to unfounded conclusions, sugar.''

''Unfounded conclusions and unqualified no's. Yep. I can see why that would make me the man you want.''

She wasn't so sure any longer. Not this way. Not with this bitterness she'd never seen coming. She reached for her red leather mini knapsack and her wallet inside, intending to settle up for the cosmopolitan and the diet soda.

Men. Never again.

With a hand placed gently over hers, Eric stopped her from paying and from leaving. His expression had softened, as had his voice when he said, ''C'mon. Let's go talk in my office.''

2

HIS HAND AT THE SMALL of Chloe's back, Eric guided his unexpected visitor across the bar's common room, past the swinging doors leading to the kitchen and into a short hallway toward a door boldly marked: No Admittance Without Proper Authority or Play-Off Tickets.

The small of Chloe's back was really small. The girl had a mouth on her, a big one, and an attitude to match. But boy, was she a curvy little thing. Made it hard to decide whether he wanted to date her or adopt her.

One thing he knew was that he wasn't going to say yes to whatever cockamamie scheme she'd come here to pitch. If she didn't want him for more than her own self-serving reasons, then screw her.

And screw him if he hadn't learned not to let himself be used.

Chloe may have thought she'd come away from their scavenger-hunt month holding the upper hand, but he'd done his share of scouting, and he knew a thing or two about Chloe he doubted she knew about herself.

As tough as she seemed, she was appealingly vulnerable. He didn't know why she protected herself with her big bad attitude, but if made her feel safer, he'd play along. At least until he learned more about what had brought her here.

Because Chloe Zuniga didn't show up out of the blue looking like a cross between a *Maxim* cover model and a soccer mom without a damn good reason. A better one than needing an escort.

He reached for the doorknob, guided her forward, moved his hand from the small of her back to her shoulder. A surprisingly muscled shoulder, come to think of it, considering she hated physical activity.

His office decor reflected the rest of the bar, which meant Chloe would no doubt be just as uncomfortable in here as she had been out there. He'd give her an A, though, for effort, because she had made a big one. He didn't think he'd ever seen her wear athletic shoes.

As he watched her take in the long wall covered with autographed photos, he couldn't help but wonder what she'd look like having worked up a good sweat. He couldn't even imagine, having never seen her with a single blond hair out of place, unless tousled on purpose for the sake of being sexy. He'd seen rational men turned into blubbering idiots by that bedroom hair and those big, violet-colored eyes.

Eric chuckled to himself. He loved tinted contacts. He loved the idea of mussing up her hair. He also loved the way she looked in play clothes. And the way she looked in his office.

He moved to lean back against the huge wooden desk he'd purchased at a rural school auction, crossed his arms over his chest and waited. He didn't have a lot of time; Jason would be needing backup soon. But Eric had a feeling that whatever he was waiting for would be worth weathering a rebellion in the ranks.

"Bagwell, Biggio, Olajuwon, Lipinski, Campbell,

Ryan, Lewis.'' Chloe named off the past and present Houston sports figures, stopped when she reached the one frame set off from the others, and gave Eric the look most gave him with they came across the autographed shrine. ''Anna Kournikova?''

Eric lifted a shoulder. ''She plays tennis.''

Chloe's only reply was a loud huff. She continued to tour his office, moving from the autographed photos to the matted and framed ticket stubs he'd collected since attending his first professional sporting event at the age of five.

He hadn't framed every stub from every event. Most he'd randomly stapled to the wall, which made for wallpaper worth reading. But once in a very rare, memorable while, a frame was called for.

He watched Chloe lean in closer to read several of the stubs, watched her stand on tiptoe to read others. Watched her lips move as she mouthed the words. She smiled, she frowned, she sighed.

He wanted to ask which of the souvenirs generated which response, but he was too busy enjoying the way her calf muscles flexed when she lifted and stretched, the way the denim cupped her backside, the way the jersey molded her shoulders.

Either she'd pumped a lot of iron over the past couple of months or he'd really been blind as a bat the few times he'd had his hands on her before. Especially that time they'd danced at Lauren and Anton's housewarming party…after he'd licked the salt from her skin, downed a shot of tequila and sucked the juice from the lime she'd held in her mouth.

God Bless America, but the woman could kiss.

Catching him in his intent study of her rear view, Chloe suddenly turned and flopped down on his office couch, which was some local designer's interpretation of a cushy baseball dugout.

Middle fingers rubbing at her temples, Chloe closed her eyes and leaned back. "I really don't know what I'm doing here."

She'd mumbled the words, and he knew she'd said them more to herself than to him, but he wasn't going to let her slide by that easily. "I think you're here to make me an offer I can't refuse."

She stopped rubbing, looked up suspiciously. "You already told me no."

He had, but she hadn't looked quite so down and defeated then as she did now. And he hadn't felt quite so compelled to offer himself up as her savior. Maybe one of these days he'd come to his senses and rescue stray animals instead of stray women. But for now...

Hands braced hip level on the edge of his desk, he crossed his ankles and made the conscious and recognizably half-witted decision to invite her confidence. He'd worry about regrets later—when he was in over his head.

"You went to a lot of trouble to get my attention, princess. You must need me in ways I've only dreamed about."

"More like in ways I've never dreamed about," she said, not even rising to his bait.

Ouch! Slam! Cut to the bone! "So, tell Dr. Eric all about it before Jason drags me back out to the bar."

Chloe took a deep breath, scooted forward to sit primly on the edge of the couch. Her face, when she looked up to meet his gaze, could not have shown less guile. "Here's the thing. I love my career. I really do. I can't think of anything that would make me as happy

as I am at gIRL-gEAR. And I don't want to lose it.
I'll do anything not to lose it.''

"Why would you worry? You're a partner. It's not
like you'd be first in line to be laid off.''

"It's not about layoffs or downsizing. Sydney
knows what she's doing. Our bottom line has never
been so black.'' Chloe tucked her hands beneath her
thighs, rocked back and forth and finished her explanation in a rush. "This is about me, my mouth
and…my habit of dating everyone who asks.''

"Oh, now. *That* hurt my feelings. I asked and you
turned me down.'' He gave her a quick wink designed
to convince both of them he was teasing.

"I'm exaggerating, obviously. I don't go out with
everyone.'' Her rocking slowed and she studied him
intently with those big violet eyes.

Eric tightened his fingers over the edge of his desk.
"Just everyone but me.''

"I didn't go out with you because, well, I have my
reasons…one of them being that you're a lot of fun.''
She paused, as if wondering how much to say, then
softly admitted, "I didn't want to screw that up.''

"Dating is supposed to be fun. Dating me would be
a hell of a lot of fun,'' he said, more harshly than he'd
intended.

Chloe straightened her back, gave a regal lift of her
chin. "I'll keep that in mind.''

"See that you do.'' It was all he could think of to
say, at bat, as he was, bases loaded, bottom of the
ninth.

"But then what happens when we finish dating?''
She waited for him to answer, and when he remained
silent, she added, "I don't want to screw up what we
have as friends.''

What *did* they have as friends? And why did it feel like he'd been clothes-lined by her assumption that they'd be "finished dating"?

Even though he knew she was right, and he couldn't see himself sharing a future with Chloe, he didn't appreciate not being given a chance.

To do what, hotshot? Prove the princess as capable of dumping on you as any woman?

"Give me a clue here, Chloe. What sort of assistance, exactly, would you be needing from Eric's Escort Service?" Maybe he could back his way into helping her out, because no matter how much he enjoyed her company, he wasn't going to act the part of any escort.

Chloe got to her feet, paced to the opposite end of the couch, then back. She worked her hands as she talked. "Over the next few months, gIRL-gEAR is scheduled to be profiled in several national publications. Sydney has her eye on the big time. She's courting designers. She's talked about taking the company public.

"Which means we're all living under a magnifying glass. We've been ordered to clean up our acts. And I specifically have been asked to dismantle the skeletons in my closet and give the room a thorough disinfecting."

"Wow." Eric nodded and absorbed and tried to fit his escort services into the lineup. "That's heavy duty."

"Which part? gIRL-gEAR going public?" She narrowed her eyes. "Or my skeletons?"

"If you have any skeletons, you've done a super job of keeping them under wraps. But then, that would make them mummies, wouldn't it?'' He waited for her to get it, then added, ''Skeletons? Under wraps?''

''That's not funny.''

''C'mon, Chloe. I can't believe it's all gloom and doom. You've been here, what?'' He glanced at the basketball goal converted to a clock on the wall above her head. ''Thirty minutes?''

''Yes. And?''

''So, you might've slipped one by me, but I don't think I've heard so much as a *dagnabbit* come out of your mouth.''

''Trust me.'' Her hands went deep into the pockets of her shorts, her gaze to the toes of her cross-trainers. ''It's only for the tight leash I have on my tongue.''

Eric leaned forward, catching the scent of sunshine in her hair. He smiled and whispered, ''Just don't let go. You'll be fine.''

''So, you've solved one of my problems.'' She held up two fingers. ''There's still my fast and furious reputation. And then there's Poe.''

''Poe?''

''A buyer at work. Her name is Annabel Lee. And she'd sell her soul for my job.''

Eric needed more information to diffuse that particular bomb. But since Chloe's reputation was one thing he knew about, he could ease at least that worry.

''You think you have a fast and furious reputation?'' He shook his head. ''In my dreams, maybe.''

A tiny smile crooked the corner of her mouth. ''There you go. Dreaming again.''

No way was he touching that comment. Ten-foot pole or twenty. ''You date a lot. It's not a big deal. If you slept around, I'd know it.''

''What do you mean, you'd know it?''

Here he needed to tread carefully. He might not be held to the same standards as a man of the cloth, but neither did he spill his guts lightly. "We run in the same circles, Chloe. And I own a bar. Trust me. I hear as many confessions as a priest. Your reputation is safe with me."

The second the words left his mouth, he knew he'd stepped into a big pile of dog doo. Chloe got a look in her eye that could only be called a wicked gleam.

"I was hoping you would say that."

He stumbled over ten or twelve words before he finally shut his big mouth. This was what he got for trying to be a nice guy. At least he knew enough to stop with the shovel before he buried himself completely.

"I have three functions coming up over the next couple of months," Chloe was saying. "Official business functions. I can't get out of any of them and I'll be representing gIRL-gEAR while I'm there."

"So go already." He knew where this was headed, knew he'd been smart to establish his just-say-no terms up front. Making like Chloe's arm candy was not his idea of self-respect. "I'm sure you can find a date. Or better yet, avoid the reputation hassle and go alone."

She shook her head. "This girl does not fly solo."

"Why not?"

"My reputation, duh."

Try as he might, Eric could not make sense of her logic. "I hope you're kidding, because I think it's your reputation that's gotten you into this mess, am I right?"

"You're not a girl. I don't expect you to understand. I can't go alone. I have to have a date. And I would be ever so appreciative if you could help me out here."

He ignored the eyelashes she batted. "And by help you out, you mean…"

She nodded.

He shook his head. "I don't know, Chloe. I'm not sure I want to be one of your statistics."

"You wouldn't be. This is strictly business. Totally up front. If I show up with the same date all three times, the industry gossips won't have a tongue-wagging leg to stand on."

Threads of common sense were unraveling all over the floor. "Sure they will. It'll just be a different leg. My leg. And I don't really care to be the object of anyone's wagging tongue."

Then again…

"Don't you get it?" She wrapped delicate fingers around his forearm. "That's the point. Sydney can hardly object if the reason for the gossip is all good. You'd be putting a positive spin on my situation. Party girl interrupted."

"First you want an escort. Now you want a spin doctor. I know it's hard to believe, but even *I* can't be all things to all women."

The imprint of her touch remained on his arm long after he'd pushed away from his desk. He'd hoped he could walk away; why had he never learned how to walk away? But he didn't get very far because Chloe was in his face, one hundred twenty pounds of enthusiasm.

"Think about it, Eric. Three dates. That's all it is." She counted them off on her fingers—one, two, three. "Three nights spent in my company, schmoozing with the media. With designers. Supermodels."

She'd called him Eric. Not sugar. "Supermodels?"

"I'd do the same for you."

Oh she would, would she? "Supermodels, huh? I tell you what. I'll make you a deal."

He had to give her credit; she didn't turn him down immediately the way he had before hearing the dirty details of her idea. She had an open mind.

A desperate open mind?

Willing to go to any lengths to save her career?

Hmm. He could see himself playing the devil to her Faust.

"What? What's the deal?"

"You get your three dates." He did the finger thing—one, two, three. "And I get my three—"

"No." She shook her head so forcefully that wisps of her blond hair caught on her lips, leaving her decidedly disheveled.

Eric liked the look. "What kind of double standard is this? I'm not allowed to say no, but you can turn me down flat without hearing me out?"

"I don't want to hear you out. Not if it's going to be about sex."

He hung his head and did his best to look puppy-dog pitiful instead of guilty as hell. "After all that talk about friends being there for each other? You've gone and hurt my feelings, Chloe."

"You're saying your deal-making efforts aren't intended to get me into bed?"

He looked up in time to catch the imperial lift of her brow. "What? And ruin this beautiful friendship?"

He wasn't about to admit what the picture of her tousled hair was doing for his imagination. Just get her out of her shoes and shorts and, yeah, he could see Chloe Zuniga in his bed, wearing nothing but her socks and that jersey hanging over her thighs and curvy bare ass.

"Okay." Her chin went up. She shook back her hair. "What three *nonsexual* things do you want in exchange for your escort services?"

"We're going to do this, then?"

"Well, it depends on what you want."

Nope. He wasn't going anywhere near that one, either; there wasn't a long enough pole. "Don't worry. I'll think of something."

"So, you don't even know what you want? This is just an open-ended deal? I'm expected to be at your beck and call while you get off on stringing me along?" At each question asked, her voice had risen. Her final query was nothing if not a screech.

"I suppose we can set a time limit."

"Damn straight we're going to set a time limit. I'd be a thousand kinds of a fool to leave myself open to the warped workings of your imagination."

Ah. Now this was the Chloe he knew and…*hmm.* Definitely didn't love. Admittedly had the hots for. "Okay, then. What? A month? Six weeks?"

She'd pulled a mini diary from her mini knapsack. "The Wild Winter Woman fashion show is my third event, and it's in the middle of May, so let's wrap up this deal by Memorial Day."

He thought of everything he had on his calendar between now and then. A huge grin started at the edge of his mouth and spread until he thought his face would split.

"What the hell are you so happy about?" Chloe groused, hoisting her small leather backpack onto one shoulder.

"Just thinking how I've always wanted a genie to grant me three wishes. And here you are."

SETTLED IN THE SADDLE of her exercise bike, Chloe wished her legs were longer so she could give herself a good swift kick in the pants.

Instead, she pedaled harder, faster, her legs pumping like pistons, and all the spent energy getting her abso-friggin'-lutely nowhere. She released the bike's handlebar just long enough to swipe a towel over her forehead.

Her sweatband had long since passed the point of saturation, but she wasn't about to stop spinning to switch it for a dry one. Not when she had an unstoppable rhythm going and hours of frustration to burn.

The television mounted in the corner of the spare bedroom she'd converted into her own personal exercise-slash-torture chamber was running a tape of *Shakespeare in Love.* But even Will's desperately romantic pursuit of Viola was not enough to distract Chloe from yesterday's fiasco.

Damn that cocky Eric Haydon, sweet-talking her into doing exactly what he'd wanted. Granting him three wishes. And how stupid of her to agree. No, not stupid. Just desperate enough to act like she didn't have an ounce of common sense…or much of a memory for details.

He was wrong.

Yesterday afternoon, once she'd gotten out of Haydon's and arrived home, she'd headed straight for her diary. And Eric was wrong. Sixteen. Not twenty.

She'd gone out with sixteen different men so far this year. Eight of them had been one-nighters, not deserving of the time of day much less any more than her cell phone number. Caller ID *was* a girl's best friend.

Puffing through the aggravation of realizing she needed a new strategy for finding that elusive happily ever after, she tried to sort out the entire dating process—or at least her personal lack of dating success.

She was not unreasonably selective, yet she didn't go out with just anyone who asked. Somehow, though, she had gained a reputation for doing just that. Which guaranteed she was asked out a lot.

By everyone, it seemed, but Cary Grant.

Her dating rules were flexible, her only demand that a man treat her like a woman. Too many took that to mean trying to get into her pants. Others assumed she wanted to be coddled and pampered and saved from herself.

She never went into a date with her rules spelled out on a cue card. But men asked, and she answered, and then all hell would break loose, depending on the man and what conclusions he'd drawn about women.

It was always one extreme or the other. The virgin or the slut. The whore or the lady.

What had happened to the middle ground?

Her looks were one problem, her vocabulary another, but she was who she was. Her upbringing had defined her; the pedestal on which she'd been forced to sit had towered miles above reality.

So she'd countered her father's insistence that she rise above the rabble by getting down and getting dirty. To her sheltered and rebellious young mind that had meant a coarse vocabulary, a take-no-prisoners personality, an unapologetic enjoyment of life's earthier delights, as well as the power afforded by passion.

Perhaps not the most straightforward approach to

life or to love, but a method that *had* served its purpose. She'd learned that being good wasn't going to get her anything she wanted. She'd also learned that what most men gave her she wanted to give back.

At the crook of her finger, they came running, bringing flowers and chocolates and baubles, and declarations of love so profusely poetic she wanted to barf. She had attention, affection, the things of female fantasy…and all of it was bogus as hell.

No man had ever taken the time or made the effort to learn that she read Tom Clancy for fun. That she'd take lemon over chocolate any day of the week. That she grew her own tomatoes in whiskey barrels kept on the patio, but killed every flower she planted.

Men. Ruled by their dicks. Every one of them.

What she wanted was chivalry.

Was the word really that anachronistic? The concept that out-of-date? And what about respect? Not only for her person, but for her ideas and opinions.

She was blond. She was built. She was not about to apologize for her love of makeup. She had a brain. She was not a bimbo. She liked men. She was not an easy score.

Why was that so hard to understand? she wondered, and pedaled even harder, faster, closing her eyes and pushing beyond the burn. She doubted her reputation or her mouth truly crossed Sydney's line in the sand.

But Chloe loved gIRL-gEAR, her vice-presidential perks and position, the cyclical industry of fashion and her partners, the five women who'd been her best friends since their days in Austin at University of Texas.

Hell, she even had a soft spot for Poe, though the other woman's ambition irritated Chloe more than a broken underwire on a brand-new bra. Poe needed the air released from her inflated self-opinion. She might have five years on Chloe, but Chloe had the heart Ms. Annabel Lee was missing.

The ringing of the phone in her bedroom slowed Chloe's cathartic pace, but she didn't stop pedaling until the machine picked up and she heard Eric Haydon's voice.

"Yo, Chloe. About that first wish."

Chloe sat up straight on the bike and listened to the recording being broadcast from across the hall.

"Be at Haydon's. Saturday morning. Nine on the nose. Oh, and the outfit you had on yesterday? Wear it."

The line went dead, then came the dial tone, followed closely by Chloe's disbelief. That was it? Orders he assumed she'd follow left on an answering machine?

And what was up with the dress code? He knew she wouldn't wear those clothes again on a dare. She certainly wouldn't wear them because he'd told her to. Or would she? After all, she'd been stupid enough to grant him three wishes.

She'd had enough exercise, and her fill of that bossy Eric Haydon. Hopping from the bike, she headed for the shower, flinging pink Lycra and spandex all over the bathroom. Once the hot water started melting her balled up muscles, she was better able to think.

Other than removing sex from the equation, she and Eric had set no boundaries for this granting-of-three-wishes business. She supposed it was a fair enough trade-off.

Eric knew he'd be accompanying her to gIRL-

gEAR business affairs. She knew she'd be doing anything Eric wanted her to do...except crawl naked into
his bed. Chloe sighed.

How terribly disappointing.

3

HAVING ARRIVED at Haydon's only minutes before Chloe, Eric leaned against the back end of his car, legs crossed at the ankle, arms crossed over his chest, and watched her pull her lime-green VW Beetle into the parking lot.

If he was a betting man, he wouldn't take better than fifty-fifty odds that she'd worn the outfit he'd wanted her to wear. Still, she was here. And that was saying something.

He continued to watch as she jerked her sunglasses from her face, the keys from the ignition. With a look between a frown and a glare, she climbed from the car, her eyes never breaking contact with his.

"Well, blow my mind. A woman who can follow orders." He grinned. He winked. Because seeing her in play clothes had just become the highlight of his day. "I think I'm in love."

"I see your mouth is making promises you don't have the backbone to keep," she said, tucking both her shades and her car keys into her knapsack and slinging it over one shoulder.

"Not promises as much as observations," he said, ignoring her dig. He pushed himself erect and headed for the passenger door, then added a dig of his own. "Unless you want me to see what I can do about paying up."

Chloe, of course, ignored him. He'd opened the car door and now stood with both wrists draped over the frame. Chloe waited, one hand wrapped around her knapsack's shoulder strap, the other at her hip, feet unmoving and eyes cutting from Eric's to the Mustang and back again.

"I take it that you want me to get in?"

"You got it."

"Do you mind telling me where we're going? Or what we're going to do? And, most of all, why you wanted me to wear this ridiculous getup yet again?"

Ah, yes. The Chloe he still didn't love…but was starting to appreciate way too much. "How 'bout you get in the car and trust that all will be revealed in good time?"

"In your good time, you mean," she groused, but she did slide down into the car's bucket seat.

Eric closed the door behind her and skirted the rear of the car, slapping his hand on the trunk on his way to the driver's side. Talk about your bad mood. He couldn't believe Chloe could really be that worried about her position at gIRL-gEAR, worried enough to bite his head off when he was the one she'd come to for help.

She'd been one of the original girls. To his mind that made Chloe irreplaceable, the same way Ted Williams would always be a Boston Red Sox, Michael Jordan a Chicago Bull, Joe Namath a New York Jet. No. There was something else going on here. But Eric wasn't going to ask her yet.

He slid into the driver's seat, slammed the door and turned over the two hundred sixty horses beneath the Mustang's hood. He shoved the five speed into reverse and whipped the car around, squealing his tires out of the parking lot and onto westbound Richmond Drive.

Chloe slid him a sideways glance. "Is the length of the skid mark a guy lays in direct proportion to his opinion of himself?"

"Nope." Eric grinned. He wouldn't be able to afford retreads if that were the case. "That's just me giving the horses their head. Gotta put the sweethearts through their paces."

"Humph. Typical man. Your car gets treated better than your date."

Eric downshifted for the traffic light a half block ahead. "How do you figure?"

"'Give the horses their head.' 'Put the sweethearts through their paces,'" Chloe mimicked, digging for her sunglasses. The sun was at their backs, but glared off the approaching cars' glass. "Your date doesn't even get a straight answer when she asks where you're taking her."

Women. Couldn't even give a guy a chance to spring a surprise. Had to be all distrusting and suspicious…though, in this case, suspicion was not unwarranted, Eric had to admit. "Trust me, princess. I know how to treat a date. And if we were dating, I'd be more than happy to show you what you've been missing."

"I know exactly what I've been missing," she mumbled. And he swore he heard her add, "Cary Grant."

Eric frowned. The girl needed help. "Tell me something, Chloe. If you can't find a man you'd like to keep company with, why don't you quit dating instead of setting yourself up for disappointment?"

She was quiet for a long minute, staring straight

ahead through the windshield. He was about to give up and turn the conversation to the weather when she finally said, "I don't set myself up for disappointment. I mean, it's not like I go into a date hoping the evening will crash and burn." She gave a careless shrug. "It just happens."

No one crashed and burned every single time. No matter what Chloe said, it just didn't happen. "How open is your mind then? Because I gotta say, you're not exactly little Mary Sunshine."

"How would you know?" she snarled. "We're not dating, remember?"

"We don't have to be dating for me to see that you have a hell of a negative attitude."

Chloe closed the front pouch of her knapsack; the jerk of the zipper sounded like she'd ripped a jagged hole in the air. "You can let me out anytime. I can get myself back to my car, thank you very much."

Eric hated to do it. He really did, but he whipped the car in a U-turn and headed back to Haydon's. He wanted her company, the company she usually offered, or had offered before she'd hit this personal downhill slide.

She was smart and she was funny. Her sharp tongue could slice a man into shreds. Her eyes could throw daggers at any part of him left standing. Her mouth could grind the fallen pieces into the ground.

But, oh, could she kiss and make it all better.

Which told Eric that part of what drove her was passion, and passion was one mother of a two-edged sword.

What he wanted from Chloe was to see the shine of the blade without feeling the sting of the razor. He had trouble enough with his own morning shave.

He shot up into the sports bar's parking lot, coming to an amazingly gentle stop.

Chloe reached for the door handle. Eric stopped her with nothing more than an exaggerated clearing of his throat.

"You have something to say?"

"Just a reminder of our deal. And turnabout being fair play and all. You don't grant my first wish, I don't feel I have to attend your first function." He frowned, paused for effect and added, "When was that, anyway?"

"Tomorrow. gIRL-gEAR is hosting an open house."

"Tomorrow? Well, I'm not sure I'm going to be available. You hardly gave me any notice."

"That's because I've almost decided not to go," she said softly, slumping down into the seat, closing her eyes and letting her head hit the window.

Uh-oh. "Did you tell Sydney you were bailing?"

"I haven't bailed yet. I've just been wondering if any of this effort is going to make any difference."

Not if you don't change your attitude, he wanted to say, but instead he offered, "I still don't get why you think you have to go to all this trouble."

She shook her head, waved him off with the flutter of one hand. "Forget it. I'm just in a lousy mood. Chalk it up to a crappy Friday."

"Another bad date last night?"

"No, actually. Last night was great. I stayed home, no one but myself for company, and watched old videos. Six hours of my favorite love stories and you'd think I'd be in a better mood, wouldn't you?"

"If you like love stories. I'd be in a coma."

"I suppose you spent all night watching a ball game

or a fight or whatever sport is in season." She made the accusation, then pulled off her sunglasses.

Eric had trouble keeping a straight face. "Actually, no. I had a date."

She opened one eye, slid him a glance, opened the other eye and turned her head enough to look at him straight on. "Do tell."

"What's to tell? It was a date."

"Dinner? A movie? Back to the bedroom?"

This time Eric shifted in his seat and did his best to face her. "That's your idea of a date?"

"Not mine, no. But that's what I'm usually offered."

No wonder she went through men like he went through running shoes, if that was the height of her dating expectations. "And you're going out with losers, why?"

She studied him for a minute, frowning slightly, her eyes that amazingly cool shade of sunset purple. Her lashes were long; he only noticed because of the way she blinked like that, so lazy and slow.

He didn't think he'd ever seen her face in the buff, and wondered what she'd look like with her skin scrubbed clean. If she'd look as innocent as she did in his imagination. The same imagination that was making hard work of the lower half of his body.

She wore her makeup well, considering she used more than a lot of women. And he wasn't sure he'd noticed until now how perfect she looked in the colors. Soft and feminine...like the bunches of wildflowers that had popped up all over the field at Stratton Park, where they were headed.

Or had been headed until Chloe got a bad-mood burr up her butt.

It probably wasn't fair of him to hijack her this way, but she'd agreed to the terms of the deal and he was looking forward to seeing her sweat. It would do her good to get rid of those built-up stress toxins.

It would do him good as well to see her get all huffy and insulted at having to play ball. He needed the reminder that they would never get along as a couple. She stirred his blood wildly, but dinner and a movie and back to the bedroom was not his idea of a good time.

He loved it when a woman understood his passion for getting out and getting physical. The ones who shared his idea of having fun were the ones he enjoyed most in bed. They didn't worry about wrinkles and tangles and makeup running in the sun and the heat.

And they brought that same energy and stamina, not to mention their strong warrior-woman thighs, to bed. He wondered about Chloe's stamina. He wondered about her thighs.

Finally, he snapped to the fact that she still had her gaze trained fully his way. "Well?"

"I'm not intentionally going out with losers. You can take my word on that."

"I thought all women had some kind of—" Eric waved one hand "—hormonal radar thing going. To lessen the chance of winding up with a jerk."

"Do all men have one? Or, if they do, does the one they have work one hundred percent of the time?"

Eric ran cupped fingers back and forth over the curve of the steering wheel. "I guess that's the better question, isn't it? My gaydar never fails me. I'm not as lucky with my laydar."

Shifting into a more comfortable, the-better-to-see-you-with position, she repeated, "Laydar?"

"Sure," he said, and grinned. "The wiggly little stick that tells me if I'm going to get laid."

Chloe rolled her eyes. "That is about the most sexist thing I've ever heard."

"C'mon, princess," he said with a wink. "Don't tell me you don't wish you had one."

She answered with a careless shrug. "I don't need one. I can get laid anytime I want."

"Now who's being sexist?"

"I'm being a realist. You want me to lie about it? Deny that men find me sexy? Well, I won't." A self-deprecating smile lifted both corners of her mouth. "I'll also admit that I can be an unadulterated bitch. But that hasn't yet stopped a guy from begging to show me heaven."

"And that would be right about the time you tell him to go to hell?"

"For all the good it does." She gave a quick shake of her head, scooping flyaway hair behind her ear, before adding, "I so don't get it. I mean, I understand the concept of coming back for more. But it's not like I'm giving out candy here. I can't decide if their egos are that resilient or if they have some sort of rejection fetish."

Eric considered her dilemma, considered, too, the shell of her ear and the tiny little Spock-like point now exposed. He gripped the steering wheel tighter. "Kick me, beat me, make me beg? Yeah. It can happen with some guys."

"But never with you." The tone of her comeback asked the question she'd stated as fact.

Time to get a few things straight. "Chloe. I never say never because life offers too few sure things. But I can say this. You will never know what I do or do not enjoy in bed until you're there to find out firsthand. Then, trust me. I won't hesitate to show you what I like, where and how.''

And then he bit his tongue before inviting her to take a trip into his fantasy. Because his imagination had taken on epic proportions, and all she needed to know he could teach her with a quick zip of his fly.

For the next few moments she remained unmoving and silent, the only sound in the car the muffled noise of the engine and that of Chloe's breathing, ragged and more than a little bit out of control.

Eric could only imagine the matching pulse beating in her wrist, her chest, the base of her throat. He could only imagine because he had no intention of looking away from her eyes. He could see her considering the possibilities. How would they fit together? Would he like her best on the bottom or on the top? Would he prefer she take control or surrender? Would he get his first? Would he even be able to make her come?

He smiled at that, not because he was a miraculous, all-powerful lover, but because he was surprised how many women had given up on orgasms. And how many men weren't man enough to take the time and figure out what a woman needed.

They weren't all built on the same assembly line, which meant where one woman needed a tweak, another needed a nudge and still another needed a nice little squeeze. All a man had to do was ask. Then figure out how to coax her to answer. Women were such amazing beings.

Finally, Chloe cleared her throat. ''Well, Eric. Sugar. I'm not sure I know what to say. I would love to know what you're like in bed, but since I'll never

be there to find out firsthand, I guess I'll die an un-
fulfilled woman.''

She was so damn good at busting his chops. Why
did she have to be so damn good?

He didn't know another woman who'd ever been
able to get his hopes up when he wasn't even looking,
only to crush him into line chalk by the time he got
up to speed.

''Remember what I said. Never say never.''

She waved a hand in front of her face. ''It's getting
rather stuffy in here. Think you could turn on the
AC?''

Eric tossed his head back and laughed, adjusting the
flow of refrigerated air. ''I would've turned it on a
long time ago if I'd known you'd be sticking around
to need it. But you were so gung ho to get back to
your car.''

''I know. I was.''

''But you're not now? What's with the change of
heart?''

She turned her head, returned her sunglasses to her
face. But not before a hint of grudging respect flashed
in her eyes. ''Nothing but that little ol' promise I made
to grant you three wishes. A deal is a deal.''

Eric rubbed his hands together. ''My own personal
genie in a bottle.''

''Just keep that rub-a-dub-dub business to yourself,'' she said, slicing him with a sharp sideways
glance.

''So, we're ready to hit the road here again?''

She sighed. ''I suppose I don't have much choice.''

''What're you talking about? You have all kinds of
choices.'' But he put the car into gear anyway, exited

Haydon's parking lot and headed again for Stratton Field.

"Sure. Like choosing between saving my job or giving it up to Poe without a fight."

Poe. Eric's first problem to tackle. Or to let Chloe talk herself into tackling. Women liked to talk. All those lips movin' and jaws flappin' seemed to jar loose whatever it was keeping their brains from calling the right play.

Give 'em a willing ear, and most of the time they worked things out just fine on their own. He didn't claim to understand how it worked. He just knew that it did.

"I guess first thing you need to decide is if the job's worth fighting for." He downshifted as they rolled up to a traffic light and stopped.

"You have got to be kidding me." She shifted in her seat, fighting with the seat belt in order to face him. "I *am* gIRL-gEAR. This is my career. My future. I can't imagine doing anything else with my life."

There it was again, that passion. He wondered how aware she was of her nature, and how it must be killing her to rein it in, to bite her tongue when her tongue had so much to say.

And it was more than her mouth. Even the way she wore her makeup fit her personality. That and the way she culled her dates, a sort of aggressive search-and-destroy for...what? he wondered. What was it that drove her?

"Then I guess that answers my question. Though I do think that part about you being gIRL-gEAR is a bit over the top."

"That coming from Mr. Sports Bar?"

Eric paused to consider the comparison. "Not the

same at all. Eric Haydon. Haydon's Half Time. Chloe Zuniga. gIRL-gEAR. Nope. Totally different arena.''

Chloe snorted. ''You can't even carry on a conversation that isn't littered with—'' she gestured dismissively ''—your sports expressions.''

Eric had never really thought about it, but he supposed Chloe was right. He did think in the lingo. But athletics and competition had been so much a part of his life that he didn't remember a day going by without it. Sorta like he didn't remember a day going by without food or sleep.

''Besides,'' she continued, ''even if I am over the top about gIRL-gEAR, it's a reflection of me. I'm fairly over the top about a lot of things. I don't think that's much of a secret. Between my profanity issues,'' she said, sketching air apostrophes with her fingers, ''and my problems with Poe, I'm a walking talking cry for intervention. Or so Sydney thinks. Having intervened.''

Eric chuckled and signaled his lane change. ''So, how long has she been with gIRL-gEAR? This Poe of yours.''

''She's not mine and she's been there a little over a year. She started as Sydney's assistant, but now she works as a buyer. When the position became available, she flexed her claws and got what she wanted. I don't think she liked working directly under a younger boss,'' Chloe said, and redirected the air-conditioning vent. ''This way she has more autonomy.''

Eric adjusted the temperature of the refrigerated air. ''How old is she?''

''Thirty, I think. And way more suited for a corporate environment. Not conventional, just...I don't know. gIRL-gEAR seems too funky an atmosphere. I can picture her in Leo Redding's law office. Though Macy's only slightly more tolerant of her than I am."

"Why's that?"

"I'm not sure I can put it into words. You almost have to work with her, see her in action. She's got this whole *Crouching Tiger, Hidden Dragon* thing going. Very composed, serene even. But you know behind those eyes she's just waiting to go all martial arts on your ass. She…simmers, if that makes any sense."

Checking the traffic in his rearview mirror, Eric couldn't help but grin. "Simmers, huh? Takes one to know one, maybe?"

"I do not simmer." Chloe pulled herself up straight in the seat. "I boil."

"Right over the top." Eric made a diving motion with his hand.

"Exactly."

She seemed so proud of her fiery nature, he hated to bring up the obvious. "So, you don't think your tendency toward, oh, I don't know, aggressive behavior has anything to do with your dating problems?"

"Why would it? It's not like I'm running them down with my car or—" she smiled to herself "—drop-kicking them over the goalpost."

"Whoa. Be still my heart." He pressed his palm to his chest and beat his fingers in a thumping tattoo.

"Don't get too excited. I don't plan to make a habit of it. Even for you."

"You enjoy being a tease?"

"I am not a tease."

He wanted to tell her to prove it. Instead, he said, "If you give the guys you date what they want to hear, then a lot of them are going to think you'll give them anything they want."

"All because I'm making the effort to be polite? To show interest, even if it's bogus?"

"Oh, so now you're a tease *and* a fake. A guy won't know if he's coming or going."

"Sure he will." Chloe paused, then added, "If he's going, it's yellow. If he's coming, it's white."

Eric choked on a snort of laughter. "That is the sort of gutter mouth comment that's going to get your ass fired."

"Because I'm female. But if we were two guys talking, I could get away with referring to any bodily function I wanted to. And I wouldn't have to worry about losing my job."

"First of all, no guy I know is going to tell that joke."

"Maybe not that one, but ones equally offensive."

Eric continued to shake his head. "Not on the job, if he doesn't want to find himself facing a sexual harassment suit."

"Well, if it makes you feel any better, I have more class than to tell that joke at work. I usually have more class than to tell it at all." Her tone was a cross between apologetic and defensive.

More than a little aggravated himself, Eric muttered, "Glad to know hanging out with me doesn't require any class."

She banged her head back against the seat. "Hanging out with you means I can relax. I don't have to censor everything I say. But I do have an understanding of what is and is not acceptable in the workplace."

"Just not what's acceptable on a date."

"No, actually. I think I am well versed in dating etiquette."

"That's right. This isn't a date. You and me, here and now."

"Duh. No. It's blackmail."

Eric took a deep breath and focused on the road ahead. He was so close to saying something he knew he'd regret. He had no business letting her get to him. She was right. This wasn't a date. It was a deal. And getting mad wouldn't do anyone any good, anyway.

"So, tomorrow? Is that going to be a date?" he asked, jumping from the frying pan into the fire. "I mean, I want to be sure I don't get out of line. That I treat you like a date, if that's what it is. Or that I treat you like one of the guys and swap smut jokes if it's not."

For several moments Chloe seemed more interested in the road flying by beneath the Mustang's wheels than anything Eric had to say. A part of him wanted to take it back. A more perverse part was glad for every word he'd said, even though her hands remained locked around the strap of her knapsack and her feet pressed primly together on the passenger-side floorboard. Her posture was straight and her voice was soft when she spoke.

"I know what you're doing. Don't think I don't. You're trying to make me behave the way you think I should behave. I get so sick of conventions. Who decided girls had to wear the ruffles and sit on the sidelines? I tell you," she added, this time her voice barely above a whisper, "I'm sick to death of sitting on the sidelines."

Eric didn't know if she was speaking literally or making another sports analogy. He wanted to find out, to explore where Chloe came from, because he was curious to find out how she balanced her bad-girl body and her baby-doll face with her mouth that belonged in the gutter.

"Well, this should be right up your alley, then. No one does any sideline sitting when Haydon's Half Time Hammers meet Big Boy's Bad Boys for the city's unofficial coed sports bar volleyball championship."

"YOU WANT ME TO PLAY volleyball? In a pit filled with dirt?"

"It's a court, not a pit. It's sand, not dirt. And it's clean."

Having plopped down on the grass outside a court squared off with a permanent barrier of hard black rubber, Eric unlaced his high-tops. "C'mon, Chloe. Get rid of your shoes and socks. It's too hard to maneuver with all that bulk."

Oh, she knew what it took to maneuver. She knew exactly. And she couldn't believe that of all things athletic Eric might choose for his wish, he'd conned her into playing volleyball. Volleyball! Screw her career. She should've stayed in bed.

She'd left her knapsack in the Mustang, realizing Eric's little wish for a sporting adventure did not include a locker room or a shower. But taking off her shoes and socks and exposing the pedicure she'd had refreshed first thing this morning to the abuse of gritty sand? She did not recall this being any part of any deal.

Volleyball. She could only shake her head.

Still, she couldn't deny that, on the drive from Haydon's, Eric had given her a lot to think about. She wasn't ready to cut him loose as a source of good conversation—or as the escort she needed. Besides, she was not completely unfamiliar with the concept of payback being hell.

As other players began to arrive and teams checked in with the league officials stationed across the court beneath a striped awning, Chloe crossed her ankles and sank to the ground. ''I've been meaning to ask you if you own a tux.''

His fingers fumbled with the lace he was loosening and he came close to ending up with a big messy knot. ''I hope you're not expecting me to come up with a tux by tomorrow. You'll be escorting yourself if that's the case.''

Chloe wiggled the toes of her first bare foot, reached for shoe number two. ''Oh, no, sugar. The tux is for the Wild Winter Woman fashion show.''

His hands stilled halfway through pulling off his second shoe. He finally looked up with one eye narrowed. ''The one with the supermodels?''

Men. Eyes rolling, Chloe nodded.

''Would that be your function number two or three?'' Eric asked, his narrowed gaze roaming down to Chloe's naked foot and smooth bare calf.

She finished stripping off her second shoe, then set about tucking both socks inside, flexing her toes, her feet, stretching the muscles of both inner and outer thighs and her calves, realizing halfway through her warmup that Eric appeared to have been struck dumb.

She moved on to working the kinks from her torso, not totally for her own benefit, either. ''Number three. Two is our first gIRL-gEAR gIRL awards ceremony and should merely require a nice suit. I'm just giving you fair warning here. Sort of like you did me when you ordered me to show up at Haydon's this morning.''

Eric had the good grace to glance up from her legs and look guilty. "I wasn't sure you'd show if I told you where we were going."

"And you were right to worry." Chloe handed Eric her shoes when he held out a hand. Then she got to her feet and brushed the loose grass from her backside. She wiggled her toes in the freshly mowed lawn, deciding gRAFFITI gIRL's Bubbling Parfait was a perfect color and that her toes felt as good as they looked.

"Damn, Chloe." Still sitting, Eric stared at Chloe's legs. "Where'd you get those calf muscles?"

Chloe looked down, turning her legs this way and that while wondering what he'd think if he saw all the exercise equipment in her spare bedroom. "These little ol' things? Why, I was born with them, sugar."

"Well, if they work as good as they look, I might just have to revise my opinion of girls like you."

Her hands went to her hips. Her chin went up and she waited for an explanation. "Girls like me?"

"Yeah, you know." He grabbed up all four shoes and stood. "Powder puffs. Cotton candy. Marshmallows."

Marshmallows? "You think I'm a marshmallow?"

"Not after seeing those legs."

"You've seen me in shorts before. And I know you've seen me in skirts."

"Yeah, but never from ground zero. Puts things into an entirely new perspective."

"Well, then. This should really rock your world." And tugging her jersey free from her shorts, she grabbed the hem and jerked the shirt over her head and off.

Eric obviously didn't know where to look. For the longest time, he kept his gaze locked with Chloe's until, at the tentative uncertainty she saw in his eyes, her heart softened and she gave a quick grin and granted him permission to ogle.

His gaze took in her full-coverage sports bra before moving down to her bare belly. The waistband of her shorts rode right below her navel and exposed the toned abdominals even Chloe recognized as music video material.

Eric let loose a long low whistle. ''Woman, where have you been all my life?''

''Right here, sugar. Under your nose.''

''If you'd been under my nose, I would've caught your scent.'' He shook his head, eyes wide with admiring disbelief. ''Where you've been is under too many clothes.''

''Think so, huh?'' Chloe moved two small steps forward, keeping hands tucked in the rear pockets of her shorts and her shoulders back. ''Would you like it if I got rid of more?''

Eric tossed the shoes—one, two, three, four—into the back seat of the Mustang through the convertible top he'd lowered when he'd parked.

''I'd like it if you'd get rid of everything,'' he said, and then he approached, stopping only when his bare toes brushed the tips of hers. He shoved his own hands down into his back pockets, mirroring her stance and, in the process, giving his shoulders an exceptional breadth.

Except at this near intimate proximity, Chloe was not as caught by Eric's shoulders or stance as she was by his eyes. They were the blue of Paul Newman and of poetry, yet flowery compliments had never come easy and too often seemed like a big waste of words.

Besides, what Eric's eyes made her feel was beyond

her ability to describe. The beat of her heart echoed in her ears, drowning out the words wanting to be said. Even a backhanded compliment might get her into too much trouble. But they'd been standing still here so long now that she had to say something.

And so she did. "Are your eyes really that blue, or do you wear contacts?"

For a moment Eric didn't have an answer, then he tossed back his head and roared. "Oh, princess. And here I was hoping that this time you weren't yanking my chain, that we were getting serious."

"Such a nice way to tell me to put up or shut up."

He looped an elbow around her neck and turned her toward the volleyball court. "That's because I'm such a nice guy."

Chloe could hardly disagree. Especially when she knew that any other guy would have insisted she do one or the other.

Warmed by the weight of Eric's arm, warmed further by the bright April sun, she shivered, reluctantly forced to admit that Eric wasn't any other guy.

And that scared her half to death.

4

"GOT IT!"

Bouncing from foot to foot in the back left corner of the court, Chloe maneuvered into position beneath the incoming serve. The ball popped against her wrists, shot up perfectly, came down for Eric's set and Jason's spike.

The ball sliced over the fist of the receiving forward and hit the sand on the opposite side. Whooping it up with the rest of Haydon's Hammers, Chloe rotated to the left front, while Lizzy, one of Eric's waitresses, stepped back to serve.

Two more of Eric's employees made up the rest of the team of six, which had managed to win their first two matches. This third game of the third match was the last of the afternoon and would determine the tournament winner.

Having breezed through check-in, though she had no real connection to Haydon's, Chloe still wasn't clear on the rules covering what qualified a person to play in a competing team. Who knew what story Eric had told the officials when he'd added her name to Haydon's roster?

And, actually, she didn't care how many lies he'd told the tourney organizers because, though she wasn't about to admit it to Eric and give him any sort of satisfaction, she wouldn't have missed today for the world. She was having a blast, more fun than she'd had on a date since, well, since she could remember.

Of course, today wasn't really a date, because she and Eric weren't really dating. But, one friend to another, he was definitely showing her a good time. And, damn the man, she thought, catching his wink from across the court, he knew she was enjoying the game and his company.

"Heads up," Jason called as Lizzy's serve sailed across the court. Pass, set, hit, and the ball skimmed inches above the net, right into Jason's block and back down to the sand on the other side.

The Haydon's team cheered the point and Lizzy readied for her second serve. The opposing forward slammed the return and Eric went flying as he reached for a save. The ball hit his wrist at an awkward angle and popped toward Chloe before she could blink.

Reflexes and adrenaline kicked in and, knees bent, she stepped forward, swung her arms up and jumped, pulling her fist back, swinging her elbow forward, making contact high above her shoulder and...*smack!*

Awkwardly, she spiked the ball, but spike it she did and, in the next second, she registered the point she'd scored and the cheers going up from her teammates.

Wow! How totally cool was that? Especially since spiking had never been part of her game. Jason met her midcourt for a high five. Lizzy shot her a grin and a thumbs-up.

And Eric. Oh, Eric.

Chloe couldn't take her eyes off his approach. His smile was crowing and wide. Sweat soaked the neck and chest of his dark navy T-shirt. His eyes flashed with excitement. His stride ate up the ground, long and powerful and determined.

The rush that sent her blood pressure soaring had nothing to do with a player's high over the point. This was about her body reacting to the look in Eric's eye, to his predatory approach, to the reality of being his prey, and the wrenching desire to be devoured.

How unfair that he'd discovered her weakness, her longing to be the light at the end of a man's tunnel. Unaware that he'd done so, he'd tapped into her fantasy of being the only thing a man had eyes for.

She barely had time to catch a breath or wipe the perspiration from her forehead before he was there and his arms were around her waist and she was airborne, her hands on his shoulders for balance as he twirled in a circle.

"Eric! Stop!" She dug her fingers deeper, gouging his muscles and loving the feel of his strength beneath her hands, loving even more the tickle and the warmth of his mouth nuzzling the bare skin of her belly. "You're making me dizzy. I'm gonna lose my breakfast all over your back if you don't stop."

Eric laughed. And he stopped, letting Chloe slide the length of his body to the ground, keeping her close and holding her tightly. "I doubt you have any breakfast left to lose, the way you're playing. You've burned off more than a few stored calories."

Her hands still on his shoulders, she looked into his eyes of beautiful blue. Her breasts tightened in response to his randy grin and the hunger his smile failed to contain. Pressed as she was to his chest, she could hardly hide her body's reaction. "Are you saying I'm fat? That I have an excess of stored calories needing to be burned?"

"Chloe, I swear. You could drive a marble statue to take up the bottle. I'm complimenting your play, princess. But if you can't take it, I see no point sticking around...though the points you're making there beneath your top are just about enough to convince me otherwise.'' He left her with a wink and jogged back to position.

Chloe stuck out her tongue at his retreating back. *Men.* Totally worthless species. Here she was, more hot and bothered over the feel of Eric's hands on her body than the physical exertion, and what did he do? Left her breathless and went back to playing his game.

And what did you expect? That he'd take you down and rip off your clothes in the sand? This was hardly the beach scene out of *From Here to Eternity.*

Ridiculous, really, how her thoughts about Eric seemed to be forever turning to sex. She was wondering too much about what he'd be like in bed, when sleeping with him would ruin any fun they might have. She so despised mornings-after.

So she, too, got back to the game, her concentration once again snagged by the strategy and the play. She kept her eye on the ball, on Lizzy's serves, Eric's blocks, Jason's passes, the rest of her teammates' sets and spikes.

Her feet never stopped moving. She bounced, she shuffled, she jumped. She scooted through the sand. She dived. She assisted, she scored. She sweated until the salt stung her eyes and burned her parched lips.

Then came the final play. She approached the net, crouched, judged her timing and shot into the air for a game-saving block. Scuffed leather hit her palms. Her feet hit the ground.

The ball barely cleared the net and, with the total lack of momentum from her puny impact, fell short of the outstretched hands on the opposite side and plopped into the sand. Cheers went up from her team-mates, and Chloe couldn't help but grin.

Yet for one brief moment she saw nothing but the past—her father in the bleachers, cheering on the sons he'd come to watch play, the sons who'd made him proud, who'd earned his affection with their sports-manship skills.

And Chloe had sat at his side, the fingers of her right hand clapping against the palm of her left, a good little beauty queen, the perfect daughter, smiling…the dam of her clenched teeth holding back a flood of resentment.

Unladylike resentment she'd buried deep in her heart for fear of losing what attention her father did show. She'd taught herself not to care, told herself she wasn't missing a thing.

Oh, but she'd been wrong.

This was exactly what she'd missed, this feeling of shared accomplishment, of belonging.

And even more so, this amazing feeling of being true to herself, of damning propriety and going for broke. Her teammates descended and she couldn't help but smile, her smile broadening at the pride-filled gleam in Eric's eyes.

Daddy! Look at your little girl now. Dirty and sweaty and a hell of a mess.

And happier than she'd been in ages.

CHLOE HAD NEVER BEEN to Eric's house.

And it was a house, a real house, she noted with approval, setting her knapsack on the antique tele-phone table in the entryway. Not a condo or a loft or anything equally trendy, though the two-story, wood frame structure was situated in a renovated historical district bordering Houston's downtown, and qualified as urban chic.

For some reason, she'd always pictured him living closer to Haydon's, as that area of the city drew young urban singles like flypaper. She liked that Eric wasn't just another fly, that he was, from all appearances, one of a kind.

Her mind wandered to the upstairs shower and a singularly spectacular soapy body.... Chloe blinked back her lust. So what if the man was built? It wasn't like she'd never seen abs before. Or like Eric didn't have an equally attractive brain.

Individuality was an appealing trait, and usually meant a fresh approach, a unique outlook, a sense of contentment, and conformity be damned. Eric seemed to have managed resisting the lemming mentality that made clones of men who might otherwise have potential.

He was also the only man in recent memory who took her crap and dished it right back. Which meant she was working harder than ever to top his wit.

But Eric's choice of a traditional home, a place where he'd invested a lot of money, a place where he obviously intended to stay, revealed more about his self-assuredness than anything Chloe had learned spending time in his company. He was confident in who he was, and she envied that.

He'd also been the first man ever to convince her to participate in sports of any kind, though not without resorting to a consensual kidnapping as the means to his end. Considering how she felt about sports and why, that was saying a lot.

For seven years—three during junior high, four during high school—she'd brought home forms for her father to sign giving her permission to play volleyball, to compete at the interscholastic level.

For seven years he'd refused, but that had never stopped Chloe from giving her all during intramurals and busting her ass to learn the game. Neither had it stopped her coaches from beseeching on her behalf.

Her father had put his foot down, insisting men preferred their women cultured and genteel, and no daughter of his was going to spout that feminist equality bullshit and display the aggressive nature of a man.

That insistence had stolen her chances for a sports scholarship. And once in college, where she'd pursued a degree in fashion—a feminine calling that met with her father's approval and terms for tuition—that insistence had hardened her heart toward the opposite sex.

It had hardened her heart, as well, toward anything and everything having to do with sports. Athletic competition represented opportunities lost, reminded her of a dream she'd been forced to abandon.

Until working with Melanie and the other girls at Starbucks during their shared senior year, Chloe had wondered often what was the point…of anything.

She'd kept up her grades to keep her father and his checkbook happy, but she hadn't been able to bring herself to attend a single sporting event during her four years at the university.

Now Eric actually had her playing. And he had no idea what he'd done.

He hadn't automatically stopped at his place following the volleyball tourney. He'd had the courtesy to first ask if she would mind. He needed to clean up and head on to Haydon's, to relieve his assistant manager before the onslaught of Saturday night's madness, he'd explained.

He'd offered to take her back to her car, no problem, but since he lived between Stratton Park and Haydon's, stopping for a quick shower first would save him time. He'd left the decision up to her.

And, as she had nowhere to be and was more than curious to see where he lived, she'd done her best to hide her nosy nature and told him to feel free. And now that she was here, with Eric upstairs in the shower, she was the one feeling free...to snoop around his first floor.

The house was large and the layout airy, as if Eric had remodeled a maze of smaller rooms into a windowpane design with four main rooms of near equal size. What Chloe supposed were areas to be used for formal living and dining were remarkably plain.

Both rooms faced the street, the front door acting as a divider between. A staircase rose to the second story from the main hallway cut down the center of the bottom floor. The furnishings were of good quality, but could easily have been purchased from the showroom floor of any department-store display.

Eric had breathed no hint of life, none of his self into either room. That made Chloe curious, even as she recognized that the kitchen and the fourth room were the ones that told her the most about him.

In what had to be the space where Eric spent most of his time, the only room on the first floor that looked lived in, a plush sectional in brushed blue corduroy formed a half-moon in front of a big screen TV.

The walls displayed a dozen framed prints, brightly colored abstract visions of sports figures in action, computer enhanced to simulate motion. Copies of *Sports Illustrated* and *Men's Health* were fanned haphazardly over the surface of a low, square coffee table.

Behind the curve of the sectional sofa was what had to be Eric's home gym. A space-age treadmill and all-in-one weight-and-resistance apparatus faced a massive stereo system. Chloe smiled, because she could so relate. Blasting music made it a hell of a lot easier to force the body through the burn.

But the kitchen where she now stood wasn't what she'd expected to find in the home of a guy Eric's age. Though, for Eric, the stainless-steel luxury made perfect sense. She knew he was responsible for a lot of the specialty items served on Haydon's menu, though he continually tried to talk everyone he knew into doing his cooking for him. So, picturing him in this room, slicing and dicing, simmering and frying, required no stretch of the imagination.

It was a chef's wet dream—gleaming silver-toned appliances, cabinet and drawer fronts in shiny black, countertops in white marble. It was also unbelievably spotless. Chloe wasn't sure even her kitchen would measure up, though she rarely used the grand space she did have for more than toasting bagels and chopping fresh veggies. Her food routine could use a little shake-up; she just never seemed to have the time.

She'd have to see about talking Eric into cooking for her one of these days, she thought, peering into his refrigerator to check out the contents. She had skipped lunch, after all, burning the energy of a carb bar while on the volleyball court. A little nourishment wouldn't hurt. Especially with her body screaming, ''Feed me!''

''See anything you'd like?''

At Eric's question, Chloe slowly straightened and turned. She'd been about to ask if he had time to whip up a late afternoon lunch, or an early evening dinner, but he stood there wearing nothing but a head of wet hair and a knee-length towel around his waist.

Her hunger shifted, stirring her blood and her interest.

She saw a lot worth liking. He was fantasy delicious, with his hair endearingly spiky and messy, as if he'd tumbled straight out of bed. His chest was lightly sculpted and bare of hair, with more than a few drops of leftover water she longed to lap from his skin.

That reaction surprised her, coming as it did from a place she hadn't thought she was ready to visit. A place, in fact, she'd told herself to avoid. But now that he was standing here half-naked, she had trouble remembering why enjoying his body was such a taboo.

His towel was actually nothing more than a wraparound length of terry cloth held in place by a wide strip of Velcro. The imaginary rip of the two sides separating zipped down nerve endings already tingling and charged.

She gestured at the refrigerator, the door standing open, the air cool on her back. Cool was nice. Cool she needed. "A couple of things look pretty good. I could go for that lemon cheesecake."

Or the bottle of chocolate syrup and your skin.

Eric moved a step closer, his smile white and beaming, his bare feet a sexy slap against the floor's black-flecked white tiles. He kept his gaze locked on hers, the distance between them growing sliver-width slim until with every breath she inhaled Chloe learned Eric's scent.

Beyond soap and shampoo, she smelled warmth and the intimate essence of skin. He lifted a hand, reached behind her into the fridge, so close she could count the freshly scrubbed whiskers he hadn't bothered to shave and, when she looked down, the thatch of hair in his armpit.

He grabbed the bottle of water he was after, his mouth lingering near her ear to say, "You smell great."

"Oh, please!" She smelled like stink and sweat. "You're out of your mind."

Grinning, he shook his head, regarding her while holding the bottle in one hand, twisting the spout with the other. "You smell like fresh air and sunshine."

"And salty sticky skin." She was glad, at least, that she hadn't played in her jersey. It still smelled marginally clean.

"You know, princess, when you were learning all my secrets during Macy's scavenger hunt, you should've asked about aphrodisiacs."

Again he leaned in close, this time nuzzling the patch of skin beneath her ear. His breath warmed her there, where he lightly blew on her neck. Then he pulled away, winked and squirted a mouthful of water from the bottle.

Oh, but this was so unfair. Chloe hadn't yet recovered from the brush of Eric's hair beneath her chin, or the smell of all that clean male skin as he'd reached beyond her for the water. And now he was teasing her, heightening her senses unbearably with a touch she knew meant nothing.

What she *did* know was that she really needed to shut the refrigerator door before the food inside suffered from exposure to the room's temperature and that of her body. But the cold air at her back was like the touch of an ice cube on sizzling skin, and she needed to ease the burn.

When the water spilled from Eric's mouth before

he could swallow, when the trickle ran from the ridge of his chin down his neck to the hollow of his throat, when a single rivulet squiggled down the center of his breastbone to his belly, Chloe could barely find her voice to echo, "Aphrodisiacs?"

"I like a woman who's not afraid to sweat. I like the taste of salt on her skin." Eric drank again, dribbled again, again drew Chloe's gaze down his nearly nude body to where the terry fabric at his waist soaked the drizzle from his abdomen.

She refused to allow her gaze to dip any lower. "You're doing that on purpose, aren't you?"

"What?" He asked the question with all innocence, then poured a stream of water into the corner of his mouth, where it wet his lower lip and a whole lot more.

Chloe wet her own lower lip with a flick of her tongue in an effort to slake her uncommon thirst. "Doing that. With the water. Like you think I'm going to clean it up?"

He set the water bottle on the kitchen counter and tore a paper towel from the roll mounted on a silver rod set into the countertop next to the stainless steel stove.

She took the towel he offered, thinking she was tempting fate way too much, with their obvious mutual attraction and her body being so hungry and Eric having so many qualities that belonged to Cary Grant.

But still she beckoned him closer and, with the towel folded into fourths, patted him dry, keeping her fingers from coming into contact with his skin.

It was hard to maintain control, especially when she wanted to touch the flesh she'd felt in the past only through his clothing. She handed him the used paper towel.

He took it, but then grinned and audaciously added, "The towel was for you. In case you needed to dry your mouth. After drinking."

"If you want me to clean you up with my tongue, you'll have to provide a more appetizing enticement." She couldn't help herself. And even after she'd delivered the dare, she felt no need for repentance or for taking it back.

So when Eric once again reached beyond her into the fridge and came away with the same bottle of chocolate syrup that had starred in her earlier fantasy, she didn't say a word. She only lifted a brow and glanced from the bottle, which Eric set on the counter, to his guilelessly wicked blue eyes, before returning her attention to the contents of the fridge.

Without a word, she added a can of whipped topping and a colander of freshly washed strawberries to the syrup sitting on the countertop. That ought to do it, she mused, breathless, finally closing the refrigerator door. After all, she'd always wanted to act out her own food fantasy à la *9¹/₂ Weeks*.

Eric briefly took in her additions to his enticement, then leaned his backside against the counter, his hands curled over the edge on either side of his hips, his feet crossed at the ankle. "Strawberry shortcake?"

Chloe took more than a slight pleasure in the labored rise and fall of his chest. Eric was doing his best to appear calm and collected, at ease, but she wasn't fooled. His hunger was stirred, and the terry wrap at his waist no longer lay flush against his thighs. His excitement was evident, and Chloe's belly clenched and released. Her thighs grew warm and heavy.

She reached for the can of whipped topping, shook it longer than required. But then the point of taking her time was not about ensuring the texture of the cream as much as it was about making Eric wonder and wait.

She squeezed a dollop onto her finger, then licked it clean with the tip of her tongue. Her gaze remained locked with Eric's as she repeated the process, only this time she offered the dessert to him.

He parted his lips and she dragged the flat of her finger down his tongue, leaving the sweetness behind. His eyes flashed at the contact, and again as she returned her finger to her mouth to lick it clean.

She moved closer, putting her body directly in front of his. Wetting first her top lip, then the bottom, she finally squirted a shot of the creamy froth into the bowl of her curled tongue. She pressed the cold foam to the roof of her mouth, where it melted at the contact with her body heat.

"Mmm," she hummed, and held up the nozzle toward Eric. He stuck out his tongue; she swirled a small peak onto the tip. And then, while the cream dissolved in his mouth, while his gaze remained focused on hers, steady and fixed, yet simmering, she shook the can again and drew a half moon over his chest, from collarbone to collarbone.

The chocolate syrup came next.

She squeezed a pool into the hollow of his throat. It ran down to spread out over the thick ribbon of cream. He hadn't moved. He'd done little more than pull in a sharp breath at the first cold contact, but the tic in his rigidly held jaw, the pulse at his temple, his fingers tightly wrapped around the countertop edge were all Chloe needed.

She knew by looking into his eyes what she'd see if she dropped her gaze down his torso to his groin. But she didn't. Instead she moved another step closer, keeping her eyes on his and bringing their bodies within inches of touching. Then she took up the largest strawberry she could find.

She dipped the point of the fruit in the chocolate pooled deeply in a bowl of creamy white. The chocolate topping was thick, but it wasn't minutes from separating under the weight of the sauce. She grinned as she circled the plump end of the fruit with the tip of her tongue, the motion ripely suggestive, especially when she sucked off every last drop of chocolate.

The veins in the back of Eric's hands, the tendons in his arms stood out in bold relief as he maintained a death grip on the countertop. *Very nice,* she thought and, her eyes at a sultry, sleepy half-mast, she pulled the fruit from her mouth, dragged it through both cream and chocolate and offered it up to Eric.

The same fruit she'd had in her mouth and teased with her lips and her tongue.

He bit into the meat, nipping lightly at the tip of her finger, which she then ran over the seam of his lips, down his chin, his neck, teasing the slight bulge of his Adam's apple before sliding through the hollow of his throat and breaking open the dam of cream.

Chocolate syrup ran down the center of his belly all the way to the terry wrap at his waist. She hooked her fingers over the Velcro and tore it away.

Eric's breath caught hard and he nearly choked on the fruit, but he managed to swallow. He also managed not to move, but to stand there naked without saying a word. Oh, how she longed to look down, to get a full view of what her fingers had brushed against. That brief contact eloquently spoke to the state of his arousal.

And she was no less aware and aching. Her panties were damp, her sex awash in a cream warmer than the topping spread across Eric's chest. But she wanted to wait and wonder. To prolong the excitement, making it hard to breathe.

Scooping up a glob of topping with one finger, she painted one well-defined pectoral white. And then she leaned forward, touched her tongue to his nipple, swirling through the sweet mess to find the sensitive disk. Eric shuddered, a tremor that ran the length of his body. Chloe knew she'd hit her mark.

Blindly she reached into the colander for another strawberry and teased the flat male nipple with the tip of the fruit. She squiggled her edible toy through the melting mess of chocolate and cream, drawing a line down the center of Eric's belly, circling his navel.

When she opened her lips over his breastbone, she was the one who was trembling, her breasts swollen and aching, her nipples hard peaks inside her jersey and bra, begging for the touch of Eric's hands. All she had to do was ask, but she wasn't finished with his pleasure.

She kissed her way down his midsection, lapping at chocolate and spots of cream that had slithered down his torso. She dropped to her knees then, sent her tongue chasing the strawberry in and out and around his navel as the head of his cock thrust upward into her chin.

She nibbled lower, nipping at the skin above his thatch of dark hair and moving her hands to his hips and behind to his buttocks, squeezing that solid muscle while she continued to feast, slipping her fingers deeper into the crevice between his legs, her lips drifting lower, blowing warm breath against the skin above his jutting shaft.

The wait was making her crazy, making Eric crazier still. He moved his hands to her head, flexed his fingers in her hair and pretended to be patient while subtly maneuvering her mouth into position.

As if she needed instruction. She knew quite well how to make love to a man, whether using her body or her mouth. Still, very few had enjoyed her oral talents. This particular intimacy was one she saved for the rare man with whom she shared a connection beyond the ordinary.

What that said about her feelings for Eric she wasn't yet ready to examine, even as she took him fully into her mouth.

Eric pulled in a sharp whistling breath and held his thighs rigid. His hands returned to the counter edge for support. He uncrossed his ankles and braced both feet flat on the floor. And still his body shuddered.

Now that Chloe had him where she wanted him, his legs far enough apart for her to get her hand between, she reached back to cup the sac of his balls and hold them down and away from his body. She wanted to take her time. She wanted Eric to take his pleasure, but only when she was ready.

With long strokes of her tongue, she measured the underside of his shaft, concentrating her attention around the ridge of his glans. She took him into her mouth, from tip to base, holding her lips in a firm O as she pulled back slowly over the head until he popped free.

A tremor ran through his body. She felt it in the hand between his legs and in the one wrapped around the base of his shaft. She glanced up briefly, long enough to get a look at his closed eyes, his raised chin and his head, pressed back against the door of the cabinet behind. He blew choppy breaths out through his mouth, and Chloe sensed his slipping control.

And so she let her fingers roam, releasing his sac to play between his legs and explore the places she loved to explore. And he let her, his body taut, his legs stiff, his penis so hard it had to cause a pleasurable pain. How could skin that soft stretch to cover such an enormously hard swell?

A swell that mirrored the one pressing with a vengeance in the region of her heart. Her heart, which wasn't supposed to factor into her association with Eric. She pushed her unwanted reaction away, recognizing the folly of too little too late and returned her concentration to working him with her tongue.

For several more minutes she teased and she played, enjoying his texture, his scent, his responsiveness and his taste. And then she could tell it was time. She knew, just as Eric knew, because he moved his hands to hold her still.

''Either you stop or I'll come.''

But it was already too late. She could tell by the change in his taste and the way his balls had drawn up into his body. She concentrated on the rhythm of her stroke and, as he shuddered, as he groaned, she drew him into completion, easing him through the ecstasy and taking him into the calm.

When she finally let him go, he handed her the damp paper towel she'd dried his chest with earlier. Then he reached for her shoulders and pulled her to her feet.

She didn't know what to say. For the first time in

Eric's company, she didn't know what to say! Not a single comment from her extensive after-sex repertoire came to mind. She was…shy. This was not a good thing. This was, in fact, very bad.

He wore an expression of sleepy amazement, his lids blinking slowly as he smiled. "Come upstairs with me and shower."

She shook her head. She had to get away. "Go ahead. I'll wait till I get home."

"You sure?" Uncertainty was evident in his tentative frown.

Her nod was quick and to the point. "I need clean clothes, makeup, stuff like that. I'll wait."

That explanation appeased him. Men rarely understood or wanted to know what went on in a woman's toilette.

Holding the terry wrap in a strategic position, he backed out of the kitchen toward the rear stairway he'd descended earlier, hesitating with his foot on the first step as if he knew she planned to disappear the minute he turned his back.

She kept a smile on her face, kept her shoulders relaxed, her stance casual, certain he'd call her bluff. *Please, hurry and get the hell out of here already!*

"Gimme five minutes." He glanced at the mess on his torso, then back to her face. "Better make it ten."

"Take your time." She shooed him away, returned the food to the fridge. She refused to look his way again until she knew he was gone.

And, once he was, she ran toward the hallway and grabbed her knapsack from the telephone table on her way out the door. Eric's house sat only blocks from one of the city's Metro bus routes, but Chloe knew she didn't have much of a head start.

Her car was parked at Haydon's. Eric could conceivably shower, dress, fire up those horses and beat her back to the bar. Maybe she'd luck out and not have to wait for a bus.

And maybe she'd luck out even further if Eric woke up to the fact that she'd left for a reason, and let her go without giving chase.

Her luck wouldn't hold beyond tomorrow, unfortunately, because she'd see him at the gIRL-gEAR open house. She would owe him an explanation, one assuring him he'd done nothing wrong, that their kitchen encounter had been her pleasure.

And, oh, had it ever. Her body still tingled and ached. And the fact that he'd asked her into his shower brought a rush of moisture to burn her eyes.

Chloe made it to the closest bus stop seconds before the bus arrived. She climbed the steps, slid her dollar into the meter and settled into the closest blue vinyl seat. She blinked to clear her vision, but regrets were blinding her already.

Not because she'd performed such an intimate act on a man who was no more than a friend, but because she'd thought only of pleasing him, not of any pleasure he owed to her.

She'd been more aroused by this one man's reaction than by direct stimulation from countless other men. And now, because of her, their easy friendship was a thing of the past.

But that wasn't what had her running scared. It was the realization that at some point, while her defenses were lowered, Eric had become more than a friend.

So very much more than a friend.

5

THOUGH THE NEXT DAY'S open house wasn't scheduled to begin until four, noon found Chloe in her office working to clean out her in box.

An in-depth marketing proposal for additions to the gRAFFITI gIRL line of medicated skin-care products was going to take more time to study than she had to spare today. And she couldn't do anything about the lab reports on the perfume trials until tomorrow at the earliest. The rest of the memos were easily handled via instructions jotted to her assistant.

Next she turned to her office e-mail, marking her calendar for the rescheduled partners' meeting now set for next week at Lauren's loft, and wondering, while she did so, if Revlon's or L'Oréal's founders had ever conducted business in gIRL-gEAR's unconventional ways.

Even if gIRL-gEAR was to one day enjoy a fraction of Revlon's or L'Oréal's worldwide success, Chloe doubted she'd be around to share the wealth or the fame. Not if she didn't start using her head instead of using her mouth. Her language was one thing.

But what she'd done in Eric's kitchen? To Eric? The very man who'd agreed to help her salvage her reputation?

This three-events-for-three-wishes business was obviously a big waste of time. One down, five to go, and she'd already proved that she had absolutely no desire to change her bad-girl ways. No doubt Eric had shared the joke with her skeletons, and the lot of them were laughing themselves silly at her expense. She could hear the bones rattling in the closet of her mind.

Oh, wait, no. That was a knock on her door. She looked up while saying, "Come in."

A man entered. Tall and broad shouldered and beautiful, with hair several shades darker than her own. Just as it had always been—well, except for the shoe-black dye job he'd given himself the year he'd gone Goth. The one and only time Chloe could remember their father laying down the belt of Zuniga law across Aidan's back end.

She was out of her chair and around her desk and in her brother's arms before he could take another step into the room. She held him tight. He held her tighter. She didn't know whose heartbeat it was she felt in her chest.

And then she looked up, met his mischief-filled gaze, and the four years since she'd seen him dissolve like mist. The dazzle of his smile rivaled the sweet feel of her own. Oh, how she'd missed him!

"What are you doing here?" She practically squealed the question as he swung her around. "How in the world did you know where to find me?"

Aidan finally lowered her back to the deep purple carpet. He cast a frowning glance around the room, which was decorated in bright candy colors. "You do business in here? And your stomach doesn't heave?"

Chloe punched his arm. "Stop making fun of my office and tell me why you're here. This is so out of the blue."

And it was so wonderful to see him. Ten years older

than Chloe, Aidan had always been her champion, her ally even while he'd been their father's favorite son.

"Blue would've been a better choice, Chloe. You're over the top with the pink." Aidan shook his head, but he didn't stop her from taking his hand and dragging him to one of the visitor's chairs.

Once they were both settled, Chloe having kicked off her shoes and tucked her feet beneath her, Aidan pulled a folded newspaper from the pocket of the tweed sport coat he wore with cowboy boots and worn denim jeans.

A write-up on gIRL-gEAR in the *Houston Chronicle*'s business section. She wondered if anyone else in her family had seen it. She wondered why she cared.

"It would've been nice to hear firsthand that my baby sister is a local celebrity." Aidan's brows arched over his deep leonine eyes.

Chloe shrugged off the charge. "Oh, please. I'm hardly a celebrity."

"You're doing something right to get your name here—" he tapped a long finger against the paper "—instead of in the tabloids."

He had no idea how close she was to becoming a tabloid headline: gIRL-gEAR Partner Blows Her Own Career.

"I'm doing all right. But I want to hear about you." She reached for his hand and squeezed. "What's going on in the world of quarter horses? You can't be doing too badly—those custom-made boots on your feet cost a bundle of hay."

Aidan studied her face for several long moments. His scrutiny unnerved her, because he'd been the only one able to see through her perfect daughter facade, the only one who'd known how miserable she'd been behind her perpetual smile.

She wasn't even sure her smile was fooling him now.

"The boots were a gift," Aidan admitted with a bit of a smirk. "A cowgirl who couldn't get enough of me."

Chloe rolled her eyes. "I see you haven't changed a bit. First it was cheerleaders. Now it's cowgirls. Is there a female alive able to resist your drawl or your charm?"

"Only my sister," he said, holding tight to her hand when she tried to pull free. "What's the deal, Chloe? You wave at me across the lawn at graduation and that's it?"

He was right. She had cut herself off from her family—all of her family—once she'd had her diploma in hand. She'd thought it the easiest way to be on her own. But now, seeing Aidan, she knew she'd been hasty when filing her emotional divorce. Still, all she could do was shrug. "I did what I thought I had to do."

"Well, you thought wrong. I'm your brother, Chloe. I'm not our father. Neither is Colin, Richard or Jay. Dad was never easy on any of us. But, yes," Aidan added, when her hackles began to rise, "he was especially hard on you."

He was hard on me because he wanted me to be her. Bitterness began to seep into this moment where it wasn't wanted. "Thank you for noticing."

"I noticed. You know I did." He reached up to cup her cheek. "And even after I left home, I kept up with what was going on. The boys told me. So I knew."

Chloe turned her head away from his touch. "You

knew what they told you. You didn't know what it was like. How hard I worked to please him. How I never got it right.''

Aidan shifted in his chair to sit forward, bracing his elbows on his knees and turning so he could hold both of Chloe's hands. He studied her fingers, her short practical nails painted in Porcelain Prankster.

She wanted to ruffle her hands through his hair the way he'd always ruffled hers. But to do that she'd have to let go. She didn't want to have to let go.

And then Aidan looked up. ''Here's the thing, Chloe. I do know what it was like. Colin, Richard and Jay…they were too young to remember. But I saw how Dad was with Mom. I saw it over and over for the ten years I had her.''

His grip tightened almost painfully. ''And I've lived with the guilt for years.''

Watching his throat work scared the hell out of Chloe. She jerked her hand away and stood, her bare toes curling into the plush carpet. ''What're you talking about?''

He continued to sit forward, he continued to study her face. ''I'm talking about leaving home the first chance I got and letting Dad treat you like he did Mom. I'm talking about reputation versus fact. Fantasy versus reality. Our mother was never the flawless ideal Dad led you to believe. That's what he wanted her to be, yeah. But what he wanted would've been impossible even for a saint. Though God knows she tried.''

Chloe shook her head in a dazed denial she wasn't even aware of making. The world as she knew it had turned into a carnival house of mirrors.

''It's true, Chloe.''

She waved him off, then cupped her hands over her

ears so she wouldn't have to hear any more. "This doesn't make any sense. He worshipped her. All I heard for seventeen years was how perfect she was."

"And she was," Aidan agreed in a reverent tone, his gaze warmed by memories. "As far as I was concerned, she was. But to Dad…" His focus sharpened. "She never had a chance of pleasing him. She was human. Just like you are."

Chloe started to pace, her bitterness welling to spill free in a flow of words. "When I argued with him about volleyball, he threw it in my face that my mother never questioned his decisions.

"When I wanted to major in phys ed, he told me she would never have pursued anything unladylike even if she *had* considered working outside the home…which she hadn't because her only interests were home and family. She never smoked or raised her voice, and she certainly didn't drink. He let me know all of that when he caught me smoking and drinking and cussing up a storm."

Aidan reached out a hand and snagged her wrist when she next passed by. "When she swore, he took away her car keys. When he caught her in his whiskey, he cut up her credit cards. When she told him that she'd enrolled in business classes at the community college, he told her she'd never pass. Why humiliate herself and him?"

Chloe had lost all feeling in the hand Aidan gripped, as well as in the rest of her limbs. Her heart, suddenly bruised and aching, had stolen all sensation. "You saw this?"

"I saw. I heard. But I didn't realize it qualified as verbal abuse until I was out of that dysfunctional house." Aidan shrugged and let her go. "It's a lousy excuse, but the only one I've got."

Chloe sank back into the chair beside her brother. "Well, fuck me."

After a minute, Aidan chuckled. "Nice, little sister. Very nice."

The words were barely out of his mouth before Chloe whipped her head around. "Why the hell did she stay with him?"

"I can think of five reasons, all under the age of ten."

Five children, and tied to a man who set impossible standards. No wonder her mother had adored Cary Grant. She had to have been miserably unhappy, forced to surrender her identity, her individuality. Having no control over a life that should have been her own first, shared with her partner second.

Chloe sighed and closed her stinging eyes, struck by the irony that, in the end, she'd done exactly what her father had wanted her to do. She'd become her mother, giving up who she was to earn her father's love.

She'd broken free, yes, but to become what? A wisecracking ball-buster her father would despise.

A woman Chloe wasn't too crazy about herself.

"I can't deal with this right now. I don't have time to deal with this right now." She shook off her tears and sat up straight. She had to get through the open house before she could even begin to deal with all of what Aidan had said.

"Are you staying at the Doubletree?" It was where she'd always known him to stay, he'd never stayed at their father's home when he'd come to town from his place near San Antonio.

Aidan got to his feet, gave her his room number. "Seven o'clock?"

"Perfect. And have your bags packed. You're coming to stay the night with me."

TIRED OF WAITING for Chloe in the gIRL-gEAR lobby and having already mingled for fifteen minutes with the rest of the open house attendees, Eric finally went in search of his nondate date.

He found her in her office, her back to her desk, her arms wrapped around her middle, one finger pressed to the tip of her nose as she stood staring out her first floor window onto Kirby Drive.

He leaned a shoulder against the door jamb, shoved his hands into the pockets of his khaki Dockers. The tails of his navy sport jacket flared around his wrists. He couldn't help but take a deep, steadying breath.

He'd never expected her to make him feel anything but the flirtatious affection so natural to their friendship. But he was feeling more now. More that he didn't want to acknowledge, because it would make him a sap. A whipped sap. And no man with any self-respect allowed himself to be whipped by a single blow job.

The thought of her mouth made him weak. But he'd long since learned that he wanted more from sex than the obvious fun. He wanted a connection, a woman to touch him in more than the physical way. He just wasn't sure Chloe was that woman. Not if she only had it in her to see man as the enemy.

If they didn't have anything going for them as a couple beyond the banter, the innuendo and the sex, then she was right that this time spent together was nothing more than a favor between friends. Eric had

hoped it might be more. He'd wanted for a long time
to discover the source of their sparks.

The gIRL-gEAR offices fronted on an east-west
cross street rather than onto Kirby Drive, so he knew
she wasn't watching out the window for him to pull
into the front parking lot. He wondered what she was
thinking because, though she faced away, at an angle,
he could sense her pensive demeanor from the stiff set
of her shoulders and hips.

She wore a flowing dress, pink, of course, a floral
print that draped loosely over her lower body, hugging
her waist and her bustline, yet teasing more than revealing most of her amazing curves. The hem, a
flouncy type of ruffle thing matching the ruffled collar,
hit just above her knees. Her legs were bare.

And that played perfectly into Eric's plans to pay
her back for yesterday's kitchen encounter.

When he'd come downstairs from his second
shower, fully dressed and ready to deal with the conversation they needed to have about what was going
on between them, he'd wavered between disappointment and relief when he'd found Chloe gone.

It really didn't surprise him that she'd hoofed it.
She'd been in a strangely prickly mood since they'd
left the park. He'd wanted, on the drive back, to ask
what was on her mind. He knew she'd enjoyed the
volleyball tourney. No denial she could possibly make
would change his opinion on that.

But she hadn't said anything at all. She'd just stared
out the car window, a funny sort of thoughtful crook
to her mouth, as if trying to remember why she'd held
such a grudge against sports in the first place. Or re-
playing the reason and finding it no longer held much
water.

Sooner or later he'd get to the bottom of yesterday's disappearance. He'd also figure out why she'd been so adamant that they keep their exchange of favors non-sexual, then had stripped him naked in his kitchen the first time they found themselves alone.

Today, however, he had his first part of their three-part bargain to uphold.

And a self-made promise to keep.

"Tell me something, Chloe."

She gave a start when he spoke, pulling in a gulp of air and shaking off the surprise before turning calmly from the window and offering him her usual chop-busting smile. "Anything you want to hear, sugar."

Facing him now, she wrapped her fingers over the waist-high headrest of her funky mesh ergonomic chair. It was a telling sort of movement in that she deliberately kept the chair between them instead of moving to the door to link her arm through his and join the reception in the lobby.

"What help am I going to be to your reputation if you hide out in your office instead of mingling and giving the press the sound bites they're here for?" He stayed where he was, his pride preferring she make the choice to come to him.

She didn't move except to tilt her head slightly to the right. The curved ends of her white-blond pageboy brushed her shoulder. "Actually, I was trying to decide if staying in here wouldn't be the smartest thing to do. Especially since any best foot I might put forward is still recovering from yesterday's sandblasting."

"A tough cookie like you? Done in by a little sand?" Eric gave a snort. "I don't believe it."

Chloe narrowed her eyes until the barest sliver of violet peeked through the slits of lashes and lids. "I am not a tough cookie."

"Princess, you are the toughest cookie I know. You don't take crap from anyone. You know what you want and you go for it." He paused, struck anew by the thought that she'd certainly gone for what she wanted in his kitchen. "Besides, you spike a hell of a volleyball. And that can't be said of a marshmallow."

"That spike was pure luck and you know it." Her mouth twisted into a cute but still only halfhearted grin.

He wanted to see her smile. The way she'd smiled yesterday on the volleyball court, full of more life than he thought he'd ever seen…even more than he'd seen when she'd been in his kitchen.

A particular truth he could've done without. So much for making a big first impression. "Maybe. Maybe not. One thing I do know is that you don't hate sports quite as much as you've been trying to convince me you do."

"Don't be so sure." She swiveled her chair back and forth, back and forth. "But don't think the way I feel means I don't know how to play."

"I know you know how to play. I was there, re-member?" And Eric still wanted to take a bat to who-ever it was who had burned this girl so badly. "So, do you want to join my team?"

"Permanently?"

"Why not? We're a sort of self-contained league. Sports bars. Restaurants. Friendly competition that has nothing to do with business. We bowl, play volleyball, softball. All in the name of fun, and the losers buy the beer."

"Ouch. A double whammy."

Eric shrugged. He was still having trouble reconciling Chloe with "permanently." "Whaddaya say?"

"I'll keep it in mind," she said, and then she frowned and asked, "Don't the members of your team have to have a connection to Haydon's? How did you manage to sneak me past the officials yesterday?"

"I told them we were lovers."

Chloe's chair came to a total stop. "You told them what?"

Eric moved into the office, closing the door most of the way with one hand, but with a gentle shove so Chloe wouldn't feel physically trapped. Like it or not, it was time for that conversation she'd run out on yesterday. "Actually, I said you and I were seeing each other, which is the truth. Especially now with the way things have changed…"

Reaching her desk, he let the thought trail off and waited for her ball-busting denial that their relationship *had* changed. What he got instead was a thoughtful silence and a lazy consideration from eyes boldly enhanced by eye shadow in shades of dark blue and pink.

Her irises were deep violet and her pupils flashed with what instinct told him was the memory of holding him inside her mouth. Eric stirred at the thought. He'd stirred every time he'd thought of her the past twenty-four hours.

But even before she'd wrapped her lips around his dick and made him come, he'd reacted much the same way. Yesterday's blow job had just put a new twist on an already tightly wound tension between them.

She rolled her chair beneath her desk, walked around the far end and propped a hip on the corner.

Arms crossed, she swung that one dangling foot, her skirt hiked halfway up her thigh…which wasn't doing much to keep Eric's mind on the here and now. He lifted his chin, kept his gaze locked on hers.

"In what sort of way have things changed?" She asked the question with all sincerity, or with such well-veiled sarcasm she had him fooled dead to rights.

Either way, she was toying with him rather than giving him a straight answer. She wanted to play? Fine. He'd play her until she begged him to stop.

He took a step forward, trailing his index finger along the edge of her desk. "Do you really want me to answer that?"

"That depends, sugar." Her voice was low, both in tone and in volume, a husky, seductive whisper complementing the low sweep of her lashes. "Do you think you have an answer?"

Oscar-caliber performance aside, her shy act was still an act. And he was not about to let her get away with ignoring what they'd done. "An answer other than the obvious? I mean, it's not like every woman who comes into my kitchen gets fed my strawberry shortcake."

She didn't even bat an eye. "Now that I find hard to believe."

"Why? You think because I'm a man I can't say no to a woman?" Not that he ever had, but he could. Though he wasn't sure how he'd feel about saying no to this one.

"You're a man. You're predisposed to say yes." Her arms remained crossed. Her foot continued to swing.

Amazing. Absolutely amazing, the workings of this

woman's mind. "Believe it or not, Chloe, not all men are ruled by the head of their dick."

"Oh, I know that." She swept her hair from her face with her fingers, then waved her hand to make her point. "Sure, you use the head on your shoulders. Then, with a little luck and enough votes to win the election, you turn the program back over to the head in your pants. Face it, sugar. From D.C. to Hollywood to Houston, Texas. Men will be men."

"You're serious, aren't you?" He crossed his arms and stared. "You really don't think a man has any control over his baser instincts."

"Not as much control as a woman has."

"Over his or over hers?"

She lifted both brows. "Both."

"You think it's easier for a woman to seduce a man than for a man to seduce a woman?" When she looked at him as if he'd lost his mind, he said, "Scratch that. What I mean is, do you really think a man can't break a woman's self-control as easily as a woman can break a man's?"

She laughed. "Oh, sugar. Don't make me laugh, using self-control and man in the same sentence like that. I have never met a man I couldn't bring to his knees."

Eric wasn't going to debate that very real possibility. "But you are rarely brought to yours."

She straightened her swinging leg, examined the skin of her kneecap. "Nope. Not a single carpet burn."

"I wouldn't be so sure." He pointed to a freckle, keeping his finger there on her skin. "If that's not carpet, then it's got to be from the tile on my kitchen floor."

Chloe pressed her lips together, taking a moment before lifting her gaze from her leg to his face. "I might have been the one on my knees, but I was also the one in control."

Well, she had him there. He had certainly demonstrated a total loss. He circled his fingertip over her kneecap. "Tell me something else, Chloe."

Chloe didn't say a word, though she did look back down to the skin-to-skin point of contact. Eric took that as permission granted to move his hand farther up her bare leg. "About that blow job in the kitchen. Why the rules about no sexual contact if you didn't intend to hold up your end of the bargain?"

For a moment, she hesitated, then her chin came up sharply. "My end of the bargain was agreeing to grant you three nonsexual favors. As in, you ask me for them first. You never asked me to sample your…strawberry shortcake. That wasn't part of our deal."

As explanations went, her logic was weak, but Eric couldn't be bothered with more questions. He was too busy taking great pleasure in hearing her voice catch, listening to her breathing grow choppy and shallow.

Control, my ass, he thought, and continued the trip he'd begun at her knee. She had no idea who she was dealing with. Not if she thought she could deliver a fast ball and catch him looking when he was ready to swing.

Reaching the loose hem of her dress, he walked his fingers beneath the edge of the material and up the smooth skin of her thigh. His hand lingered, and when she didn't move a muscle, when she didn't say a word, when she didn't let go of the breath he'd heard her pull in, he took a bold step into her space.

He moved his hand in a slow caress up her thigh to her hip, watching her pupils widen, her lips softly part to draw air into her lungs as he approached the strip of elastic that served as the waistband of her thong.

Touching her skin was like feeling that slide of whipped cream and chocolate all over again. A sensation of exploring the forbidden, sharing the rush of blood and the rise between his legs with the very woman making him ache.

His palm skimmed over her belly and she adjusted her perch on the edge of the desk, spreading her legs a bit wider, her weight balanced between the one foot she had on the floor and the hand she'd braced flat on the desk at her side.

She lifted her chin. Her eyes drifted shut with the arousal that shuddered through her. Anyone peering into the office would see their heads close together in quiet conversation.

What no one could see were Eric's fingertips scraping across the thong's material, his knuckles brushing through the barest strip of hair hidden beneath.

He pulled the thong lower, his index finger dipping down to find her hidden bud and hovering there before sliding to the side of the tight swell and pressing hard.

Her eyes flew open and she looked over his shoulder, her lower lip caught by even white teeth as if to hold back sounds rolling from her belly to her throat.

He heard them all, and he wasn't having any of this looking away business. His dick was throbbing, caught between his shorts and his stomach. But even that satisfaction mattered less than looking into Chloe's eyes while making her come.

He kept his hand in her panties, but lifted his finger away. She squirmed and arched, seeking the return of his touch. A smile drew up a corner of his mouth. He could hardly imagine the intensity of taking her to bed. And it would happen. But not now, not here, not in this room.

This, he thought, rubbing his finger down one ripely swollen lip of her sex and up over the other, taking what he needed of her juices spreading between to ease the friction of his way. This was all that he could think about now. This giving her pleasure like no pleasure she'd known.

Again he reached her clit. Again he stopped, teased with a single butterfly kiss of his finger to her flesh. The hand she wasn't using to support her weight moved to his between her legs.

But he wasn't having any of that, either. Not until he had more than her body's attention. "Look at me, Chloe."

She gave a tiny shake of her head. "I can't."

He made as if to pull his hand free from her hold and from her panties. But her fingers, so small, so cool, so insistent on his, made it hard to stick to his guns.

"Chloe. I'm not going anywhere. I'll give you exactly what you want." To make his point, he stepped closer, moved his lips to her ear and slid one long finger through her wet folds to the mouth of her sex, then deep inside.

She stifled a cry. His erection seized up; the ache became unbearable, the need for release a tension with a life of its own. His plan was going awry.

The sweet reality was she was responding to his touch, *his* touch, her juices flowing for him, her hand holding him and wanting the pleasure he could so easily give. He wasn't sure he wanted to make her wait as much as he wanted to make her come.

He fingered her again, this time slipping both his middle and his index fingers deep into her heat. He used his teeth lightly on her earlobe, bathed the nips with the stroke of his tongue.

"You like that?" His fingers eased in, pulled out. His thumb took care of her clit. "You want more?"

"I want you to make me come." The words were breathed more than spoken.

He felt rather than heard her desperation. One finger pressed forward into the pillow of her G-spot. Her fist tightened over his hand and she shuddered from the inside out.

"Is that what you want? Or maybe this is more of what you need?" He circled his thumb around the hard knot of nerves jutting from between the folds of her sex and drawn as tight as his own erection.

When she whimpered in answer, he found the will to move away and make his demand again.

"Chloe, look at me. I want to see you come. I want to watch your eyes flash. I want to taste it on your skin." Who was he kidding? "I want to bury my face between your legs and smell you. I want you on my tongue."

At that, her gaze cut to his. "Some kind of sweet talker, aren't you, sugar?"

But she kept the eye contact, not even looking away when he slowly started to stroke, moving his fingers to the rhythm of her short choppy breaths. Her eyes expressed everything she was feeling—the fire, the ache, the surprise that she was giving up so much of what he was making her feel.

Putting so much trust into his hands.

What he saw was almost enough to make him believe she was reaching for more than her own completion. That she was giving him a release from his cynicism that anything about this encounter was smart.

She pulled in a sharp breath. He felt it jerk her body away, and then he felt her climax. The walls of her sex clenched around the fingers he had buried deep inside. Moisture rushed down his hand to soak the triangle of her thong.

He vibrated the edge of his palm into the divide of her swollen sex, his fingers feeling her spasms fade even as he pressed his thumb down against her knot of tight nerves. Her own fingertips gouged the back of his hand as she held him still for her finish.

Finally, she exhaled. Her body relaxed even as her disposition stiffened. Seconds ago she'd pulled him close; now she pushed him away, removing his hand from her clothing and straightening the drape of her skirt.

Despite the flush in her cheeks, her brows arched elegantly, dismissively. She cleared her throat. "Well, now that you've gotten that out of your system, why don't you wait for me in the lobby, sugar? I'll be out in a minute."

Eric couldn't believe it. He was standing here with his dick on the verge of exploding, with Chloe's cream all over his hand. He'd just concentrated on giving her the orgasm of her life, and had had a hell of a good time doing it. And now she was blowing him off?

He folded his arms across his chest. "In case you didn't notice, princess, I didn't get anything out of *my* system. Not that I'm complaining. Having you come in my hand was hotter than being inside most other women."

Her deepening flush said she wasn't nearly as cool as her expression implied.

"Still," he added, stepping on eggshells, "you might want to work on being more…"

"Appreciative? Admiring? Full of slavish adulation?"

He frowned. "I'd settle for plain old-fashioned being honest. For some reason you hate to admit that you lost control just now. And that's a damn shame, Chloe. Because if it feels so good for us to lose control separately, think what it would feel like to hold nothing back when we're together."

Walking away after that comment was as difficult for him physically as it was emotionally.

But her turbulent expression made it easier to bear.

6

LAUREN HOLLISTER HAD never forgotten a thing she'd
once known about feeling self-conscious. Still, that
seemed like another lifetime, and she no longer
thought twice about standing alone in a crowd with
nothing but her musings for company.

Here at the open house, she felt completely at home.
She'd already visited with most of her friends, met and
mingled with the firm's employees, spouses and sig-
nificant others in numbers equal to that of the media.

Lingering now near the lobby's receptionist station,
she sipped her champagne and people-watched, getting a secret little kick out of witnessing the profes-
sionalism projected by her gIRL-gEAR partners.

To think these were the same women with whom
she'd discussed bikini waxes and hair-care products
and flavored condoms, with whom she shared tales of
sex gone wrong as well as sex gone right, with whom
she indulged in chocolate and margaritas…though the
latter two definitely not at the same time. Or either
one when she was on a diet.

Like the rest of the gIRL-gEAR partners, Lauren
was confident in who she was and what she wanted
from life. She loved her work in multimedia design
and especially loved being part of the team at gIRL-
gEAR, though she was, admittedly, constantly amazed
by the company's success.

Lauren was lucky, as well, in her friendships, including what she shared with Macy Webb—a friendship that went beyond those bounds. Their bond was that of sisters, and Lauren didn't know what she would've done without her best friend's support over the past two months.

Breaking off her relationship with Anton had been one of the most difficult things Lauren had ever endured. She'd thought the pain of the loss would ease with time. She'd thought wrong.

She'd known that Anton would be here today. Neville and Storey, his architectural firm, had done the remodeling of the gIRL-gEAR office space. She'd known he would be here, but had yet to figure out if that knowing had made it easier or harder to come, to mingle...to see him approached by one woman after another. To see him give each his undivided attention which was so like the Anton she knew.

No, Lauren didn't mind standing alone in a crowd, but now that Macy and Leo had run off—ostensibly to see that her office was in order, though Lauren wouldn't be surprised to find the two of them in one of the rest rooms making whoopee—leaving Lauren at loose ends, she was having trouble keeping her eyes off of Anton and Poe.

Whatever had Sydney been thinking, hiring that woman? A rhetorical question if Lauren had ever asked herself one, because she knew the answer. Annabel Lee's qualifications could've earned her a gIRL-gEAR partnership if there were any to spare, not that the six founding members had ever talked about taking on a seventh.

If the issue was brought to a vote any day but today, Lauren would truly have to weigh what was best for the firm against her own personal feelings for the woman, as well as consider the dynamics of bringing Poe into the long-standing inner circle of six.

If a vote was taken today, however, Lauren's vote would have to be no, because Poe couldn't keep her hands off of Anton. And though Lauren's head had made the decision to end their relationship before it tumbled further into nowhere, her heart had not yet given him up.

Shaking off the unproductive thoughts best saved for what time she decided to earmark for pipe dreams, Lauren drained the remainder of the champagne from her glass. Her own companionship was growing desperately depressing, after all. Now, where was that Web design columnist who'd wanted to talk to her earlier?

''If you're standing here all by yourself for a reason, I'll leave you alone. But if you don't mind the company, then I'd like to stay.'' At the sound of Nolan Ford's voice, Lauren turned and looked up into the steely-gray eyes of Sydney's father.

At six foot one, he was an inch or so shorter than Anton, though he shared the same lean swimmer's build. His hair was cut fashionably short and was dark, a color between brown and not quite black.

The lines spilling out from the corners of his eyes spoke of a life made of mergers and buyouts and initial public offerings. A life that had made him a millionaire. A fantasy life that very few lived and right now appealed to Lauren in ways she'd never imagined.

Until faced with a very appealing reason to stay, she'd had no idea how close to the edge of running away she had come.

''Hello, Nolan,'' she said, and smiled. A smile more

genuine than any she'd delivered so far today. She even breathed a strangely appreciative sigh of relief. "I'm surprised to see you here. I didn't know Sydney allowed you in the office."

Nolan chuckled, one hand holding an empty highball glass, the other tucked deep in the trouser pocket of at least three thousand dollars worth of double-breasted Armani. A tiny bit of gray touched his temples, though Lauren was sure she remembered he was only forty-three.

"What you're seeing is role reversal in action. The good child. The bad parent." Nolan stopped a passing server and offered Lauren another flute of champagne.

She accepted. "Thank you. And, yes. Knowing Sydney? I'd have to agree that good describes a lot of what she's about. But whether or not you are bad? That I'll have to take your word on."

Nolan cupped Lauren's elbow and directed her toward the bar where he ordered a simple club soda and lime. "I suppose bad is in the eye of the beholder. And since Sydney has a case of tunnel vision where I'm concerned…"

He let the sentence trail off, and Lauren so wanted to ask, but Sydney wouldn't. Whatever was between Sydney and her father would stay there until she took their laundry public. "Well, even if you two don't see eye to eye, you do share a remarkable talent for business."

"Like father, like daughter. She might not like the way I handle my dealings, but she can't deny that she inherited my work ethic." He gestured with his drink, making a toast in Sydney's general direction, before turning back to give Lauren a wry smile and his full concentration.

She felt the impact of his gaze and it caught her off guard. For a moment she feared stumbling over her recovery, but she managed to find her verbal footing. "You're proud of her. That's good to see, considering the way things stand between the two of you."

"You're right. I am proud of her." Nolan swirled the liquid in his glass. The ice cubes clinked against the clear crystal. "But I'm well aware that Syd would reject the comparison if she heard me make it. Hell, she'd reject her paternity if she could."

Lauren tried to recall what, if anything, she'd learned through the years about Sydney's mother, but it seemed the only parent she remembered hearing mentioned was Nolan. She even cast a curious glance toward Sydney, hoping it might jar her memory.

But the jolt she received was less about old recollections and more about recently suffered sorrow. Seeing Anton's attention was still captured by Poe, seeing the other woman's hand resting on his shoulder, her fingertips lightly tapping his neck above his shirt collar, Lauren was reminded most of all of her earlier desire to scratch the other woman's eyes out.

She turned back to Nolan, certain her sympathetic smile wasn't entirely convincing in its sincerity. "I'm sorry for the way things are between you and Sydney. I'm sure your estrangement can't be easy. Especially since your involvement in gIRL-gEAR keeps the two of you in contact."

He lifted one Armani-clad shoulder as if to shrug off Lauren's concern. "It's just business. I like to keep an eye on my investments."

"I'm sure Sydney understands that." Though even Lauren didn't believe it for a minute. If Nolan was keeping an eye on anything, he was keeping an eye on his daughter.

"Understands?" He arched a well-shaped brow, meeting Lauren's gaze over the rim of his glass as he drank. Once he'd finished, his mouth gave a self-deprecating quirk. "More like alternately accuses me of not trusting her or of spying."

Why had Lauren never noticed how easily he laughed at himself? And how his ability to do so made him that much more attractive? She grinned, determined to enjoy herself and his company. "And I'm sure you're guilty of neither."

"She's my daughter. I'm guilty of both."

At that, Lauren laughed. "Well, if you've been spying lately, then you've got to be applauding her for the work she's put into organizing our first gIRL-gEAR gIRL competition."

"She has been busy, hasn't she? I understand donations were enough to fund the entire scholarship."

"With money to spare. The response from our vendors was amazing. And the girls who entered..." Lauren shook her head, still blown away by the originality and creativity of the entrants. "Absolutely incredible talent. You should see some of the designs that were submitted. What am I saying? You'll see them at the awards ceremony. You are coming, aren't you?"

Again, Nolan spared a glance at Sydney, frowning slightly as he said, "I'm sure Sydney wishes I wouldn't."

"You have to come." Lauren tilted her head to one side, not sure why she felt compelled to add, "I insist."

Once again cupping Lauren's elbow, Nolan turned her to face him while putting his back to the rest of the room. "Not that it's any of my business, Lauren, but you do know that one of your co-workers is moving in on your territory, don't you?"

Lauren kept her eyes on the bottom of her empty flute—she didn't even remember tasting the champagne—instead of glancing beyond Nolan toward Anton and Poe. "Anton and I aren't together any longer."

Nolan squeezed her elbow before letting her go. "I'm sorry. I had no idea."

Lauren gave a small careless shrug and tossed back her hair. "I wouldn't expect you to know. But don't worry about it. The split was amicable enough. Anton and I are still on speaking terms."

His gaze holding hers, Nolan finished his drink, then continued to consider her silently as he returned his glass to the bar. Lauren brushed off what was a strange discomfort. She wasn't sure what it was Nolan was trying to see. Or if he was looking for the answer to a question he hadn't yet asked.

Finally, needing a viable distraction, something to do with her hands besides threatening to crack the crystal, Lauren set her empty flute next to Nolan's glass on the bar. "I suppose I'd better make a last mingling circle through the room. It's been very nice seeing you again."

Nolan waylaid her by gently trapping her hand beneath his on the bar. "Lauren, would you have dinner with me?"

"Now? Tonight?" Lauren wasn't sure she could remember how to breathe.

He smiled, nodded, leaned forward and whispered into her ear. "Now. Tonight."

"Well, actually, I'd love to." To hell with mingling. To hell with business. To hell with Anton and Poe. She'd just been asked out to dinner by *the* Nolan Ford.

"Great." Nolan glanced at his watch. "I'm going to borrow Sydney's office and make a couple of calls while you mingle. Why don't I give you, say, twenty minutes, and then we'll find a nice seafood dinner and an even better bottle of wine."

Lauren doubted she'd be able to swallow a single bite. "Sounds perfect," she said, because it did.

CHLOE DECIDED THAT even if she managed to restore any public semblance of respectability to her reputation at this afternoon's open house, the save would be offset by her loss of dignity in private. Eric's refusal to keep his distance was wrecking her legendary cool.

Every time she turned, he was there, on her left, on her right, seeming to anticipate her every move and making sure he was there for any assistance she required. He was taking his escort duties too far.

Annoying it was. Chivalrous it was not.

Chivalry required he go away and not remind her constantly, repeatedly—with every touch of his hand to the small of her back, to her elbow; with his insistence on leaning toward her and whispering into her ear—both observations of the room's goings-on and naughty reminders of where he'd had his fingers and his thumb. Of what they'd done in her office.

What they'd done in her office came from no movie she'd ever seen, and she'd been caught totally off guard by the passion, seized by a desire she'd never known. Her hunger had stemmed from a lust that was primal and raw.

A lust for nothing, she told herself, but the physical

bliss that had shuddered from the center of her body. Her own personal earthquake, she thought, and chuckled under her breath at the comparison that was all too incredibly *spot on.*

"Hey, I thought it was my job to humor you," Eric said, his lips almost brushing the shell of her ear, his warm breath stirring her hair.

Chloe lightly shivered and rubbed her hands up and down her bare arms for warmth, certain her nipples were now hard enough to be seen by everyone in the room. "It seems to me what you've been doing is more a case of humoring yourself."

"If that was the case, my hands wouldn't have been on *you.*"

They stood to the left of the receptionist's station in the lobby of the gIRL-gEAR offices. Each of the partners was there, caught up in conversation with various members of the press. This reception was important to Sydney, Chloe knew. Important to the partners as a whole, yes.

But Sydney had a more personal stake on the line involving the company's start-up and her relationship with her father. Those details hadn't been shared, for whatever reason. And until Sydney was ready to talk, Chloe respected her privacy, both as a friend as well as a partner in business.

And it was the latter that concerned Chloe at this moment—this very moment Eric had chosen to start again with the suggestive one-liners that were making her regret she'd ever hatched this scheme.

She considered the bubbly champagne in the flute she was holding. "Your idea of cleaning up my image is going to cause me more trouble than I'm already in."

"Only if we get caught." Eric's dimples deepened and his oh-so-proud-of-himself attitude flashed in his blue eyes as he locked his gaze on hers from over his own flute and drank.

"Well, we didn't. And we won't. Because that is not going to happen again."

Eric's expression went from cocky to crestfallen. "You mean we both get one turn at bat and game's over?"

"Look, Mr. Sports Metaphor." Chloe gestured with her flute, not the least bit fooled by his poor-pitiful-me act. "You're here because of my reputation."

"Which I told you would be safe in my hands." He moved one of said hands to the center of her back, drawing tiny circles between her shoulder blades.

Chloe shivered. His touch was like a hot plate. Coils of heat radiated in ever expanding loops until she was sure she would melt into the lobby's deep-purple carpet. "I think I'd be a lot safer if your hands kept their distance."

"I think you'd be a lot safer if you mingled." He leaned down closer to add, "Standing back here with me is not the best way to avoid attention. You have people curious."

"Curious about what?" she asked, though she was hardly unaware of the pairs of eyes checking her out.

"Oh, you know." He drew a finger the length of her spine, from her nape to the cleft of her buttocks. "What it is you find fascinating enough to allow me to monopolize your time."

She was afraid, at the moment, that if anyone asked, she'd have to admit it was his finger. And, unfortunately, he was right that she needed to mingle. Even more unfortunately, she wasn't sure she could do so and hide the lingering remnants of what she was feeling.

Heat still infused her face. The lace of her bra scraped the sensitive skin of her breasts. Her panties were uncomfortably damp, which meant that anytime she moved her legs she remembered.

She'd give anything to wash Eric and this entire day from her mind. Better yet, blow off this unholy alliance.

But giving up now would only leave her exactly where she'd started. One more one-nighter to add to her fast-and-furious reputation. Except this would be her second date with Eric, wouldn't it? If what they were doing could even be called dating, which it wasn't. And not just mindlessly fooling around, which it was.

"What are we doing, Eric?"

Her question snagged his attention as she'd hoped. He studied her face while she brought her drink to her mouth and took a sip. She had to admit his navy jacket did wonderful things to his bright blue eyes, which in turn, focused solely on her as they were, did wonderful things to her senses. All of her senses.

She could still feel the brush of his knuckles through her panties, hear the catch in his breath the moment he'd brought her to climax. She could still see the swell of the erection she had tasted only yesterday.

His finger began a slow reverse trail up her spine. "What are we doing as in why are we standing here instead of mingling?"

She shook her head, still holding the flute, running the rim back and forth over the seam of her lips.

Eric twisted his mouth into a thoughtful grimace. "What are we doing here as in why didn't we stay in your office where we could be writhing naked by now?''

''Would we be?'' She considered him carefully, frowning slightly, letting her tongue dip into the bubbles of the champagne. ''Writhing naked if we were still in my office?''

''Look at me like that again and I'll be writhing here where I stand.'' He toasted her with the flute he held, bringing his own drink to his mouth.

''How am I looking at you?''

Eric pulled in a deep breath, his eyes flashing brightly as Chloe continued to play with her drink, looking up ingenuously from under her lashes.

''Ah, Chloe. I wish I had time to explain exactly what you do to me with those eyes, even when you're doing it on purpose. Like you are now.'' Having called her bluff, he winked.

Well, poo. ''How did you know—''

''There you are, Chloe,'' sang out a voice Chloe could have gone the rest of the day without hearing. ''I have been looking for you everywhere. The reporter from *Go Teen* wants to talk to you about gRAFFITI gIRL for their fall preview issue. I gave them my outlook, of course, but I don't yet know the specifics on the colors.''

For a very good reason, Chloe thought. Then she took a deep breath, gave Eric a smile that said *This is what I was talking about.* Finally, she turned toward the approaching, or would that be descending, Annabel Lee.

Chloe hadn't been exaggerating when she'd told Eric that Poe had martial arts written all over her. Two or three inches taller than Chloe, the Asian-American woman was all fire and flash.

Her skin was fine ivory, her black hair a study in slashes and sharp angles framing a face both sultry and mysterious. She was a beautiful woman, Chloe had to admit. But Poe's career drive was like fingernails down the chalkboard of Chloe's own aggressive nature.

The two did not blend into a seamless team.

"Poe, I'd like you to meet a friend of mine, Eric Haydon. Eric, this is one of gIRL-gEAR's buyers, Annabel Lee."

Poe eyed Eric. Eric eyed Poe. Chloe could only watch and wonder why she'd bothered to get out of bed this morning.

After shaking Eric's hand, Poe crossed her arms over her chest and raised a confident brow. "I don't think I've seen you with Chloe before, Eric. But it is hard to keep track. Lucky girl has so many friends."

Chloe's temper rolled to the tip of her tongue, but Eric put the brakes on her first bad words of the day with nothing but the smile he delivered straight to her. A smile that said *Leave this to me.*

A smile Chloe felt in the core of her heart.

"Says a lot about her, don't you think?" Eric asked, a protective emotion flashing through his eyes as he moved his gaze from Chloe to Poe. "But since I've known her longer than even I can remember, I'd say I'm the lucky one."

Had another man ever lied for her—not to her, but for her—so beautifully? If Eric wasn't careful, Chloe might start to believe his spin herself.

She patted him on the shoulder and gave Poe a sweet smile. "Eric's not safe to release out into the general public. I have to keep him locked away."

Poe tapped a long pale finger on her bare forearm,

her arms still crossed and pressing her breasts toward the low-cut keyhole neckline in her dragon-red sheath. "I'm quite certain I haven't met a slave before. Shouldn't you be wearing a black rubber suit and licking her feet?"

At that, Eric gave a healthy laugh. "Ah, Miss Lee. I can see you are every bit the firecracker Chloe led me to believe."

"I take that as a compliment. From both of you." She turned her head, glanced to her right. "Chloe, the reporter is near the front door talking to Kinsey."

Chloe glanced over, searching out her partner's long blond hair. Kinsey Gray, no doubt, was chewing off the reporter's ear with her always uncanny predictions for the next fashion season.

"Thanks, Poe. I'll work my way over there." Chloe started to turn away, but she couldn't stop one last dig from falling off the end of her tongue. "You're welcome to come along and hear what Sydney and I have planned."

"I appreciate the offer, but the information will come across my desk soon enough." Poe lifted her chin, her interest caught by something beyond Eric's shoulder. "Besides, I have something I need to discuss with Sydney. You two enjoy the rest of the afternoon."

The other woman spun gracefully away, and Chloe leaned to peer around Eric's body to see what had Poe on the prowl.

"Oh, puh-leez."

Eric followed the direction of Chloe's gaze, blowing out a loud snort once he, too, saw who had snagged Poe's attention. "Should we warn him?"

"Who, Anton? I doubt that he's so torn up after

dumping Lauren that he can't take care of himself."
Besides, Chloe thought, keeping her observations to
herself, Sydney was on hand to look out for Lauren's
interests.

"C'mon, Chloe. You can't tell me the man isn't
suffering. He looks like shit on a stick."

"Yeah. He puts on a good act." And that was another thing. If what Lauren had with Anton wasn't true
love…Chloe glanced around the room, finding Lauren
at the end of the bar in conversation with Macy Webb
and Leo Redding…and Nolan Ford. Interesting.

"Act? What're you talking about?" Eric kept his
gaze trained across the room as he leaned in low. "The
man doesn't even have a clue that Sydney and Poe are
talking to him. He doesn't know anything but Lauren."

"Hmmph." Chloe did wonder. "That would make
him capable of human emotion."

"Men can be, you know."

"Sure," she said with a snort. "Lust, pride, anger,
greed, envy, gluttony and sloth."

"Right. I saw the movie *Seven*. And I also saw
9½ Weeks."

Chloe continued to cut her gaze between Anton and
Lauren until Eric moved to block her line of sight,
forcing her to look up.

"So?" was all she could say. They didn't have to
talk about this here and now, did they?

"So, I'm just wondering how much of what you
project is an act. And how much is the real Chloe
Zuniga. Life isn't like the movies, you know."

"That coming from a man who thinks in sports met-
aphors? Don't point a finger at me, sugar, unless you
can face the three pointing back at you."

Eric looked as if he had much more to say, more that came from a place he wasn't ready to reveal or revisit. A place responsible for the ticket-stub wallpaper in his office at Haydon's. And the need to immerse himself in what for most was a pastime, but for Eric was all-encompassing, from career to home furnishings.

But then his cocky attitude chased the vulnerable glint from his eyes. "Instead of pointing fingers or standing here arguing about whether Lauren or Anton is putting on the better act, why don't we work on your spin since, last I knew, that was the reason I was here."

Yes. That had been the original reason, hadn't it? So when had she come to terms with Eric's insistence that their relationship had changed? And that she wanted him here with her now for reasons not so easily defined?

"Fine," she said, returning her empty flute to the tray of a passing server and resisting the urge to grab a refill or two or three. She was in deep trouble as it was. She didn't need to compound her sins by washing away her worries with wine.

She needed to keep a clear head in order to convince herself she was not falling in love.

7

_____

NOT SURPRISING TO CHLOE or any of the partners, Macy Webb was the last to arrive at the loft she used to share with Lauren for the partners' meeting on Thursday night of that same week. The agenda: to discuss the upcoming gIRL-gEAR gIRL competition.

Having snagged Leo Redding, one of the sexiest single men in the city, Macy had every rhyme and reason to be late to work, to meetings, even to her own funeral.

Chloe, sitting cross-legged in the center of the sofa, didn't even pretend to suppress her envy. "Glad you could drag your butt out of bed to join us."

Macy plopped down in the yellow-and-red-plaid chair, where she still looked at home and still looked like she was about sixteen years old.

She blew Chloe a kiss, even while shrugging an apology at Sydney. "Leo's stuck at a deposition. And you have no idea how many connections Metro makes between here and the condo."

Returning from the kitchen, Lauren walked in on the conversation, carrying a tray loaded down with six glasses, a bucket of ice and a dozen cans of diet soda. She set the load down on the low table she'd added since Macy had moved out. "You could've taken a cab. Or called me to come pick you up."

"You coming to pick me up would've taken twice

as long this time of night. And I'm not going to spend money on a cab when for only a buck—'' Macy held up one index finger "—I can get a ride *and* a show.''

"Eww.'' Melanie grimaced as she leaned from the sofa's corner cushion to reach for a soda, the headset of her cell phone attached to one ear. "That is exactly why I hate the bus. I always feel like I'm risking life and limb.''

"Mel, you are such a wuss. And a techie wuss, which is even worse.'' And she was—a totally girly-girl with more technical knowledge than half the guys Chloe knew. But Chloe loved her for it.

"Watch out who you're calling a wuss, girlfriend, or you might come into the office one morning and find your computer's been hit with a virus.'' Melanie screwed her face into a visage of pure evil. "A really nasty bug. An ugly ol' worm.''

"You gross out over riding the bus, but get all orgasmic over worms and bugs?'' Chloe shook her head. "You scare me, Mel.''

"You should be scared. Very scared.'' Melanie stuck out her tongue.

Chloe did the same, but went one better and blew a loud raspberry.

"Oh, very nice.'' Sydney, walking by, ended up in the direct line of the spray. She reached over and wiped the back of her hand and wrist on Chloe's shoulder.

"She's got to let loose somewhere, Syd.'' Adjusting her glasses on the bridge of her nose, Melanie drew her knees to her chest and sank back into the corner. "All this business of cleaning up her act is turning Chloe into a crank.''

"What do you mean, turning her into? When has

she not been a crank?'' Macy asked, joining Chloe in another round of childish tongue play.

Chloe finally gave it up and huffed. ''If I'm a crank, it's because I'm being forced to deny my nature.''

''I saw you with Eric during Sunday's open house.'' Kinsey picked up a soda from the table and sat down on the floor. ''You're definitely in denial, but it's not about your nature. Your nature was doing its best to indulge.''

''I was going to mention that, Chloe.'' Sydney grabbed a soda of her own and moved to stand behind Macy's chair, where she'd left her briefcase earlier. ''I suppose you have a good reason for this new attachment you have to Eric?''

''Hey, hey. One at a time, if you don't mind. Even a crank can take only so much abuse.'' Chloe chugged her soda straight from the can, no glass, no ice. She'd kill for a shot of bourbon. ''Eric is a friend who's doing his friendly best to make sure my reputation for indiscriminate dating doesn't get any worse. That's it.''

''How do you figure dating such a womanizer is going to do your reputation any good?'' asked Lauren, who'd managed to squeeze into the plaid chair beside Macy.

''It's a temporary exclusivity. He's acting as my escort to prove I can stick with one man, thereby giving me an air of respectability.'' She kept the three nonsexual favors part and the two unplanned sexual encounters to herself. Spouting her own canned spin was bad enough.

''You may be exclusive, but I wouldn't be so sure about Eric,'' Kinsey said. ''I saw him the other night at the Daiquiri Factory.''

"On a date?" Chloe couldn't believe how hard it was to ask that question with a level voice and a straight face. Or how it set off a burn in her stomach.

Kinsey shrugged. "I don't know that it was a date. He was with a big group. But the women on either side of him? Neither one could keep her hands to herself."

Chloe shrugged and silently swore that next time she saw Eric she'd kill him, then set him straight. "Like I said. This is temporary. And he's acting."

"If he's having trouble keeping it zipped, this arrangement is going to blow up in your face." Sydney circled the chair, now full of Macy and Lauren, and moved to the free end of the sofa. "But I do appreciate that you're making the effort."

"You know, Chloe. I could rig up a WebCam at Haydon's if you wanted to keep an eye on Eric while he's working." Melanie twisted her mouth as she thought. "Of course, I'd have to think up some story to tell him."

"Thanks, Mel, but a WebCam wouldn't do me any good anyway, unless you wired it into his pants." Chloe's comment elicited a round of groans and giggles. "And that would be a case of too much information, I'm afraid."

"Oh, speaking of too much information." Sydney turned her gaze on Macy. "Could you and Leo please confine your bathroom antics to bathrooms other than the ones at the office?"

Macy's blush barely registered beneath her just-back-from-a-hedonistic-Acapulco-weekend tan. She did manage to cringe. "Leo swore he locked the door."

Sydney's shapely blond brow lifted. "Obviously any man with a tush that cute cannot be trusted."

Macy's blush deepened. "I'll tell him you sent your compliments."

"Oh, fine." Chloe could only shake her head. "Macy does the bathroom boink and earns compliments. I get Eric to act as my escort and I get nothing but grief."

"Okay, Chloe. Eric has a great ass, too." Melanie's critique sent the girls into another round of whoops and whistles.

Chloe buried her face in the arms she'd crossed over her updrawn knees. Hopeless. Totally hopeless. All this talk of boinking and butts was not the way to keep a straight face. Not when thoughts of Eric's naked body and the many ways she could enjoy his offerings were never far from her mind.

"Ooh!" Melanie leaned over, lifted a lock of hair away from Chloe's face. "Chloe's blushing."

"This is not blushing," Chloe said, straightening up in her seat. "This is the color of my blood pressure skyrocketing under stress."

"What stress?" Kinsey asked.

"The stress of trying to be who I'm not," she grumbled. Hadn't she been doing just that for most of her life? When was she ever going to get to be who she was without worrying that her behavior might offend or displease?

"Oh, it's not that bad." Kinsey waved one hand, her many silver rings flashing. "It's just a redirection of your focus and energies."

Chloe glared. "I swear, Kinsey, you'd better not go all cosmic on me."

"Anyone going cosmic, or *anywhere,* for that mat-

ter, just forget about it. We have work to do." Having
dug six bound portfolios from her briefcase, Sydney
passed one to each of the women and kept one for
herself. She perched on the edge of a sofa cushion,
surrounded by the group.

"These are the six scholarship finalists. Each of you
will find the profile of the contestant you selected from
the first round of entrants you judged. You'll also find
profiles of entrants the rest of us chose. The awards
ceremony is next Saturday night, which gives us over
a week before deciding who will be our first gIRL-
gEAR gIRL."

"We're not judging just on these profiles, right?"
Macy asked, flipping through the pages. "We do get
to see the final round of designs, and meet the girls
on Saturday."

Sydney nodded. "Also, the finalists have all been
contacted and have sent in videotapes. I'll have a television set up in the conference room by tomorrow."

"Cool. We can use these portfolios like program
guides for taking notes," Macy added.

"Exactly. The portfolios have been put together to
help you get to know each of the girls. They include
the original questionnaire the girls filled out, the ba-
sics, really, on who they are, where they come from,
etcetera," Sydney clarified.

"You'll also find their essay explaining why
they've chosen fashion as their field of study, as well
as the pictures and descriptions of their submissions
in the school wear, casual wear and business-wear cat-
egories. The formal wear they'll model live at the ceremony."

Lauren nudged an elbow into Macy's side. "Macy,

if you'd come to the office once in a while you could keep up with what's going on.''

Macy pouted. ''Hey, I have e-mail.''

''Then read it, because this was all spelled out months ago when we established the scholarship competition.''

''Go easy on her, Syd,'' Lauren said. ''Months ago her mind wasn't mush from being in love. Now every brain cell is hopelessly devoted to Leo.''

At Lauren's comment, Chloe began humming the chorus of ''Hopelessly Devoted to You,'' the Olivia Newton-John version from the movie *Grease*. Melanie joined in with the words, and Lauren followed, both scrambling to their feet and swaying back and forth, hands together beneath their chins as if in prayer.

Macy added her voice to Chloe's hum, a sort of doo-doo-doo mouth instrument that Kinsey echoed another octave higher. Sydney could only sit and wait for her once again unruly crew to finish their ode to men.

Chloe decided it was time Sydney loosened up. Pulling her to her feet, Chloe linked their hands together, swung their arms to and fro, finally drawing Sydney into a circular dance around the room.

And then, as the impromptu girl group reached the end of the song, Sydney joined in, her voice clear and strong and full.

Melanie stopped singing long enough to gasp, ''Sydney! Why haven't you ever told us you could sing?''

Sydney shrugged one shoulder and barely finished the end of ''Hopelessly Devoted'' before launching into the middle of ''You're the One That I Want'' by shaking her finger and belting out, "You better shape up."

Lauren and Melanie again joined voices to provide backup, echoing the words, "I need a man," and Kinsey adding a lot of what sounded like high energy doo-wop.

Chloe, by now, had stopped dancing and had perched on the arm of the sofa. She watched the antics of her friends with a smile on her face. What did she have to worry about?

She had friends who loved her, friends she loved in return. And she'd get through this temporary crisis of career and of self with their help. What more could a girl ask for?

Even as she fortified herself with the strength of her friendships, she looked over to catch the strangest look on Macy's face. It was almost as if she were pulled between staying and having fun with her friends, and wanting to rush home to Leo.

A month ago Chloe's cynical side would've reached across the room and given Macy a shaking. But right now, what Chloe felt for Macy was kinship.

Because the person Chloe wanted to see more than anyone else in the world was halfway across town, serving up chips and salsa and cold draft beer.

A WEEK HAD PASSED since the partner's meeting, and almost two full weeks had crawled by since Chloe had last heard from Eric. Rather, since she'd last *seen* Eric Sunday afternoon a week ago at the gIRL-gEAR open house.

She *had* heard from him. He'd called. Twice at the office. Three times at home. Never for any particular reason. Only, as he'd told her, to say hello, to check up on her, to see how she was doing.

The sort of things friends called friends to find out.

Chloe wasn't used to having a man call just to talk. Men called. And men talked. But rarely did the conversation end before they'd ask about getting together, then ask about the bee that had flown up her butt. Because lately she hadn't been particularly kind when saying no.

She sighed, realizing how long it had been since she'd even cared about going out with anyone, and wondering why Eric never called to do more than talk. And why that should bother her in the first place, when all she wanted from him was the friendship he was giving.

Most of all she wondered why she was wasting time letting her mind wander, and procrastinating when she'd promised herself she wouldn't leave the office today until she'd answered the letter on her desk.

She'd printed out the e-mail submitted through the Web site to gRAFFITI gIRL's feedback forum. Each week she did her level best to answer every letter she received, often combining similar queries and offering one cover-all-bases answer. It was the only way to keep up with the volume of mail requesting makeup and accessory advice.

Lately, the number one topic was the prom. And Chloe had to stop herself from popping off and telling the girls that dolling up to impress a boy was such a waste of time. But she managed to keep her mouth shut and remember that a lot of the dolling up was done to impress—and out-doll—other girls.

Whatever. It was all so pathetically shallow, anyway. Especially when Chloe considered the letter she could quote verbatim sitting on her desk, the letter whose author would not be going to any prom. The letter that was less of a search for skin-care advice and more of a cry for help.

Chloe wasn't sure she had it in her to answer.

Her office phone, colored like a cherry lollipop, chose that minute to ring. The distraction was welcome, even more so when she picked up and heard Eric Haydon's voice on the line.

"Did I catch you at a bad time?"

"You caught me needing a break." She needed time and a clear head to answer the letter.

"Kinda late for a break, isn't it? I figured you'd be about ready to head home."

Chloe glanced to the right of her office door where, hanging on the wall, which was papered with a textured white weave, the bright purple clock, three feet long and shaped like a wristwatch, told her she'd been here eleven hours already.

"What can I say? A girl's work is never done."

"You the only one still there?"

Chloe listened. "No. Someone else is here. Either Sydney or Poe, I imagine."

Eric chuckled. "You want I should rescue you from the clutches of the dragon lady?"

Smiling to herself, Chloe began to doodle in pink ink on the letter she'd yet to get out of her mind. "I think I'm okay. Poe's been fairly mellow this week."

"A dragon prone to mood swings. Hmm. At least promise me you'll keep out of her fire-breathing range."

Chloe sketched a long tongue of flame. "Why, Eric. Sugar. I'd almost think you cared."

"Just keeping an eye on my end of this bargain. I

don't want you toasted to cinders before I even get my second wish.''

What she didn't want to tell him, because it would mean she believed it herself, was that even remembering the exquisite stroke of his fingers set her to smoldering. ''You'll get what's coming to you as soon as I get mine. Saturday night is the gIRL-gEAR gIRL ceremony. Then I have the Wild Winter Woman fashion show in another couple of weeks.''

''That's what I wanted to talk to you about.''

Chloe didn't even wonder if she'd imagined the slight hesitation in Eric's voice. She knew. And she waited for him to tell her he'd changed his mind and was dumping her before they'd reached the end of their bargain.

''I know I'll see you this weekend. But I really think I should get my second wish before you get your second shot at my escort service.''

Hmm. Typical greedy man. ''Not that we agreed to take turns here but, okay. You can go next.''

''Great,'' he said, and this time what she heard was both relief and anticipation. A tiny flutter tickled the pit of her stomach.

''Chloe?'' he asked, so seriously, so properly and politely, that she had to respond in kind.

''Yes, Eric?''

''Would you like to go out with me Friday night?''

''You mean, on a date?'' This was his second wish? A date?

''Yeah. I was thinking of dinner and a movie.''

''I see,'' she said, drawing the letters *E-R-I-C* into the dragon's devouring flame. ''Forgive me for doubting your boast, but I seem to remember you bragging about how much fun you'd be to go out with. And then you ask me to dinner and a movie?''

"Aha! But I didn't say a word about taking you back to the bedroom."

Chloe remembered telling him that the bedroom was usually part of any date she was offered. She wondered why he hadn't offered. "Would you if I wanted you to?"

Eric was quiet for more than a few beats of Chloe's heart. ''What are you suggesting here, Chloe?''

"I'm not necessarily suggesting anything, sugar. Just doing a little bit of thinking out loud."

"Well, do you want to turn up the volume? Because I'm on my cell and I'm getting lousy reception."

Chloe laughed. "If you're not picking up, it's because I'm not broadcasting. Forget I said anything. Now, what about this date?"

"To hell with the date. Let's talk about the bedroom.''

"And, just like a man. He blows off the romance the minute he sees a chance to score. Is your laydar standing at attention?''

"Actually, no. Right now I'm all-ears. What's going on with you, Chloe?''

She sighed. She *was* out of sorts and he'd sensed it, and that had her sighing all over again. And wanting to use him as a sounding board. Which was a sign she was thinking of him as more than an escort.

"I'm working on answering a letter Macy forwarded me from the site. A girl, asking for advice, and I'm at a loss."

"And you're taking it out on me."

"I hadn't intended to, but maybe I am. And I apologize. One thing about my reputation—I've never been known as a tease."

"That would lead me to believe you're not teasing."

Was she teasing? "About taking you to bed?"

"Wasn't that what we were talking about?"

"I thought we were talking about going out on a date."

"A date. Right. Lost my head there for a minute."

Chloe settled back in her chair, swiveled from side to side, her bare feet propped on the lower drawer she'd pulled open. "Thank you."

"For what?"

"Being a good sport. Not pressing the point."

"I don't do the kick-me, beat-me, make-me-beg routine. I think I told you that."

He had told her that. He'd told her at the same time that she'd never know what he liked in bed. And now she wanted to know. She wanted to offer him that pleasure.

She was *so* in over her head. "You did tell me that. But it's nice to know you don't talk out of both sides of your mouth."

He was quiet for a minute, as if gathering his thoughts, digesting her response to his actions, before giving her more to consider. "I'm pretty much a straight-up guy, Chloe. What you see is what you get. You may find it hard to believe, but there are a lot of us single nice-guy types out here."

"You're right. I do find it hard to believe. Because the only ones I've met are already taken."

"Ouch. That hurt."

She really had to quit doing that. Opening mouth and inserting foot. And thinking of Eric as a shoulder for dumping her relationship woes. "Hey, until a few months ago, you were taken."

"Past tense being the operative here. Feel free to think of me as available."

She couldn't think of him as available. He was the closest thing to Cary Grant she'd found. And thinking of Eric as the fulfillment of her fantasy would mean not thinking of him as a friend. And right now, she needed him to be a friend.

No matter how much she was considering taking him as a lover.

HAVING HUNG UP THE PHONE after agreeing to go out with Eric on Friday night, and having wiped from her monitor every attempt she'd made at a congruous reply to the letter she needed to answer, Chloe was staring at the second hand of the clock on the wall when movement in her doorway brought her head up.

"Poe. Hey." Chloe forced herself to smile, when her insides were snarling. The last thing she needed tonight was a snarky confrontation.

Especially when the other woman looked like she'd just pulled her teal-colored pants and long-sleeved swing top from a dry-cleaner's bag, while Chloe's own hip-hugging knee-length skirt in pale pink shantung desperately needed a good pressing.

"Do you mind?" Poe gestured toward one of the brushed velvet, deep-grape visitor's chairs that faced the room's big desk.

"Sure." This was strangely out of character, Chloe mused. Poe stopping by for no obvious reason. "What's up?"

"Honestly? I'm exhausted, but I just can't face going home." She wilted into the chair, crossed one long leg over the other, flattened her hands on the seat at her hips, dropped her head back against the head rest and closed her eyes.

Chloe was never sure what to expect from the other woman, but this collapse would be about the last thing on the list. "That looks more like defeat than exhaustion."

"I need a wife."

"Is that a proposal?"

Brow arched, Poe peered through one eye before closing it again. "Hardly. Even if I were lesbian, you wouldn't be my type."

Oh, but was *that* feeling mutual. As was the feeling of being overextended. Though a wife wouldn't be Chloe's first choice to help shoulder the burden. Maybe an assistant for her assistant, to start.

She hadn't realized Poe was snowed under as well. Though taking care of her duties as buyer while keeping her eye on Chloe's job would make for a heavy workload, wouldn't it?

Office politics aside, Chloe couldn't help but wonder who *was* Poe's type.

"Anton Neville," Poe said. "What can you tell me about him?"

Well, now. Chloe could tell the other woman any number of things about Anton, since he'd been part of her circle for over a year. But she wasn't about to betray her friendship with Lauren. Not until Lauren had cut Anton loose for good.

Her elbows on the arms of her chair, Chloe rolled her pen between index fingers and thumbs and swiveled from side to side. "We've worked together how long now, Poe? Without sharing a single detail of our personal lives? Isn't this woman-to-woman bonding coming a bit late in the game?''

And had she really just used a sports cliché? *Eww. Ugh.*

''I thought we were keeping the woman-to-woman bonding on a need-to-know basis, since need-to-know still seems to define our working relationship as well.'' Eyes still closed, Poe laced her hands over her middle. ''I've decided I need to know.''

''About Anton?'' Chloe asked. ''Or are you back-handedly hinting that we need to work on our professional relationship?''

''About Anton, yes. But it might help ease the turbulent atmosphere around the office if we agree to calm any brewing storms rather than whipping the waves into a frenzy. Which I do. At times on purpose.''

Shaking her head, Chloe snorted, tossed her pen to her desk. ''I can't believe you're admitting it.''

''Why not? I'm tired. And it's not getting me anywhere, since you whip the waves right back.''

Even though the constant antagonism was getting on her nerves, Chloe wasn't ready to call an unconditional draw. ''Fine. I'm willing to make the effort. If you'll tell me one thing first.''

Poe raised her head, raised both brows and waited.

''Why are you after my job?''

For a moment Poe met Chloe's gaze, then she let her eyes drift shut. Her lips, painted a deep dark red, drew wickedly upward. ''Why do you think it's your job I'm after? How do you know I'm after anything? That I'm not just playing mind games?''

''I'm not sure it matters. The end result is that it's making for some seriously bad karma beyond that of our working relationship.'' Chloe had enough going on making nice with Sydney. She didn't have energy to waste deflecting this psychic vampire.

"I'm kidding." Poe waved a hand. "Of course I want your job."

Now that they finally had *that* out in the open, Chloe picked up her pen again and scratched the tip against the paper on her desk. "Why mine and not Melanie's? Or Kinsey's, even?"

"Melanie's is easy. I am not the least bit interested in technology beyond what it can do for me. And the gift line?" Poe gave a careless sigh. "I can only get excited about half of the products."

Both were reasons to which Chloe could relate. "And Kinsey's lines? You can't tell me you don't get excited about clothes. I've seen what you wear. And if nothing else, I hate you for the size of your closet."

"Kinsey's lines are great. And I've worked with her and Eleanor, one of the junior buyers, on selecting the products to showcase. But I don't wear the clothes. Which means I'm not the best choice to grow the lines."

At least she was honest. More honest than Chloe would've expected. "And my lines?"

Excitement seemed to jump from Poe's smile into the room's very air. She gripped the chair's armrests so hard that Chloe was afraid the material would show puncture wounds once Poe let go.

"God is in the details, Chloe. Have you ever heard that expression? The clothes, the hair." Poe shook her head. "They're nothing but a foundation. Add the jewelry, the bag, the right scarf or belt and the picture begins to take shape."

Chloe had long since stopped doodling. Now, listening to Poe spit fire, Chloe sensed a strange sort of epiphany building, the beginning to an end, which made no sense in any light. All she could do was continue to listen.

"But it's what you can do with a face…" Poe paused, as if unsure she could define her enthusiasm, or put her passion into words. And then her gaze cut to Chloe's. "I have something I want you to see."

Poe got to her feet and headed for the door. She didn't look back to see if Chloe had followed. But Chloe was intrigued enough to have done just that, walking down the hall and into Poe's office to find the other woman spreading open a portfolio on her desk. A photographer's portfolio, black velvety pages framing six five-by-eight portraits.

Chloe had kicked off her shoes while talking to Eric, and she made her way softly across the deep purple carpeting to the black lacquer desk. The portfolio had been turned so that the portraits faced her, right side up. Six studio head shots, the lighting varying from blindingly bright to shadow.

Each portrait was of Poe, but Chloe wasn't sure anyone unfamiliar with the other woman would know that. The hair styles were radically different in each, and none that Chloe had ever seen Annabel wear. And the makeup… As cynical as she was, Chloe found herself awed.

She knew exactly what Poe meant when she talked about what could be done with a face. And why she would make a better gRAFFITI gIRL ambassador than Chloe even wanted to be.

"You model. I didn't know that."

"Few people do. For a very good reason." Poe flipped to the portfolio's next page.

"Does Sydney know?" It was the first question that came to Chloe's mind as she studied the four eight-by-ten nudes.

A wry grin pulled at one side of Poe's mouth. "No one knows."

Chloe turned back to the portraits and continued to study them for a few moments longer, as they were what she most wanted to see. What she had been invited to see. Not out of arrogance, but a shortcut explanation as to why Poe coveted Chloe's position.

Funny, but Chloe no longer felt quite so threatened. Or antagonistic.

"Can I ask you a question, Poe?" Chloe didn't wait for permission, but went ahead. "You started here as Sydney's assistant. Now you're working as a buyer for the main line of gIRL-gEAR clothing. Why?"

Poe's brows came together in a thoughtful V. "Because I have a lot of habits to support. Like eating? And keeping a roof over my head?"

"No. I mean, why aren't you modeling? These photos are amazing."

"They are good, aren't they." Poe tapped a manicured nail against one portrait set against a white background, her head and shoulders limned with a vague shadow.

Her face was heavily powdered, her hair coiffed geisha style. Her mouth was set in a perfect moue. But it was her eyes that told the tale, glinting with a mischievous fire that hinted at even more naughtiness than did the imprint of a woman's lips on her cheek.

"This is actually my favorite. Even more so than the nudes, which I have to say are about as good as the female body gets."

She stated it matter-of-factly, with absolutely no

pretense, but still Chloe laughed. "And you don't have a single shy bone, do you?"

A strange smile came over Poe's mouth. "Actually, I'm very shy. And I know that I overcompensate and come across as having a huge ego. Not many people can reconcile what I know must seem like a multiple personality disorder."

Chloe lifted a brow. "You do have your moments. But you still haven't answered my question. If you don't model, why the portraits? I can't imagine you not being able to find work."

"The dilemma of being too distinctive. My look has only limited appeal. I do get work, but I turn down even more. I don't want to be the token Asian chick." She slapped a palm on the open portfolio. "I want to be hired because my face is the only face that will work."

Chloe crossed her arms over her chest. "Isn't that a classic case of cutting off your nose to spite your face?"

"I suppose it is. But it all comes down to what I want."

"What do you want, besides my job?"

Poe closed the portfolio, leaned to slide it back into the kneehole of her desk. She quickly straightened her paperwork and logged out of the computer network. Chloe just stood and waited, knowing the other woman's stall tactic was as much about strategy as anything. Strategy she understood.

Once Poe had gathered her purse and circled the desk, she said, "Let's walk back to your office."

"Sure," Chloe answered, and headed that way.

"This is going to come totally out of the blue," Poe said, shutting off her office light once Chloe had left the room, "but what I've wanted more than anything for as long as I can remember is to be a forensic anthropologist."

Chloe stopped in the middle of the hallway. When Poe walked past, Chloe shook off her surprise and continued on to her office. "Next time you're going to blow me away, can you broadcast a warning?"

"That's the reaction I get every time. I haven't yet decided if I'm insulted or charmed." She turned into Chloe's office without a backward glance.

"That reaction shouldn't surprise you. A forensic anthropologist is about as far removed from a fashion buyer as it is from the moon." Chloe returned to her desk, but remained standing with her chair at her back.

"It gets better. I wanted to specialize in reconstruction, to be a forensic sculptor. In taking a skull, or what pieces were available, and rebuilding the face."

That obsession with faces again. The picture of Poe was taking shape. "What stopped you?"

Poe stood with her arms crossed, the thin strap of her purse hanging on her shoulder, that slender finger tapping against her sleeve. "Life, money. Family. Twists and turns and obligations."

"You still have time."

"I know. And that's what the modeling work is for. Using my face and my body to get what I want. Which makes me a first-class whore."

"What're you talking about? It makes you savvy and resourceful. And, yeah." Chloe picked up her pen and twisted the barrel. "I'm starting to see why cosmetics and accessories would ring your bell."

"Exactly. Why not indulge my fascination?" Poe gestured expansively. "Modeling pays for the credit hours I'm taking. gIRL-gEAR pays the bills. Your job would make paying the bills a lot more fun.''

"You know I'm not going to lie down and let you have it.''

"I wouldn't expect you to.''

Chloe concurred. "And I could go to Sydney with what you've told me and ask her to find a place for you in marketing. Or even in customer service and sales.''

"You could, but you won't.'' Poe moved to the center of the room and stood between the two visitor's chairs, a hand on the back of each. Her eyes flashed, but with respect rather than defiance. "You're too much like me, Chloe. You want to be the one to fight your battles. You don't want to be rescued. You have too much pride. And that makes us worthy opponents.''

Chloe thought of being rescued, thought of fighting her own battles, thought of Eric and wondered what he'd make of her having this long overdue conversation with her nemesis…who wasn't such a fire-breathing dragon, after all.

"Opponents make for lousy co-workers. Besides, I wouldn't be very loyal to the company I helped found if I let my position fall into your hands, knowing you think of your time at gIRL-gEAR as a temporary career layover.''

One of Poe's angled brows lifted. "Do you plan to stay with gIRL-gEAR forever?''

"I can't answer that. But I can say I'll give the company one hundred ten percent while I'm here.''

"As would I. In fact, I'll go for one hundred twenty. I would never shortchange any position I'd busted my ass to achieve. Why would you think that I would?''

Frustration and exhaustion battled in both sides of Chloe's brain. "Maybe because I haven't gotten to know you."

Poe tapped her index fingers against the headrests of the chairs. "Should we call a truce? You accept that I'm not going anywhere and I accept that you're not going to let me get away with anything?"

"Those are rather broad terms, don't you think?"

"Perhaps, but now we know better where the other stands. We're not flying blind. Maybe we can even collaborate." Poe's mouth twisted with ironic humor. "Down the road, of course."

"No," Chloe said as inspiration struck. "Not down the road. Now."

"Now as in this moment?"

Chloe picked up the letter and handed it to Poe. "Here's your chance to put your money where your mouth is."

Setting her purse in one of the chairs, Poe dropped into the seat of the other and began to read.

Dear gRAFFITI gIRL, I need your advice, please. All of my life I've known that I'm ugly. I see my reflection when I pass a mirror, though I try my best not to look. I used to think it didn't matter to my parents what I looked like. I used to think they loved me anyway. But now they're getting divorced and are arguing over who I'm going to live with. Neither one of them wants to take me. I know that if I looked better, I wouldn't be so embarrassing to have around. If you could tell me which products I could use and which of your colors would make my face appear less disgusting, I would be ever so grateful.

Poe slumped back in the chair, hung her arms over the sides and let the letter fall to the floor. "You have to answer this, don't you? Where do you even start?"

"I was thinking of starting with the parents."

"Can I come along? My hands haven't been registered as deadly weapons, but we can lie and say that they have."

Chloe leaned back in her own chair and studied the woman who sat on the other side of her desk, wondering if Annabel Lee might actually prove to be a more formidable friend than she'd ever been a foe.

8

DINNER COULD NOT HAVE gone any better, Eric decided, congratulating himself on the evening he'd put together as he settled next to Chloe in the theater seat. They'd eaten at Biraporetti's earlier, before the usual Friday night rush hit the combination Italian grill and Irish bar.

The tiny white Christmas lights wrapped around the tree branch jutting out from one of the restaurant's walls had flickered in Chloe's eyes while they'd waited for a table at the bar. The television screens behind the bar had flickered as well.

Eric had been able to watch the baseball game over her shoulder while they'd sat drinking the bar's special champagne cocktail called a Sicilian Swirl, made with peach juice and a shot of Chianti. Like he'd said. The night, so far, from the time he'd picked her up at her apartment until a few minutes ago, when he'd led her by the hand into the theater, was cookin'.

Chloe had dressed in her usual color tonight, though this time the pink was part of a pink-black-and-white camouflage pattern that gave a bad-ass attitude to her short-skirted halter dress. The fun part was that she wore knee-high boots that matched. A cocky little chick from head to toe.

Or so she appeared to be. Eric knew differently, and took more than a little credit for the fact that her hard outer shell was beginning to crack. Her side of the phone call, when he'd called to ask her out, had been proof enough of that fact. He was also beginning to better understand this deal she'd been willing to make. Her three nights for his three wishes.

She was into some serious reflection about her job with gIRL-gEAR and had wanted to see herself through the eyes of an outsider, check out the view from someone who had no stake in the company.

He had a feeling that what was going on with Chloe was more than keeping to Sydney's straight and narrow. He just couldn't yet put his finger on what it was. Though he'd come close a couple of weeks ago with his hand up Chloe's dress.

When he'd arrived at the open house, Chloe'd been hiding out in her office, which even *he* knew wouldn't sit well with the boss. But she'd seemed too caught up in whatever she'd been thinking to care. And then she'd blasted out of nowhere with all that crap about using sex to control a man.

That would be a cold day in hell. In fact, if anyone had been doing any controlling, he'd certainly set Chloe straight that afternoon. She didn't have to know he'd damn near come in his boxers just watching her face. One more breathy shudder and he would've unzipped and plunged deep.

No. She wasn't the tough cookie she'd been trying—for as long as he'd known her—to convince everyone, including herself, she was.

The Cary Grant film retrospective started at seven, and the River Oaks Theater being right down the block from the restaurant, they'd been able to relax and enjoy one another's company during dinner, the way a couple should relax and enjoy when out on a date.

And this was a date.

In fact, if not for their three-for-three deal, he wouldn't have put off seeing her again for so long. But he'd had to wait for the perfect opportunity to present itself so as not to waste one of his wishes. And if he hadn't happened to glance through a copy of the *Houston Press* left open on the bar at Haydon's, he'd have totally missed out on this one.

Chloe might've complained that dinner and a movie and back to the bedroom was a lousy idea of a good time, but Eric planned to make sure he proved two out of the three could make for a hell of an evening given the right company.

And that he was the right company.

Glancing beside him at Chloe's dimly lit face, her closed eyes, he rode a powerful wave of emotion that had nothing to do with lust.

The bedroom part they'd get to, but not tonight. That was the only absolute he'd set for himself. He wanted to get Chloe naked in a bad way. How could he not, after he'd had his hands all over her, and she'd had her mouth on him? But tonight it was not going to happen. Not even if she begged.

Tonight was all for Chloe. Not for gIRL-gEAR. Not for her career. Not for her potty mouth or her problems with Poe. Tonight was for the woman she was, the woman who needed to be reminded of everything she had to offer a man besides her knock-out body.

"Can I open my eyes now?"

Eric laughed.

He'd forgotten he'd told her not to look at the theater marquee or the notice of times and listings or the movie posters hanging in the lobby. He'd kept his hand over her eyes, in fact, part of the time.

It was possible that she'd heard the ads and knew exactly what she was about to see. But if that was the case she was doing a bang-up job of hiding her excitement. Unless, of course, she wasn't excited.

Eric frowned.

Chloe's lashes fluttered and swept up, her gaze wide and expectant. Eric relaxed his frown. "Sorry. Guess I was kind of enjoying having you dependent on me. Makes me feel all warm and fuzzy inside."

She moved her head back as if to pull him into focus. "Having me dependent on you gives you the warm fuzzies? I would think clinging females would give you a major pain in the ass."

He grinned and winked. "All females do that, some time or another."

"Careful, buddy. Your mother is female. Show a little respect."

Impossible, considering he'd never known his mother. But that was a subject best avoided. "Are you going to share that popcorn or do I have to get my own?"

She slapped his hand away when he reached toward her lap. "You said you didn't want any popcorn. That's why you bought the Milk Duds."

Yeah, but that was before the bucket of popcorn had been sitting where it was sitting. "I changed my mind. I'll share if you'll share."

"Humph," she muttered, then shushed him as the lights went down and the curtain rose.

When the original preview trailer for *The Philadelphia Story* began to play on the screen and Chloe got her first glimpse of Jimmy Stewart, Katherine Hepburn and Cary Grant, she seemed to forget all about Eric's wandering hand.

She didn't even appear to be breathing. She didn't move a single muscle, even the ones it took to blink. And Eric would have noticed had she batted an eye. His gaze was focused on her face and not on the black-and-white action of the trailer. And then she smiled. A killer smile that hit him where it hurt.

She was beautiful. A fact that he'd realized for as long as he'd known her, but for some reason had never fully appreciated until the past few weeks in her company. Even now, with only the flickering film for light, he could see what he'd been missing.

It was her vulnerability that was doing him in. The soft edge to her hard insistence on continually busting his chops—and those of anyone who crossed her. She tried so hard to be tough. And she was tough. He'd seen her play volleyball. He'd seen her stand up to Poe.

But he also saw what he imagined her girlfriends saw—the traits that drew their loyalty and affection, and solidified the friendships that had endured not only the years, but the stresses and hardships of working together and building the business of gIRL-gEAR.

Those were the traits that brought him back even after it seemed she'd whacked him off at the knees. She had a lot going for her. But she had just as much going against her. And he couldn't help but think that her attitude about men was going to be what eventually ruined their friendship or their chance at anything more.

He needed to have fun with a woman, and Chloe never failed to show him a good time. He needed great sex, which he knew their eventual coming together would bring. What he didn't need was to fall for a woman struggling with "issues." He'd promised himself at the first of the year no more damsels in distress.

A soft noise brought his attention back to the movie. *An Affair to Remember,* he thought the marquee had said this one was. Apparently a classic, though he wasn't much into these old productions. Even the ones that had been made in color…or was this one colorized? Hard to tell, the print was so grainy.

He turned to ask Chloe, figuring she would know, finding that she'd grown perfectly still at his side, her hand hovering over the bucket of popcorn in her lap, her eyes wide and unblinking as she stared straight ahead.

And then he heard it again, a cross between a sniffle and a sob, so tiny, nearly imperceptible. Had he not seen the hitch in her chest he might not have realized she was the one who was crying.

Chloe crying. What the hell was there to cry about? Oh, he wasn't up to dealing with this. Nope. He wasn't. But he did shift in the old-fashioned seat and lean toward her, slipping his arm around her shoulder.

He didn't even have a chance to pull her close because she was moving his way on her own, tucking her shoulder up into his armpit, her head into the crook of his neck.

She was cold, that was it. Her bare arm was dimpled with goose bumps. He rubbed his palm up and down her skin. She was cold and probably premenstrual, what with the crying coming from nowhere.

And the sappy movie wasn't helping, not that he'd paid much attention to what was going on between Cary Grant and the actress. But now it looked like someone had died, and there was an old lace shawl that meant something to Grant's character.

Eric brought his lips close to Chloe's head and whispered, "I'm sorry."

She looked up, her expression one of confusion, her eyes wide and wet and intoxicating in the inconsistent lighting thrown by the film.

"For what?" Her question was mouthed more than spoken.

"I should've picked out something more upbeat." He nodded toward the screen, lowered his whisper another notch. "But I knew you liked this stuff. I thought it would be fun. I didn't think it would make you sad."

"Don't be an idiot." She reached over and laid a hand on his cheek, her soft touch at odds with her name-calling. She leaned even closer and whispered, "I'm not sad. I love this movie. It's so romantic."

Romantic he didn't know about, since he hadn't been paying much attention to the story unfolding onscreen. But even now what was happening with the film was nothing compared to what was happening here, with Chloe's breath heating the skin just below his ear. Where even now she seemed to be nuzzling with her nose.

A soft nuzzling. A gentle brush of her cool skin to his warmer, rougher cheek. He really should've shaved. But the bristle of his beard didn't seem to be a problem. Chloe hadn't backed away. And when he shivered at a touch from the tip of her tongue, she cuddled even closer.

"You're missing the movie," he muttered, and she responded, "I don't care," tearing him up as she said it. He wanted her to stay right where she was. He wanted her to climb into his lap. He wanted her to turn her attention back to the screen and leave him alone with his honorable intentions.

He pulled back to look into her eyes, to see if she'd stopped crying, if she was using his cheek to hide her tears or just as a toy for her tongue. And if he hadn't been sitting against the wall, with a dozen legs between his seat and the aisle, he would've popped up and out for a soda he didn't need.

What he saw cracked open with frightening ease his vow to avoid all damsels in distress. It bashed his resolve to leave her at her front door at the end of the night. Ripped apart his determination to pay attention to the rest of the film so they could talk about what they'd seen later, over drinks.

As it was, he couldn't pull his gaze away from her face. And when she raised her head, her eyes questioning, her lips trembling and seeking, he lowered his mouth to hers.

It was the first time they'd kissed, and he knew he'd remember it forever because she tasted like salt and warm buttered popcorn.

They'd once shared a kiss meant for show while under the influence of an audience and too much tequila. But this wasn't that kiss. This kiss was real, possessing more true intimacy than the sexual encounters they'd shared.

Her lips were soft and tentatively searching, as if she wasn't sure he'd want to accept the sweet offer of her mouth. As if she was afraid he'd turn her away. He'd never known a woman so contradictory, so confounding, or a woman he wanted to kiss more.

He settled his mouth over hers and answered her unspoken question. The kiss was nothing more than a brush of contact, a moment of simplicity and innocence. But it stabbed Eric in the gut with its sharp insistence that simplicity and innocence weren't what they appeared to be.

Chloe had never been innocent. He knew virtually nothing about her past, but he tasted her strong desire to be wanted, her deep, piercing need for acceptance. And he knew. As her tongue touched his lips and moved into his mouth, he knew.

It didn't matter that she claimed to know men, that she professed to have experience in relationships, that she said she knew all about romance. Eric knew better. He knew the truth. Her mouth told him.

With the gentle, rubbing press of her lips to his and the tender caress of her tongue, her mouth told him.

She was simply looking to be loved.

THE BALLROOM at the Renaissance Hotel looked like it had been pulled straight from the Web pages of www.girl-gear.com for the following night's gIRL-gEAR gIRL competition.

The hotel's event organizers had worked with the partners to decorate in the company's color scheme of lime-green and orange, hot-pink and bright yellow.

Two tablecloths in contrasting colors draped every table. Centerpieces had been designed with bright green foliage and a cluster of hothouse blooms in orange, yellow and pink.

Confetti in the shape of a tiny *g* littered the floor, the tables, even the chairs. Chloe knew she'd be shaking bits of it from the black feather boa fringing the knee-length hemline of her dress for the entire life of the garment.

Sitting at a huge circular table for twelve, she flipped through the program introducing the finalists vying for the title of gIRL-gEAR gIRL. Marketing had done a super job putting together the souvenir brochure for the evening's event.

All six of the finalists had appeared onstage earlier to deliver their introductions, along with an oral presentation detailing the influence of fashion on their lives. Each girl had since returned to model the formal ensemble she had not only designed but constructed from the inside out.

Whether a dress or a combination of separates, every seam, every buttonhole, every piece of trim had to be the work of the contestant. Even the accessories had to be handcrafted. Footwear was the only exception, though each of the finalists had extended her creativity to her feet as well.

Now all that was left to be done was the scoring and the tabulation. And the first gIRL-gEAR gIRL would be crowned.

All in all, Chloe was totally amazed. Amazed and more than a bit envious. Not by the girls' imaginations and talent, but by the fact that here they were, seventeen or eighteen years old, knowing exactly what they wanted to do with their lives.

At that age, being forced to study fashion instead of phys ed, all she'd known was that what she wanted to do with her life was never going to happen.

She wasn't sure about her partners, but she definitely had a particular favorite among the girls. A favorite who probably wouldn't win the competition once the scores were tabulated. But the girl—her name was Deanna—touched Chloe's heart in ways she'd thought herself untouchable.

Deanna's talent for fashion wasn't in question. She had all the right answers, as well as the body and the face. There was one thing, however, that Chloe was certain would keep the girl from walking away with the highest score.

And that was her demeanor. Her slacker-speak. Her punk-ass attitude. An attitude that was nothing but show, a cover for her insecurity, a red herring to draw attention from her lack of self-esteem.

Chloe recognized so much of herself in Deanna it hurt.

Oblivious to the distress churning in Chloe's stomach along with the rosemary chicken, the rest of her tablemates chatted quietly, the five partners pouring over the score sheets in the portfolios they'd had now for over a week, the men waiting the arrival of the evening's dessert.

In addition to Eric, who sat to her right, Chloe shared the table in front of the stage with Melanie, Kinsey, Sydney, Lauren and Macy, along with their dates. It was a sort of boy, girl, boy, girl reenactment of the scavenger hunt pairings.

Macy, of course, sat as close as she could to Leo without actually climbing into his lap. Melanie had brought Jess Morgan, who Chloe really did like and thought perfect for Mel. And Kinsey had invited Doug Storey.

The last two pairings, however, had Chloe and the others shaking their heads.

Sydney's date for the evening was Ray Coffey, which wasn't so strange in and of itself, because the two were known to go out from time to time. But tonight they'd barely spoken. Ray looked mad as hell and Sydney totally pissed off and as uncomfortable in his company as the rest of the table was with Lauren apparently dating Sydney's father, Nolan Ford.

Not only because Sydney and Nolan barely spoke

to one another these days, which had made for an awkward dinner for all, but because at the table behind,
Poe sat with Anton Neville. Chloe shook her head.

"You're being too quiet."

Chloe looked up at Eric just as he presented her
with a bite of the lemon sorbet the waiter had delivered, along with the rest of the guests' chocolate
mousse.

She accepted his offering, trying to remember when
she'd told him of her preference for lemon desserts,
wondering how richly he'd greased the waiter's palm.
Then she realized five pairs of female eyes were
trained her way.

She thought about sticking out her tongue but knew
that exposing a mouthful of smeared, melting lemon
would not earn her any Sydney points. So she smiled
sweetly and went back to marking her score sheet.

"C'mon, princess," Eric urged. "Talk to me."

"I hate it when you call me princess." Chloe
slammed the portfolio against her thigh and poked Eric
in the shoulder with her pencil's sharp point. "Why
do you have to call me princess?"

Eric pushed his chair back a foot from the table,
braced his elbow on his thigh and then leaned into her
space. "Tell me why you hate it and I'll tell you why
it fits."

"It does not fit," she muttered, unsure why she was
so irritated tonight, and denying that it had anything
to do with Eric's tenderness at the movies last night.
Or the lemon sorbet. "I am not some goody-goody
little spoiled ingenue."

"That's not what the word brings to mind." Eric
ran his index finger up and down the tender skin of
her bare inner arm.

Chloe shivered because she was cold. Not because his touch was nothing more than the barest whisper. Or because his knuckle brushed the swell of her breast. He stroked his thumb into the pit of her elbow and she finally pulled away, too aware of other places she'd felt his touch.

He was being way too sweet, making her crazy with all this kind and gentle crap when she was in the mood to growl. "Then think of another endearment if you have to use one at all."

"Sure thing. Peaches."

"No."

"Lamb chop."

"No."

"Doll baby."

She considered the expression. "Is that the best you can come up with?"

"Works for me." This time he scooted his chair a foot closer to hers. "Doll baby."

Eyes at half-mast, she cast a glance to the side. "Are you trying to sit in my lap? Because it's absence that makes the heart grow fonder."

Eric laughed and draped an arm across the back of her chair. He pretended interest in her scoring process. "So this really is all happening live, huh?"

"Right before your very eyes." She indicated the score sheet bound into the back of the portfolio. "Now that the girls have all done their thing, we grade them on a complicated point system. The results will be compiled by our accountant while everyone finishes dessert. So, if you don't mind…"

Tapping the portfolio still open to Deanna's profile, Eric leaned farther into Chloe's space. "Is she your favorite?"

He smelled warm and comfortable, and Chloe hated herself because she wanted to burrow into his body beneath the blankets on her bed. She could barely think to answer his question for fighting the urge to tickle his neck with her nuzzling nose.

Why did he always make her think about sex? And not just about having sex, but enjoying sex. Wanting his body because no other body would do. Last night, after that kiss, she would've given him anything. But he hadn't even asked.

What kind of guy kissed like that and then didn't ask for sex? "I like this one, yes. And, no. It's not because she has an eye for color."

"You mean an eye for pink." Eric's wandering hand was back, fingering the thin strap holding up the deep-cut bodice of Chloe's hot-fuchsia, flapper-style dress.

"She has good taste. She knows what to wear with her coloring. That's all part of the picture." God is in the details. Where had she heard *that* before?

"There's more, though, isn't there? I've watched you turn back to this one over and over."

Chloe wasn't sure she could give Eric a coherent reply without revealing her entire life story. He didn't need to know that she and Deanna shared a motherless upbringing. Or that the identity Deanna found in fashion, the seventeen-year-old Chloe had found in sports.

And now here was this girl, on the cusp of realizing her dream, her father in the audience looking nervous and ready to puke, while Chloe had followed the same path with one hundred percent resentment for being forced into a field of study in which she had no interest.

Chloe had the career this girl would kill for, and

she couldn't have cared less. How was she supposed to explain *that* to Eric?

Pencil in hand, she lifted his fingers, which hovered too near her cleavage, and returned his hand to his lap. Then, leaning forward, she passed her portfolio and completed score sheet across the table to Sydney.

Sitting back, Chloe slid a sideways glance Eric's way. "You're getting awfully touchy-feely."

"All part of the escort service, ma'am. I'm showing my dedication to you." This time he shifted the arm draped over the back of her chair, his fingers moving to her nape and tugging on the tiny hairs on the back of her neck. "Besides, you're fun to touch and feel."

"Dedication to me?" She ignored the touch-and-feel part. She was already feeling too much. "That's why you were sharing your affections with any woman you could get your hands on the other night at the Daiquiri Factory?"

"What's this?" He pulled back as if to see her more clearly. "I've been spied upon? And I'm now the victim of rumor and hearsay?"

"The information was passed on to me by someone who saw you there sharing your...dedication." Her glare dared him to deny the charge.

"Oh, yeah?" he said, and frowned. "Who's telling these tales on me?"

Because Kinsey was all the way on the other side of the table, Chloe cut her gaze to Melanie, the next best thing, sitting, as she was, on Eric's other side. His hand still at Chloe's hairline, Eric turned to Melanie.

"Hey, Mel," he said, and she looked away from her conversation with Jess.

"Hey, Eric."

"You've been feeding Chloe rumors about me, I hear."

Melanie shifted her position and studied Eric over her tiny black rectangular frames. "I haven't been feeding her anything. Kinsey, however, has been giving her the truth."

"Is that so?"

"Yes that is so," Melanie said, obviously gearing up to give Eric an earful.

Chloe made a halfhearted attempt to rein in her friend. "It's okay, Mel. He's not going to listen to you any more than he listens to me."

"What do you mean, I don't listen to you?" Eric's gaze cut from Melanie to Chloe and back again. "What am I missing here?"

This time Melanie lifted her chin, looking over her frames and down her nose. "Chloe filled us in on your role in her grand plan to repair her reputation."

"Yeah? So?"

Melanie rolled her eyes. "So. What good is your arrangement going to do her if she's the only one keeping it exclusive?"

"Exclusive?" This time Eric's head made a slow swing in Chloe's direction. His eyes flashed and the heat warmed more than the surface of her skin.

She started to tell him that if he'd had half a brain he would've understood that her plan wouldn't do a bit of good if he continued to date anything with breasts. But she didn't want him to know she'd given him that much credit.

Neither did she want him to know that thinking of him with any other woman raised her hackles.

She didn't get a chance to tell him anything, however, because he'd turned to Melanie, offered an, "Excuse us,'' and now had his hand wrapped around Chloe's upper arm and a look in his eye that dared her to give him any shit.

When he insisted, she got to her feet, because she didn't have much of a choice, he held her so tightly.

But the primary reason she did as he ordered was because her body refused to tell him no. Her nerves were firing heated rounds from the point of their innocent skin-to-skin contact to other places she remembered the touch of his fingers.

What was going on with him? And why couldn't she breathe?

''Chloe?'' Sydney called from across the table. ''The results will be back in fifteen minutes.''

Nodding, Chloe opened her mouth to lay the blame for her departure right where it belonged. But the guilty party took full responsibility with his devilish dimples and a charming, ''I'll have her back in a jiff, Syd.''

And then Eric propelled Chloe from the table near the stage area to the exit at the rear of the rectangular room. Fortunately, they had the width rather than the length to cross.

Once out in the hallway, he slid his hold down her arm to her hand, pulling her along behind him as he glanced at alcoves and blind turns and dead ends, and tried every door he passed.

''Eric, damn you. Slow down before I break my ankle.'' But Eric was intent, and Chloe sensed the desperation in his grip and in his silence.

And the rapid beat of her heart was less about adrenaline and more about anticipation and awareness and the arousing sleight of hand he played in her palm with his fingers.

Her body pulsed, and even more than she wanted to jerk him to a stop and demand answers, she wanted to wait and find out what he could possibly want so badly that he was turning into this wild man.

The unlocked door he finally found opened onto a narrow mechanical room. He flipped the light switch; the bulb sputtered and buzzed.

He pulled her inside, locked the door and stared down so intently she backed up, hitting the door with one heel, then the other. His breathing was rough and labored as he dragged a hand back over his hair, shoved his other to his waist.

The thrill of the unknown had Chloe's own chest rising and falling hard. "What the hell—"

The hand he slammed into the door above her head cut her off.

9

"YOU WANT TO EXPLAIN this exclusive crap Melanie's talking about? Because I don't remember that being any part of any deal you and I made."

Chloe narrowed her eyes, jerked her chin higher, her shoulders straighter. She pressed her body into the solid door at her back, needing the sense of being grounded in even that weak reality before she hauled off and slapped Eric silly.

Whatever was about to come tumbling down was going to have a more substantial impact than a house of cards.

Steam wouldn't be coming from his ears otherwise.

"What's to explain? It's what Melanie said. Your whoring around isn't going to do much in the way of helping my reputation. I thought you would have figured that much out on your own. But I guess I should have spelled it out for you."

Steam wasn't even the half of it.

"Whoring around?" His jaw visibly taut, his eyes narrowed to irate slits, Eric raised the intensity in his voice, though it remained a coarse whisper. "Hanging out with a bunch of friends, some who happen to be female, is whoring around? This from the woman who dates everything in pants?"

"Not everything in pants," she said, vilely pleased to see her barb gouge and stick.

Eric's nostrils flared. ''That's right. You don't date me. But you want us to be exclusive while we're not dating. That's bullshit, Chloe. Total bullshit. I never signed on to be a monk.''

Chloe crossed her arms over her chest. Something was going on here that was way beyond her understanding. But it was clear Eric was in no mood to calm down and explain.

And, quite frankly, she was well equipped to cover her own fast-and-furious ass. ''You know, let's just forget this whole thing. I don't know why I ever thought it would work. I've never been able to count on anyone but myself, so why should this time be any different?''

She tried to move, to step away from the door and leave the room, leave Eric and his problems here where he could bang and pound and piss and moan to his heart's content. But he refused to budge, standing in front of her, hovering, doing what he could in the way of intimidation.

Which didn't do him much good at all. Chloe didn't do intimidation.

But she was curious and, though she hated to admit it, concerned. Not for herself, but for Eric. This wasn't like him at all, not the Eric she knew. And she knew him well. Better than any man whose company she'd kept for any length of time.

Why had she been so soft, letting him get to her?

''Look, Eric. I don't know what the hell is going on with you, but I've got a program to get back to. So, if you don't mind…oh, wait. Even if you do mind, get your attitude the hell out of my way.''

She shoved against his chest. He didn't say a word. He didn't move away. If anything, he leaned in closer, so close Chloe realized that his irises were actually rings of blue in at least a half-dozen shades, that his pupils were pitch-black and dilated with heat and arousal.

An arousal that she felt like a kick to her solar plexus. He wanted her. Desperately. He had to have her now, right now, here in this moment. "Eric?"

His head came down. He pressed the side of his nose to the side of hers and leaned his weight into both hands braced against the door above her shoulders. "Do you want to be exclusive, Chloe? Do you want to date? Like a couple? And not see anyone else? Is that what you want from me?"

What she wanted was for him to pull off her panties, drag his pants to his ankles and fill her like she'd never before been filled. But dating? Exclusively? Letting Eric see who she really was beneath the surface of his doll baby princess? She didn't know. She just didn't know.

What she did know was that her body had never hummed with this much electricity. Nerves sizzled on the outside of her skin. Eric's breath was warm on her cheek, his lips soft where they barely touched the corner of her mouth, resting there, as he was, waiting, patiently waiting for her answer, with his body so taut she feared he would snap if she touched him.

She touched him anyway, laying both palms on his chest and sticking her tongue out just far enough to touch the tip to his lips. His entire body quivered and stiffened. She felt his restraint.

And then his mouth was on hers and this was not the kiss he'd given her at the movies. Or any kiss she'd ever imagined Eric giving. His lips pulled at hers and his tongue demanded. And he hooked one forearm behind her neck to hold her still.

It was mouth-only contact, and it wasn't soft, but ravenous, as if he'd gone hungry longer than his body could stand. His mouth was firm, his tongue hard, stroking against hers, measuring hers.

She returned his every movement, stroke for aggressive stroke, sucking at his tongue, devouring his mouth, drawing his lips, first one, then the other, between hers, and nipping lightly with her teeth. She couldn't believe how much she wanted this man. This one man.

Her hands kneaded his chest, her thumbs searching out his nipples, the tiny centers as hard as her own. Eric groaned, the rumble rolling out of his body and into Chloe's mouth and both of her hands.

She rubbed harder, pressing with her thumbs and the heels of her palms, finding the erogenous zones buried in the muscle. Eric's shudder, his grunt, his hiss of breath were music, and she played him harder. She pressed in massaging circles until her own panties grew damp.

And it was about that time that Eric buried his face in the crook of her neck, ran his hands down her back to the tops of her thighs and lifted her from the floor. He backed farther into the long narrow room. She wrapped her legs around his hips and held on.

Turning, he set her on a low tabletop littered with nuts and bolts and scraps of electrical wire. She leaned back, lowering her upper body toward the surface of the table, then bracing her weight on her elbows behind her.

What he did then had Chloe almost coming undone. He reached back with one hand to hold her heels together at the small of his back. His other hand crawled between her legs, one finger slipping beneath the crotch of her panties.

He snugged a knuckle into the opening of her sex, drew it up her slit to the hard knot of aching nerves. And then he pulled his hand away, brought it to his nose and inhaled.

"I love the way you smell," he said, and she could see her juices glistening on his skin. When he brought the same knuckle to his mouth and sucked away her wetness, all she could do was close her eyes and let her head fall back.

"I love the way you taste," he said, and she felt her skirt being raised to her waist, felt air on her bare bottom.

"I love that you don't wear panty hose," he said, snapping one of her garters on her thigh. "But more than anything I love that you wear these thongs that are made of nothing."

Rip! The crotch of her panties fell away. He lifted her ankles to his shoulders, and she couldn't even think to gasp, exposed as she was under the light that glared examining-room bright.

Eric took a short step back, leaned down and forward and worked his shoulders beneath the bend of her knees. And the kiss he delivered to the hood of her clit sent moisture dripping from the mouth of her sex into the crevice of her bottom. She ached and she burned and she couldn't stand the suspense.

He nuzzled lower, his nose exploring the crease where her thigh met her torso. He sniffed her scent from one leg to the other. She wanted to beg, but bit her tongue, focusing on the warmth of his breath on her skin and the pressure points where his fingers held open her thighs. The light bristle on his face tickled and she shivered.

His tongue played around the edges of the strip of hair left after she'd shaved, and he pressed down with his chin, rubbing back and forth over the hard ridge of her knotted nerves. Her pleasure bordered on pain.

She could hardly stand his touch. It was too much. It wasn't enough. She was open and she was ready, everything below her waist bare and exposed. And Eric was way too intent on taking his time.

She wanted to reach for his head and guide it between her legs. She wanted to feel the suction of his lips over the bud of sensation so tightly aroused. She wanted to feel his tongue, his fingers, slipping inside.

More than anything she wanted to feel his solid length. She knew how hard he could grow, how swollen, how the ripe head of his penis stretched his skin taut. She wanted to touch him.

Instead she touched herself, moving her hands to her breasts, pinching at her nipples, which had grown pebble hard. Squeezing the mounds of flesh together, she imagined Eric above her, straddling her on his knees, sliding his cock between, sliding it into her mouth.

She tipped her head back farther, lifted her hips to his mouth and moaned. Eric stopped. And she sensed him looking up as he blew warm breath the length of her slit before he moved forward and covered her hands on her breasts with his own.

He didn't even hesitate, but tugged down the bodice of her dress until she spilled free. And then his tongue was there and his lips, sucking and stroking, nipping, while his hands pinched and squeezed. He teased one nipple with light flicks of his tongue, and she raised up, wanting more.

The teasing wasn't what she needed. She needed it hard. She needed it rough. She lifted her hips and scraped her naked sex over the fly of his pants. Eric groaned deep in his gut, the sound vibrating against her skin.

And when he tugged sharply on the nipple he held in his mouth, she swore she felt her sex pull taut. "If you don't have a condom, I'm going to kill you."

Eric didn't say a word as he reached into a pocket with one hand, not even into his billfold but straight into the pocket of his pants, as if he'd tucked the condom there, expecting to get lucky.

He was about to. He stood up, tore open the packet. Chloe tucked her chin to her chest and opened her eyes, watching as he unbuckled his belt, as he freed the catch on his suit pants and pulled his zipper down.

His boxers were a sexy white designer cut and not doing him a bit of good as he sprung free from the opening as soon as given a chance. He shucked the clothing down his thighs, and Chloe could only watch as he rolled the condom over his cock, his balls already drawn close to his body.

"Hold on, princess," he said, his mouth and chin damp and red. "This is going to be wild."

What the hell was she supposed to hold on to? But then it didn't matter, because his thumb was at her sex, judging her wetness, drawing the slick moisture down into the crevice of her bottom, where he stayed to play, pressing against her tight rear opening as he filled her vagina with one long stroke.

Chloe cried out. And he stopped, his penis stretching her open, one thumb pressed to her clit, the other to the crevice of her bottom. She thought she was going to die. The three points of contact had her aching to move, but she stayed still, savoring the feeling of that first filling thrust and the anticipation of what else was to come.

Her sex twitched, her bottom clenched. Eric increased both pressures, the pad of his thumb rubbing teasing circles over her rear opening, pressing lightly until she relaxed, and then he began to move, slowly stroking, pressing her clit, teasing her bottom, circling both points while his cock slid in and out.

She milked him and he groaned and shuddered to a stop. He looked into her eyes then, his diamond-hard, flinty and as hot as she'd ever seen a man's be. His mouth was pulled into a grim straight line, as if the struggle for control cost him plenty. She ran her tongue out over her lower lip and invited him to come.

''Are you ready for this?''

She gritted her teeth and nodded, so ready to explode. He wrapped his arms around her thighs and then he let himself go, his hips driving forward again and again. The angle of his thrusts rubbed the base of his shaft where she most needed the contact.

She came silently because she couldn't wait anymore. Shudders tore through her. Her hands clenched. Her head thrashed. Her hips lifted, crushing her sex as hard as she could to his body.

With each contraction of her orgasm, she gripped Eric's erection, working to pull him farther inside, wishing she could get either her hands or her feet behind him to urge his body deeper. But she needed her arms for balance, her bottom was barely on the edge of the table, and her legs on Eric's shoulders were all that kept her from tumbling to the floor.

She was helplessly dependent. Eric was in control.

His eyes narrowed, burning with the knowledge that she'd taken her pleasure and taken it with him. Knowing he could take his time, take her over the edge again. That he could arouse her further, heighten the thrumming of nerves already exposed and raw.

He slowed then, pulling his cock all the way out until only the head remained buried inside. He pressed forward in one long, leisurely motion until he was fully engulfed. He repeated the process. Again. And again. Each time increasing the speed of his thrusts. Each time hitting bottom sooner, harder. Until he pumped with the stroke of a piston.

Chloe watched all of it, the clenching of his thighs, the grinding of his jaw, the slick slide of his penis in and out of her body. She hadn't counted on the return of her arousal, but seeing the way he drove himself into her, the way he wanted her, the way he couldn't wait any longer...

She sobbed. Spasms rocked her body to the rhythm of Eric's thrusts. A guttural howl ripped from his throat and he came. Chloe felt the warmth. Even through the latex she felt his semen's heat. She squeezed him hard, pulling him deep, drawing out her own orgasm until her shudders ceased.

Her legs slowly slipped from Eric's shoulders, her knees sliding down to hook over his elbows. He didn't back away, but kept his arms wrapped around her legs, his fingers imprinting her inner thighs. He remained hard and buried in her body, and she had no choice but to look up.

"If you're waiting for permission to leave, then permission granted."

"I'm waiting for an answer to my question."

Question? When had he asked her a question? "Remind me, as I seem to have lost my mind."

His face remained a hard mask. "Do you want us to be exclusive?"

How was she supposed to answer that when he had her bound to him? Every time she moved she felt his possession. "Yes. Until we finish this Faustian agreement."

Eric eased his body free, eased her legs from his supporting hold. He slipped an arm behind her and helped her to sit on the edge of the table. He rid himself of the condom, adjusted his clothing and looked her in the eyes.

Chloe could barely move. Her back ached, her hip joints screamed. Her inner thighs throbbed. Her sex burned. Her conscience stung, and any control she'd once had had long since ceased to exist.

Working her dress down over her hips, her straps back over her shoulders, she slid from the edge of the table onto shaky feet, stood and smoothed her hair. She prayed for Eric to keep his mouth shut and leave without saying another word. But her prayers had rarely been answered.

He put his hand on the doorknob, paused and turned to meet her defiant gaze. "Let me tell you something, Chloe. The reason I call you princess is because your ivory tower is so damn high. You make it hard for a man to get close to you, much less claim you as his."

She lifted her chin. "And now you've breached the tower, you think you own me? That you have a say over how I run my life?"

"Is that what you think I want, Chloe?"

"Isn't it?" When had a man ever wanted anything less?

"No, I don't want to own you. I want to know you. There's a helluva lot left for me to learn. And I mean to learn it, princess. All of it." He stepped into the hall and reached back for the door, his gaze hardening. "No matter how many walls I have to scale."

For long moments after Eric left, Chloe stared at the closed door. But no matter how hard she pressed a hand to her heart, she couldn't stop its flutter of foolish hope.

CHLOE REFUSED TO PANIC.

She remembered having rushed past a ladies' room during Eric's earlier mad dash for privacy. And she scurried there now, before anyone could see her.

Before Eric, who was pacing the hallway—thankfully at the far end and in the other direction, rubbing a hand over the back of his neck and looking down at the floor—could say anything more about what had just happened, and add to her regrets.

Or to her hopes.

Her face was an absolute mess. Her lipstick was completely gone, or else smeared across her cheeks and her chin. Her foundation was damaged beyond any repair she could make with a compact. And what was left of her blusher was a joke.

Her mascara had fared better, though it left her with a serious case of raccoon eyes. And she hadn't even gotten to her hair. Her brush, along with her makeup, was in the tiny black feather-boa bag she'd left hanging on her chair, thinking she wouldn't be gone from the ballroom for more than a minute or two.

She'd never expected to find herself dragged off like a cave woman by a caveman.

She stared at her reflection, thankful the ladies'

room was off the beaten path and empty. She couldn't face seeing anyone just yet. It was hard enough to face herself. What she'd just done was exactly what she'd promised herself and sworn to Sydney wouldn't happen.

She'd jeopardized the very career she was trying to save by walking out on the gIRL-gEAR gIRL awards for a quickie. And she couldn't begin to understand why.

She never went into a sexual relationship without using her head before using her body. And sex, as a rule, came in one of two flavors: Sinfully Sweet Fun or Power Trip Delicious.

The intimacy she and Eric had just shared was beyond her ability to define. Her head hadn't factored into any part of their joining, yet she'd felt more than bodily connected. She feared she had put her heart on the line. Eric's accusations had cut to the bone and his words continued to sting.

Experience had taught her not to involve emotion, and to avoid give and take. Giving was too tied into giving *up* for her comfort. After so many years of being told what to wear, how to behave, where to focus her studies, she was finally *in control of her life*.

Every single aspect of her life. And no one was going to take that away by convincing her they loved her and, because they loved her, knew what she needed, what she wanted.

Who she was.

She turned on the faucet, the rush of water a drowning sound ridding her of old memories and those still fresh, still sticky and new. Damn Eric Haydon and his ivory tower promises.

Knowing she wasn't going to be going anywhere

until she did what she could to fix her face, she
splashed warm water onto it and, resigned to using the
liquid hand soap, had just started scrubbing her forehead when she heard the bathroom door open.

Taking a deep breath before taking her medicine,
she lifted her head, opening her eyes just enough to
peak through the bubbles and get a glimpse of Melanie
Craine in the mirror.

At least it wasn't Sydney. Or Eric, Chloe thought,
hoping to avoid facing both of them.

She finished cleaning her face, then rinsed her skin
free of soap and rinsed it again. Melanie hopped up
onto the far end of the counter, handing Chloe several
paper towels once she'd turned off the water.

She straightened, patted her face dry, grimaced at
the reflection in the mirror of her splotchy red skin—
the result of the harsh soap, the rough towels, her embarrassment and the abrasion of Eric's beard.

That last was harder than anything to look at because of the undoubted repercussions, both personal
and professional. And professional she had to deal
with first. She turned her gaze to Melanie. Melanie,
the doll who hadn't forgotten Chloe's purse.

"I owe you for this." Chloe went straight for the
tiny bottle of moisturizer. "How did you know where
to find me?"

"Your guard dog is sitting on a bench outside the
door." Melanie crossed her feet at the ankles and
swung her legs. "You might want to tell him that Pep-
permint Peony is not his color."

Chloe squeezed her eyes closed. Perfect. A walking,
talking billboard advertising her bad timing and loss
of judgment. "So everyone has seen him and knows?"

"Actually, I don't think so." Melanie caught

Chloe's purse before it slipped into the sink. "You managed to pick an out-of-the-way rest room."

A light at the end of the tunnel? "Do me a quick favor?"

Melanie nodded, watching as Chloe worked the lotion into her skin. "Stick your head out there and tell him to beat it." When the other woman's dark brows lifted in question, Chloe added, "And tell him I'll call him when I get home."

Melanie hopped down from the counter's edge. "Didn't you two come here together?"

Shaking her head, Chloe dug into her emergency makeup bag for foundation. "He met me here. He's only my escort. We're not dating. Remember?"

Melanie's reflected expression echoed her disbelieving, "Yeah. Right."

But she stuck her head out the door, anyway. Chloe listened to the mumble of voices, not able to make out any specific words. But Eric's tone of voice was enough to convey his displeasure at being blown off.

She wasn't blowing him off. She really wasn't. But she could deal with only one disaster at a time. And Sydney had to come first. If only Chloe could figure out how to diffuse that bomb before it dropped.

Melanie returned, hopped back onto the counter, dragging the hem of her short dress in the second sink.

"You're going to ruin that silk."

But Melanie, being Melanie, and thinking on a technical plane, couldn't be bothered with Chloe's fabric care tips. "He left, but he wasn't happy about it."

"So I heard." Chloe paused, makeup sponge hovering above her nose. "You told him I'd call him, right?"

"I did."

"And? I'm not in the mood to pull teeth here, Mel. What did he say?"

She shrugged. "He'll be waiting."

He'll be waiting? "That was it?"

"We didn't take time for a long chat. I thought you wanted him gone."

She did. She didn't. "I know. I'm sorry. I'm not at my best right now."

"Now I find that hard to believe, seeing your post-orgasmic glow." Melanie's arched brow dared Chloe to deny the obvious.

So Chloe told only half of a lie. "This is not a glow. This is the result of washing my face with industrial-strength cleaner."

"And Eric was wearing your lipstick because you were doing his colors?"

Chloe returned the foundation to her bag, dug out her powdered blusher. What was the point of beating around the bush when the obvious was so damn obvious? She attacked one cheek with the brush.

"Okay, yes. I'm wearing a head-to-toe postorgasmic glow. Eric and I just screwed our brains out." She attacked the other cheek. "Was it worth ruining my face and my panties? You're damn right it was. Was it worth screwing up my career?"

She left the question hanging. She needed time to think, to make more than a few decisions about what she was doing with her life.

"Panties, huh?"

Chloe sighed.

"Your career is fine."

Chloe snorted. "Sure. You can say that. You're not the one who ran out on one of the most important nights gIRL-gEAR has ever put together. I let everyone down.''

''I told Sydney you were sick.''

Snapping her compact shut, Chloe cut her gaze from the mirror to Melanie's face. ''What do you mean, sick?''

''It was obvious to everyone at the table that you weren't your usual self. You sat through the entire meal and program without tossing off a single smart remark. Then Eric dragged you out of there right after you ate that lemon stuff.'' Melanie shrugged. ''Since the rest of us had chocolate, it was an easy enough bluff.''

Chloe's heart thudded. ''You really think anyone, Sydney especially, bought that I'm sick?''

''It's worth a shot. Eric's gone. You can say you sent him home, which is the truth.''

''Yes. But it doesn't say much for his character, does it? Leaving his sick date all alone?''

''You're not all alone. I'm here. And I helped you send him home. Besides, this is your career, Chloe. If you have to choose between gIRL-gEAR and hot sex…'' Melanie let the sentence trail off, picked it up a second later. ''It's not really a choice at all, is it?''

For all that she wanted to agree, Chloe found herself unable to do anything but twist the wand back into her mascara, leaving her eyes halfway bare. She looked over and met Melanie's gaze. ''What if it's not just hot sex?''

Melanie blinked, blinked again, then slowly scooted off the edge of the counter and leaned against the wall. ''You are kidding, right? You and Eric? Wait. You and anybody? Since when is this mission to clean up your act the real thing?''

"It's not. Never mind." Chloe went back to fixing her eyes.

Melanie edged closer. "Don't tell me to never mind. You wouldn't have asked that question if you weren't seriously wondering."

"That's just it. I don't want to think about what I'm thinking about. I don't want it to be on my mind. I want to get through the Wild Winter Woman fashion show and be done with this escort business."

Except she owed Eric one more wish. And even then she wasn't sure she'd have settled anything in her mind. Or what so strangely felt like her heart.

10
_____

ANTON NEVILLE STOOD facing the converted freight elevator that would take him up the four floors to Lauren's loft. He took one last drag on the cigarette he didn't want, dropped the butt to the concrete walkway and crushed it beneath his boot.

What the hell did Lauren think she was doing with Nolan Ford?

She'd moved out of Anton's place six weeks earlier, claiming he was a control freak, that he couldn't deal with her sexuality or her sexual past, that he was too uptight and had never taken the time to get to know her the way he would have if he'd loved her.

Anton could have thrown the same accusation into Lauren's face. But he hadn't. Because they'd both been guilty as charged. He was man enough to take what was coming to him. He wasn't going to ask her to come back.

He had been going to suggest they start at the beginning, that they take things easy and slow and forget they'd ever tumbled head over heels. He'd been going to suggest all of those things because he couldn't believe Lauren had thrown away the year they'd been inseparable.

But now he wasn't going to suggest anything.

Not when she was seeing Nolan Ford.

Anton shoved his hands in the pockets of his baggy

designer suit pants of dark brown corduroy. He'd left his jacket and his tie in his Jaguar when he'd parked in the garage adjacent to the loft.

After the gIRL-gEAR gIRL ceremony, he'd dropped Annabel at her place and had been on his way home. He'd enjoyed her company and was quite sure she would've been happy to make sure he ended the evening a very satisfied man.

But he wasn't in any frame of mind for a new involvement. Not when he hadn't yet given up the old.

He hadn't been aware of any conscious decision to stop and see Lauren. But old habits were hard to break. And now that he was here he didn't know whether to leave or to take the ride to the fourth floor and see if she wanted to…get a cup of coffee and talk.

The thought of finding her in the throes of drinking coffee with Nolan Ford was what finally turned Anton away from the elevator and back toward the garage. Thinking about Lauren with another man was bad enough. He didn't need to give witness. And so he was walking away. Except two steps down the hallway, he heard the elevator motor engage.

He hesitated, waited for his heart to regain its usual rhythm. *Thump-thump. Thump-thump.* And he stopped, turned back, listened to the mechanical bellow and groan as the car made its way to the ground floor.

He had his hands in his pockets and his feet spread wide, prepared to come face-to-face with the laughing couple, and ready with the excuse of having stopped by for a DVD he was certain he'd left here and had promised to drop off for his teenage brother in the morning.

But when the door creaked open it was Lauren, alone, and she was taking out the trash.

She wore thick white socks and had shoved her feet into clogs. Her sweatpants were purple, worn and baggy. Her hair still tumbled to her shoulders in the same big curls he'd wanted to get his hands on all night.

She hadn't yet scrubbed the makeup from her face. Her eyes glittered. Her skin glowed. She was incredibly beautiful. And the T-shirt she wore was a concert souvenir she'd bought him weeks after they'd started dating. Even if Nolan *had* been standing beside her in the elevator, she was still wearing Anton's shirt.

He took the black plastic bag from her hands because he wasn't sure he'd be able to find his voice. Lauren fell into step at his side and walked with him down the hallway to the back door and the building's Dumpster. Her feet made a shuffling, scraping sound that echoed off the high brick walls.

"Did you have a good time this evening?" she finally asked, and her voice echoed, too, breaking the uncomfortably awkward silence.

Pretending his sudden appearance wasn't unusual suited him. "I did, thanks. Did you?"

She nodded, gave a slight smile. "It was fun to finally see the program come together after all the work we put into it."

"That was a good thing gIRL-gEAR did, awarding those scholarships. And you picked the perfect girl for the job." He frowned. "I'm sorry. I've forgotten her name."

"Deanna Elliott."

"Deanna, right." He hesitated for a second, then went ahead with what he wanted to say, even though the issue had long been a bone of contention. "She seemed as passionate about fashion as you've always been about art."

"Are you dating Poe?" Lauren asked, exchanging one bone for another.

"We've been out, but we're not dating." He pushed open the heavy steel door that opened onto the walled-off section behind the lofts and contained the building's Dumpster, loading dock and maintenance shed. A lone streetlight illuminated the big asphalt square, and the night was cool and misty.

Anton tossed the bag in with the rest of the trash and returned to the door Lauren held open. "What about you and Nolan? Are you and the old man serious?"

Lauren released the heavy door. It slammed shut, the reverberating echo ringing in Anton's ears.

"Nolan is not an old man."

"Relatively speaking, I suppose not. But he's got, what, twenty years on you?"

"Seventeen, if it's any of your business, which I don't think it is." She turned and started her shuffle and scrape back down the hallway to the elevator.

Anton wasn't going to let her slough off the subject as easily. "So what *is* going on with you two?"

"Does it really matter, Anton? I don't remember us agreeing to stay in touch and keep tabs on each other's lives and loves."

"Is that what Nolan is? A love?" Anton hated the weakness that caused him to ask.

Lauren wrapped her arms around her middle. "Nolan is a friend. A supportive friend who shares my passion for art."

Anton kept himself from asking what other of her

passions the older man shared. He hadn't come here to get into a sniping match and he didn't really want to know. "Right. And since he seeded gIRL-gEAR, he no doubt thinks pouring all your energies into the company is what you need to do. Instead of, oh, say, exploring what else is out there. What bigger and better things you might do with your degree."

Another long-standing argument that had played a part in Lauren's decision to break off their relationship. But she replied, "Actually, he's made me realize that what I want to do is go back to grad school."

And that surprised him. Pleased him on one hand, caused a sharp pang of resentment on the other. "You never even hinted that you wanted to go back to school when we were together."

They'd reached the elevator now and stopped. Lauren delayed hitting the button that would retrieve the car. She looked at him instead, frowning slightly, as if trying to see something she'd missed before. Or something she'd hoped had since disappeared.

"I didn't know it myself. Leaving gIRL-gEAR was not something I wanted to think about. That I did know. But I hadn't considered going back to school while working."

"Why that particular change of focus? School instead of a career change?" He liked that she was talking about taking her career forward. He just found it curious, since she'd been so adamantly against any change all those nights they'd argued.

She gave a thoughtful shrug. "It seemed to make sense. I won't be giving up a career I love, but I'll be keeping future options open."

Which was all he'd ever wanted her to do. Did she

now think differently about him? Or had she still not figured out he had her best interests at heart?

"Nolan agrees that it won't be easy—"

Bitter, Anton shoved his hands to his hips. "I should've known. This is Nolan's doing."

"No. It's my doing," Lauren said, raising her chin.

"But you've talked it over with him."

"The same way I would have talked it over with you if you hadn't been so set on me looking beyond gIRL-gEAR."

Had their relationship really been so lacking in communication? "I never suggested you leave immediately."

"You never suggested I do anything *but* leave, Anton." Lauren appeared on the verge of pulling out her hair. "We never discussed other options. You put down your foot and told me what was best for me."

"I suppose Nolan gave you those options." Anton practically spat out the other man's name.

"As a matter of fact, he did. I talked to him about what I would need down the road if I wanted to move into marketing or even into film." A grin touched the corners of her mouth as she drew an imaginary theater screen in the air. "Art Director, Lauren Hollister. I like the way that sounds."

Anton ground his teeth. "You could've talked over your ideas with me."

She shook her head, her gaze finding his. "No. You weren't open to anything but things being done your way. I hadn't even thought of film until Nolan brought up the subject."

"Well, I'm glad you've found someone willing to humor you."

"I don't know what you're talking about," she said, and frowned. "Nolan isn't humoring me."

"He's giving you what you want to hear. What would you call it if not humoring?"

"Friendship. Caring. Interest."

Anton snorted, recognizing that what he was feeling was about as shitty as his attitude got. But it still didn't stop him from saying, "You sure his interest isn't in finding out what you have in your pants?"

Lauren only stared, then huffed in disgust and smacked her palm against the elevator call button. "I think you'd better leave now. We've said all there is to say."

The elevator arrived. The door opened. Lauren stepped inside. The moment stretched.

Apologize, Anton ordered himself. *Tell her how you feel before it's too late.* But his emotions were a jumbled mess, inexplicable even to himself.

So he let her push a button and refuse to meet his eyes. He let her leave, believing he was a first-class prick. He let her go back to her loft and evolving career and a future that didn't include him.

When the elevator door closed, he would've kicked the damn thing, but he didn't want Lauren to hear the sound of his frustration echo up the shaft. Instead, he turned slowly and headed to the parking garage, his steps heavy.

For the first time in memory, the sight of his gleaming black Jaguar failed to give him a rush. He unlocked the driver's side and slid behind the wheel, wondering if it was too late to pay a return visit to Annabel Lee.

Her reception would be warm. She would probably banish this cold emptiness inside his chest.

But she wouldn't be Lauren.

Acknowledging defeat, Anton fired up the engine and screamed out of the garage. Hell, who needed a woman? His buddy Jack Daniels could warm him up just fine, with far fewer complications.

CHLOE DIDN'T THINK she'd ever been so glad to get home. Halfway across the living room, she tossed her purse to the sofa and kicked off her shoes. The strappy pink heels went flying, leaving her three inches shorter and closer to being able to relax.

She needed to shower, to wash her face again, to wash away her encounter with Eric and the rest of the disastrous night. No matter what Melanie claimed, Chloe wasn't sure she'd convinced anyone she wasn't feeling well even if, by the time she'd actually made her way back to the near-empty ballroom, she'd been feeling like ten-day-old garbage.

Melanie had done her best to cover, but Chloe knew she was going to have to clear the air with Sydney herself. It was hardly fair to use Melanie even if the sick-as-a-dog story had been her idea. Chloe was a big girl and needed to swallow whatever bad-tasting medicine Sydney spooned up.

She padded across the thick, cream-colored carpet of her dark taupe-and-mauve living room through the dining area and into her apartment's nice big kitchen, complete with breakfast nook and walk-in pantry. The complex where she lived was downtown and upscale, and being on ground level meant she was one of the lucky few with a patio courtyard.

After staring blankly into her refrigerator and deciding what she really wanted was a glass of wine—which she didn't have, so she'd have to settle for a beer—she reached for a cold Corona longneck and a lime.

With stocking-covered feet slipping on the tiled floor, she carried both to the butcher block island in the center of the kitchen and pulled open the drawer where she stored her bottle opener and paring knives. She pried off the bottle cap, sliced the lime, squeezed the juice from a single wedge into the golden brew and lifted the bottle to her mouth.

As her chin came up, her head tilted back and the bitterly cold liquid flowed into her mouth, her gaze naturally rose until she found herself looking down the line of the bottle and out the patio door.

Eric sat on the black, wrought-iron bench that was the focal piece of her courtyard garden. He leaned forward, his knees spread wide. His elbows were planted on his thighs, his fingers playing with a long blade of monkey grass.

He drew the shoot between thumb and index finger, from end to end, holding the base in one hand until, with the other, he reached the narrow tip. He repeated the process. Stroking long and slow. Base to tip. One end to the other. His eyes remained fixed on Chloe's even when he moved the frond to his mouth, pulling it between lightly pressed lips, then blowing.

The grass fluttered to the ground.

Chloe lowered the bottle slowly, the cold glass beginning to sweat in her hand, the smell of lime a tangy contrast to the smell of the barley and hops. Against the cool floor, the soles of her feet grew damp, as did the pits of her knees, the creases of her thighs at her groin.

What had initially begun as fear, a sharp metallic fright stinging her skin and hampering her ability to breathe, was turning into a wave of sweet expectation, wonder, anticipation and want.

How could she want him again so soon, already, when she'd had him only hours ago? When she'd since sworn to redirect her priorities and make reparations and amends and take control of the direction of her life?

And now here was Eric, his blue eyes unrelenting as he held her gaze, his expression as tender as it was intense. And everything inside her, every part of who she was, knew she would not recover from him easily.

She saw in him so much of what she wanted—was there anything about him she didn't want?—and yet she'd never truly thought to find her fantasy man, or considered what the fulfillment of her fantasy would mean.

She'd never recognized the threat to her control, the desire to give herself up completely to this man who refused to look away, whose vibrancy and sharply tuned focus warmed the air shimmering around her as surely as it heated her skin from the inside out.

He got to his feet then and Chloe swallowed hard at the picture he made, the uncertainty of a little boy lost, of a delinquent caught breaking and entering, and the determination of a man who'd come to claim what was his.

Chloe felt her restraint crack and chip away. How was she supposed to fight a battle she'd already lost? She set down her Corona, then placed both palms flat on the butcher-block surface, her fingers curling over the edge and seeking purchase. But the solid block of wood offered her nothing in the way of a solid foundation.

She was on her own.

The suit Eric still wore was a deep-charcoal-gray pinstripe cut in classic lines. He'd since rid himself of his tie, and his white shirt gaped open. Chloe swore that even from here she could see the pulse beating in the hollow of his throat.

The patio was lit by sconces on either side of the door and the replica of a gas streetlamp that stood at one corner of the bench. There was enough light to see the moisture in the air. Eric had to be cool. A fine sheen of mist covered his hair and his shoulders.

Chloe wanted to beckon him inside, but she wanted even more to wait for him to make the first move, like William Hurt in *Body Heat.* The tension between them crackled, the electricity in the air that of a summer storm, sharp and biting and hot.

She breathed as deeply as the anxiety-driven compression of her chest would allow. Oh, how she could taste the heat of her own rushing blood.

And then Eric moved a step forward, and a second, the third bringing him within arm's length of the sliding glass doors. Chloe prayed she hadn't locked the latch when she'd filled the bird feeder this afternoon. Or that Eric, somehow, had entered through her front door, releasing the catch when he'd stepped outside.

But he had to have come over the courtyard fence. A proverbial scaled wall. And she realized the lengths he'd gone to to be here, to see her.

To have her.

Her knees shook. Her thighs trembled. Her heart seemed to pound in her throat. And then he reached for the door and shoved. It slid open along the tracks, and Chloe wanted to cheer. One long step and he was inside and crossing the dimly lit dining area, his footsteps determined but nearly silent on the tiles.

And then he was in the kitchen, and his nostrils flared as he caught her scent—whether perfume or arousal, she had no way of knowing. But it hardly mattered any longer because he was there, and his hands gripped her shoulders as he backed her into the refrigerator and lowered his head.

His mouth wasn't rough, but it was demanding, of her surrender and her acknowledgment that he would not be walking away. Thrilled into submission, she parted her lips and met his seeking tongue, slipped her hands beneath his jacket and skated her palms up the shirt on his back. His skin beneath the fabric was deliciously cool, and she shivered and pulled him into her own body's warmth.

For a moment she wished she still wore her shoes so he wouldn't have to bend so far to meet her mouth. But then she realized their difference in height placed the fly of his pants just below her navel. And the press of his erection into the soft give of her belly stole her breath.

His lips teased hers. He played with first the top and then the bottom, then sucked on the tip of her tongue. His movements were alternately soft and hard, daring and subtle, sweet and savage, questioning and bold.

Chloe was certain she'd never known more physical sensation from one single kiss. It was more than the involvement of lips and tongue and teeth. It was the vibration of Eric's heartbeat thudding against her hands. The cold tile floor beneath her bare feet. The hum of the refrigerator at her back. The heat of his fingertips where they bruised her shoulders.

All of this amplified by his sweet, sweet mouth. And then suddenly he wasn't so sweet anymore. He was wildly moved to mate. Chloe hadn't known a man's hunger could so suddenly spring to life until he seemed to be nothing but living desire.

Eric's hands, desire's hands, were seeking, searching, slipping over her shoulders, down her arms, across her belly, up to her breasts. He kneaded, squeezed, and she moaned into his mouth. He ground harder, desire ground harder, mouth to mouth, erection to belly, and then the heel of his hand moved to the mound between her legs. No preliminaries, no gentle coaxing. Just a kiss that became sex, with no romance between.

All Chloe could do was spread her legs, giving desire room to explore. He went straight for the hem of her dress, hiking it up, digging beneath, finding the responsive warmth he was seeking, and driving his fingers deep.

Chloe gasped at the shocking invasion. She gouged her fingers into his biceps as he pushed in and out with the whole of his hand. She was stretched wide-open and his fingers hit every hot spot of her sex.

His thumb rubbed hard circles around and around the bud of sensation swollen to a tight knot and aching for the contact that would send her over the edge. Already tonight he'd inflamed her this way, and she wanted to return the same maddening torture.

So she sent her hands to the fastenings of his pants and went to work on belt, metal catch and zipper, shoving his suit pants and his boxers down his backside, then moving to his front and stretching the elastic of his waistband and allowing his sex to spring free.

Again he was hugely swollen, erect and jutting upward. The taut skin of his glans fairly glistened, as did the moisture beading at the opening in the tip. Chloe wanted to lean down and take him in her mouth, but Eric didn't allow her the time.

He stole even the pleasure of touch, bending down for the pants he'd kicked free and the condom he'd stashed in the pocket. Chloe was determined to do this much at least, and grabbed the packet from his hand.

She rolled the rubber the length of his shaft, slowly and with teasing intent, touching her tongue to the bow of her upper lip and watching her handiwork rather than Eric's face. She sensed the heat of his gaze but refused to answer the visual, visceral pull.

This encounter was all about sex—one hundred percent physical sensation; no eye contact, emotion or meaning allowed—and she was going to take charge. She refused to let feelings come into play as she exacted revenge for the uncertain confusion his earlier possession had sparked.

Standing on tiptoe, she lifted her other leg, wrapped it around his body, dug her heel into the back of his thigh. Hands met between bodies, his spreading her wetness, hers guiding him into alignment. He laced his fingers through hers, then drove his body forward, trapping their hands between.

At that—the joining of their bodies so intimately, with hands so casually clasped—she couldn't help but look up.

"I couldn't wait for you to call." His eyes gazed down with the most tender of emotions, all things kind and gentle and caring and warm.

And Chloe couldn't take it. She couldn't handle what his expression revealed. She pulled her hand free of his, moved it around to his backside to prompt him to move. But he remained unmoving. Immobile. His body buried deep with no place to go unless he did as she asked, as she demanded with the squeezing and prodding of fingers and hands.

Still he remained motionless and impaled. Still she urged him into action, growing desperate and emotionally frightened by his insistence on making her wait. She wanted to slap him, to shout. Instead she growled in frustration and scratched her short nails over the small of his back.

He leaned his forehead to hers and whispered, "Shh. I'm right here. I'm not going anywhere."

"That's the problem. You need to move."

"I will," he said, and subtly shifted, rubbing up and into her core, which he'd so easily inflamed.

She hated that he held this power over her. That he could make her crazy with a look and nothing more. That he was able to touch her and take her apart until she wanted to scream with pleasure. And cry at the frustrating loss of her cool.

"Maybe you could get to it sometime soon?" She snarled the question, smacked her palm to his backside.

Bending his knees, he slipped the one hand still between their bodies down underneath their slick joining to play between her legs. His fingers tickled the skin of her thighs, moved to tease the edges of her sex, where his shaft remained buried to the hilt.

That one hand incited her to whimper. And at her sound of surrender, his other hand came up to cradle her face.

"Chloe, I lov—"

"No!" She cut him off with her shout, then pressed her fingers to his lips. "No, you don't. You can't. Please." A sob burst free and she hated herself for the weakness. "Just make me come. That's all I want."

Eric closed his eyes. His jaw worked to repress the words she knew he wanted to say. When he looked at her again, his expression showed a battle between anger and hurt. Neither sentiment did a thing to set Chloe at ease.

"Not a problem, princess." Eric's mouth twisted. "One orgasm coming right up."

And then he began to move. Before she could protest or tell him to get the hell out of her house, he started to slowly thrust, to withdraw, to push forward, to pull away. He knew her too well, knew how to strike the head of his match to set her fire ablaze.

Her body took over, refusing to listen to her mind or her principles or even her common sense. The friction of Eric's movements brought her to the edge and sent her tumbling over.

No man but Eric had ever so perfectly met her physical needs.

Even while she hated him, she loved him.

11

MONDAY, MIDMORNING, Chloe checked her reflection in the mirror of the ladies' room down the hall from her office. The lighting was, of course, perfect, the room's design conceived by Anton Neville's firm, with input from all six of the gIRL-gEAR partners.

Today Chloe had chosen to dress more conservatively than usual. Her suit was a pale pink leather, the straight skirt hitting midthigh, the short-sleeved top double-breasted and waist length. Her stockings were a pale cream and her stacked-heel pumps a bright fuchsia.

She'd applied her makeup deftly as well, carefully blending the shades of blues and purples on her eyelids and going with a pale pink frost on her lips.

Tugging the hem of her top into place and smoothing the lines of her skirt, she took a deep breath and blew it out slowly. She was worrying too much over her appearance, when she saw Sydney every day, and cosmetics and clothing weren't half as important as the confession she needed to make.

Yes, the women were partners, but Sydney held a controlling interest and had the final word when it came to the firm's business. When it came to personnel issues, as well. And since Chloe had professional issues to discuss with the woman at the top, she'd taken her appearance seriously, because she wanted to be taken the same.

She left the ladies' room and headed up the hallway to the office at the end. Sydney's space was no larger than the other five offices located on the executive side of the building, but her space did sit in the primo corner, as befitting her position as CEO.

Chloe rapped her knuckles against the door and peeked into the office, which was decorated in rich shades of peacock blue and olive. "Do you have a minute?"

Sydney looked up from the spreadsheet she'd been studying. "Sure. I need a break. These numbers quit making sense about an hour ago."

Moving into the office, Chloe sat in the chair opposite Sydney's desk and crossed her legs. "Numbers haven't made sense to me since first grade, and one plus one equals two."

Elbows propped on her desk, Sydney settled her chin into the cradle of her laced fingers and smiled. "I think I knew that about you when you kept making wrong change at the coffee shop."

Chloe couldn't stop the upward quirk of her mouth. "And here I thought you had me pulling the espresso because I made less mess with the grounds than everyone else."

"Oh, yeah." Sydney screwed up her nose. "I forgot about that. I have a bad habit of remembering things the way I want to see them until I'm reminded of what actually happened."

Here we go. Chloe took a deep breath. "That's why I'm here. To remind you."

"About the espresso?"

Chloe shook her head. If only it were so simple. "About the gIRL-gEAR gIRL ceremony."

"You got home okay, I hope? Melanie said you weren't feeling well. I should've called to check on you over the weekend, but I've been up to my ears with the designers who are sending samples for the Wild Winter Woman fashion show." Sydney gathered her hair back into a tail at her nape and rubbed the base of her neck with her other hand. She met Chloe's gaze with a questioning lift of an elegant brow.

"I wasn't sick. I was with Eric. I shouldn't have let Melanie cover for me," Chloe said as her foot begin to nervously swing. "Though, by the time she found me, it's true that I wasn't feeling my best."

Sydney continued to rub at her neck, moving her hand into her hair to massage the base of her skull. Chloe had no idea what the other woman was thinking. No idea if Sydney was about to lower the boom or if she was still processing what Chloe had said and deciding how painlessly to drop the ax.

Instead of doing either, she let go of her hair and leaned forward, lowering her voice as she asked, "What *is* going on with you and Eric? Because this can't all be about your reputation. Not that I thought that plan would hold water."

Chloe's foot stopped swinging. "What makes you say that?"

"Because I don't see Eric Haydon ever being content in the role of your escort, temporary or not."

"You mean he'd expect me to live up to my reputation?" And wasn't that just exactly what she'd done?

Sydney's brows drew together as if she were trying

to grasp Chloe's response. "Chloe, you banana. The man is in love with you."

Chloe's eyes drifted closed and she let her head fall against the back of the chair. She couldn't deal with this now. No matter that Eric had been but a breath away from telling her before she'd stopped him with her fingers to his lips.

Sydney cocked her head to the side. "He probably won't tell you, you know."

Of course he wouldn't now. Even Chloe knew that a man had his pride. "He won't tell me because it's not the case at all. I'll admit he has the hots for me. Hell, I'll admit I have the hots for him."

"I think you admitted that when you let him drag you out of the dinner."

Chloe uncrossed her legs and sat forward primly. She was here about gIRL-gEAR, not about Eric. "I owe you an apology, Syd. You and the others. I haven't held up my end of the agreement we made about keeping our closets clean."

Sydney sat back, her fingers gripping the curved ends of her armrests. "What do you want me to do, Chloe? It sounds like you're here for more than an apology. In fact, I've thought for a while that you haven't been as excited about gIRL-gEAR as you were at the beginning."

Chloe gave a huff of a laugh. "And here I thought I'd done such a bang-up job convincing everyone otherwise."

"It might have worked if you'd first convinced yourself," Sydney said, dispensing the sort of wisdom Chloe was coming to recognize as the truth.

"I do love gIRL-gEAR, Syd. Don't get me wrong. If I'm unhappy it's because of what I have going on personally.'' Chloe screwed up her mouth. ''Sort of a pre-mid-midlife crisis.''

After several thoughtful seconds, Sydney released a long, pent-up sigh. ''You know, Chloe, it's not easy being the boss. I have to put aside our friendship, including all the juicy stuff I'm dying to hear about Eric, to consider what your lowered enthusiasm might mean to the company.''

Chloe quietly laughed. ''Not to change the subject, but I have never thought about you as the juicy stuff type.''

Sydney stuck out her tongue. Then she smiled. And then her humor turned wry. ''It's my all-business-all-the-time demeanor that fools people.''

''I'm not sure you're fooling Ray,'' Chloe remarked, struck with the thought for not the first time. ''I was watching him the other night. And something tells me he knows what lurks beneath.''

''Unfortunately, he does know, though I've always hoped he'd forget.'' Sydney picked up her pencil and tapped it against the spreadsheet on her desk. ''Did you know that I went to high school with Ray?''

It was Chloe's turn to squeeze the metaphorical orange. ''I had no idea. Neither one of you has ever even hinted that you have a past.'' When Sydney appeared on the verge of a squirm, Chloe added, ''It wouldn't be a lurid past, would it? One still skulking about in your closet?''

Sydney's chin went up. ''I do not skulk. And neither do my skeletons.''

''You keep them under wraps, right? And that would make them mummies?''

''That's terrible,'' Sydney said, with both a frown and a chuckle.

"That's what I told Eric," Chloe said and, after both women were quiet for a minute, softly added, "Can you give me some time? To work this out? Trust me. It won't be long, because I'm starting to get on my own nerves in a bad way."

Sydney got to her feet and circled her desk, her long, peach-colored skirt hugging her hips as she walked, her classic camp shirt in a geometric pattern of peach and black silk delineating her narrow waist.

She settled into the chair next to Chloe and mirrored her head-back, legs-crossed pose. "How about I give you my friendship? Unless I see a noticeable downturn in your department. Then I'll have to hang you out to dry."

Spoken like Nolan Ford's daughter, though Chloe would never voice the comparison. "Just make sure I'm not wearing leather."

"It's a deal." Sydney held out her hand and Chloe laced their fingers together, swinging their joined hands between their two chairs until Sydney turned her head. "You want to get some lunch?"

Chloe considered her stomach, which seemed to have settled. "On two conditions. We go to Mission Burritos and you fill me in on all the juicy stuff about you and Ray Coffey."

ONE OF THE PERKS of owning Haydon's Half Time and keeping involved in the local sports community was getting to know several of the city's professional athletes on a first-name and buddy basis.

Palling around with the players wasn't about boosting his ego or his in-the-know reputation. The interaction, however, allowed Eric to feel part of a brotherhood he'd belonged to all of his life.

He'd been headed for a career in baseball, had attended University of Houston on a full scholarship, had been the pro scouts' favorite son ever since pitching his high school team to three consecutive state championships.

He'd been ejected from his dreams of a pro career by a torn rotator cuff that three surgeries hadn't been able to fully repair. He'd thought of coaching; hell, he still thought of coaching.

But being on the field, day in and day out, was asking a lot of a man whose dream had been painfully ripped from his future by the shoulder socket. Eric harbored no resentment, but neither did he see any point in rubbing salt where salt wouldn't do a bit of good. He'd learned a long time ago to walk away and leave his past in the past.

Tonight Haydon's had been closed for a private party, a couple's wedding shower Eric, with Chloe's help, had hosted for a rookie member of the Houston Astros he'd known from his days of college ball.

Strange, the twists and turns life took. Here Eric was, content with the life he'd made for himself, feeling no bitterness toward his buddy for achieving the professional success of which Eric had dreamed.

What he did envy, however, was his buddy's relationship with his woman.

And it had taken Chloe Zuniga, of all females, to turn Eric on to what was missing in his life.

His house felt amazingly empty when he went home at night. The big downstairs rooms echoed with silence. The television only provided impersonal voices, chatter to listen to, and he found himself talking back a little too often.

But even more quiet were the rooms upstairs, the

bedrooms he used for storage, the ones he'd left empty. And, most of all, the one where he slept alone. He was tired of sleeping alone. He was tired of living alone.

And the companionship he craved was not the sort to be satisfied with an overgrown, mixed-breed, big-footed mutt, even if he did have a puppy-perfect back-yard.

No. While he was here in Haydon's kitchen clean-ing up the party remains, the companion he wanted was in the bar, sitting on a stool, her head resting on crossed arms, taking the nap she claimed to need after working her ass off as his co-hostess.

Chloe Zuniga could deny she had feelings for him until the Red Sox won a pennant.

Eric knew better. It wasn't the seeing to drinks and hors d'oeuvres and staying on top of the caterers for ice and trash detail and linens and clean crystal that had tapped the bottom of her energy well.

She was beat up by emotion, her exhaustion a result of the bombardment of happy couples, the whispered questions about their relationship, the congratulations on snagging one of the city's most eligible bachelors.

Eric had heard Chloe's insistence that they were nothing but good friends. But he'd heard the rest of the talk, too—talk that had hammered away at her re-sistance to admitting that what they shared had long since moved beyond friendship.

Sure, they were friends—the best of friends as a matter of fact. Intimate friends, though he wasn't sure lovers was an accurate definition. The sex they'd en-joyed had been too intense, too combustible to be free of consequences, but not tender enough to be called making love.

She hadn't let it be.

Oh, he'd given her the orgasm she'd begged for that night in her kitchen and, yeah, he'd gotten his, too. And then he'd left the way he'd come, through her courtyard, though this time he'd opened the gate and walked out. One wall at a time was plenty.

He'd seriously thought about not coming back, not seeing her again, blowing off his last wish and her Wild Winter Woman fashion show. He'd been hurt. He'd been pissed. But he was a man of his word, or he was nothing.

And Chloe's cold shoulder, her fingers pressed to his lips, even her trembling body and quiet sob of release, hadn't told the same truth as her eyes.

In the end, her eyes were what he'd listened to. What had convinced him that her ivory tower was tumbling down. He'd read more than physical gratification in those eyes and, by God, from now on he refused to cheapen himself and the woman he loved.

No matter his past reputation, Eric Haydon was no longer an easy lay. His princess would not be getting him naked again until they were in his bed and he could make love to her the way she needed to be loved. With heart and soul as well as body.

Resolved, he stored the last of the food he'd come to the kitchen to put away, and headed back into the bar. Chloe was right where he'd left her, with her head down on the bar…asleep. And snoring.

He couldn't believe it. His princess snored.

If he hadn't already been a goner, she'd just sent him on his way as she sat there, ankles primly crossed to one side, her deep-rose-colored dress softly draped over her legs and lap, the tiny cap sleeves hugging her shoulders.

He'd turned out all the lights in the bar earlier, once the last of the guests had left, leaving on only the two that lit the swinging doors into the kitchen and the one that glowed from the hallway to his office.

It was enough light to see how relaxed Chloe's face was in sleep. Her lips were lightly parted and drawn into a bow. Strands of her hair fluttered in her face with each exhalation of breath.

Eric eased up onto the stool next to hers, wanting nothing more than to watch her sleep, preferably on the pillow next to his. Her expression appeared so gentle, so pure, and this was the part of her he loved the most. The part he didn't understand her reasons for hiding.

He reached out and with one finger tucked the fallen strands of hair behind her ear. She frowned at the contact, shifted slightly, then slowly opened her eyes. Her frown deepened.

"Don't do that." He drew his finger down the tiny crease between her brows. "Your face might stick that way. Didn't your mother ever tell you that when you were a kid?"

She blinked once, twice, then raised up, propped her elbow on the bar and cupped her head in her palm. "I didn't have a mother when I was a kid. In fact, I've never had a mother, period."

Whoa! He'd known she'd been pretty much raised by her father but... "What do you mean, never?"

She covered a tiny yawn, shook her head lightly. "My mother died in an auto accident before my first birthday."

Trust Chloe not to milk his sympathy in past discussions. She was too tough for that. Eric tucked back her hair, which had again fallen free. "Why didn't your father ever remarry?"

"Are you kidding?" She lost the frown for an expression of mocking disbelief. "Where would he find a woman as perfect as the wife who'd given him five children? Who'd never smoked or drank or raised her voice? Who was beautiful and gentle and content to be the happy homemaker?"

He studied Chloe's face, the way her cynicism remained, the way her gaze never wavered. "You're serious, aren't you?"

She shrugged. "It's the truth I grew up with. I only recently found out it was a lie. She couldn't measure up to his impossible standards when she was alive, so he created a paragon of virtue after her death. After a few years, I think he actually believed it himself. He sure as hell made me believe I was inferior."

Oh, now this was interesting. It wasn't a past lover, but her father who'd made it damn near impossible for Chloe to trust men. "How did you find out?"

She straightened where she sat, stretched, then draped her upper body over the edge of the bar. "My brother recently came to town and told me."

"Yeah? Which one?" He knew she had four, but that she rarely saw them.

"Aidan. The oldest. The cowboy." Her fond smile said he was also her favorite.

"Cowboy." Eric snorted under his breath. "Why didn't I know that, Chloe? Why don't we both know more things like that about each other?" He toyed with the drawstring tied into a bow beneath the baby-doll top to her dress. "Don't you think it would be a good idea if we learned?"

She pulled the silky strings from his hand. "You've

had your three wishes. I have the Wild Winter Woman fashion show to get through and then we'll go our separate ways. I think the best idea is to keep focused on our deal.''

That damned deal again. A devil's bargain. ''You scratch my back and I'll scratch yours? Is that it?''

''Do you have an itch that needs scratching, sugar?'' Her eyes were still sleepy, her smile relaxed, her posture a limber melting of tired muscles and bones. She looked like she harbored a sexy secret, and when she reached out a hand to share, Eric tensed.

She scraped her short fingernails down his thigh to his knee. The sensation was less the abrasion of a chalkboard and more the downward pull of a zipper. Eric was not going to let this happen.

He knew what she was doing, could see in her eyes the offer she was going to make. She didn't want to talk about what he wanted to discuss, so she was turning the channel, switching stations, working to tune him in to her broadcast instead.

He should have jumped up from his stool right then, but he couldn't leave without seeing how far she planned to take him. Or how far he'd let her get before he told her no. Because he would tell her no.

''I can do better than that, you know.'' She pushed up from the bar, then from the bar stool. Trailing her nails in a reverse direction until she reached his hip, then drawing them up his torso to his shoulder, she circled to stand at his back.

He'd long since lost the jacket he'd been wearing, and his white oxford shirt did little to deaden the effect of her touch. Her fingertips pattered along his shoulders to his neck, where she skimmed her nails into the hair cut close at his nape. She scratched and rubbed, finally cupping her hand and massaging his tired muscles. He couldn't help but groan.

"See? You like it when I scratch your itch." She whispered the words close to his ear, her breath a tickle of warmth across his skin.

"I never said I didn't like it. When did I say I didn't like it? Liking it isn't the problem, Chloe."

"Then what *is* the problem, sugar?" The question rolled off her tongue and she cupped the shell of his ear.

He pulled in a shuddering breath. "The problem is that I can't do this anymore."

Her hands paused in their working of his shoulders, but she quickly resumed her pace. "I don't get it, Eric. What can't you do?"

She'd called him Eric. He could deal with her calling him sugar. But when she said his name it made it hard to keep her at a distance. "I'm going to lock up the bar. I'm going to drive you home. I'm going to walk you to your door and, if you're lucky, I'll kiss you good-night. But that's it. No more getting naked."

For a moment, she hesitated. Then she leaned forward to run her hands from his collarbone to his pecs. Her breasts pressed firmly into his back. "You know, sugar, we never have gotten naked. Not together. Or at the same time. I think we should do something about that, don't you?"

Eric took the biggest breath his lungs would hold and slipped out from under Chloe's arms, turning on his stool to face her. He spread his legs, pulled her between, linked his arms behind her back to hold her still.

He knew from the spark reflected in her eyes that

his own burned with the fire eating him alive. "Are you sure you want to know what I think?"

Her flirtatious, come-on smile was uncharacteristically unsteady. "Of course I want to know what you think. I also want to know what you feel like—" she ran her hands up his thighs "—what you smell like—" she leaned toward his neck and inhaled "—how you taste."

He managed to survive her seduction with only a slight adjustment to his fly and his shorts. Now it was his turn. And he hoped she was ready.

"What I think, Chloe, is that I should kiss you. Kiss your eyebrows—" which he did, one then the other "—the tip of your nose—" he kissed her there, too "—the corner of your mouth—" here he had the most trouble sticking to his game plan because he knew her mouth was so sweet "—before I nuzzle your neck."

He drew the line at any more physical contact, beyond the fact that his hands were still pressed to the small of her back. He wasn't made of stone, though in another minute he'd be hard as a rock. The look on Chloe's face didn't help. Her eyes were soft and dreamy, and the play of her lips and tongue spoke of her own obvious arousal.

Eric lowered his head, catching a hint of her floral perfume and the clean scent of her skin as he whispered close to her ear, "What I think is that I should tug down your dress and dip my tongue into your cleavage. Then I think I should peel you out of your bra and work you over with my mouth."

Chloe released a breathy moan, pressing her upper arms together and lifting her breasts for his attention, while walking her hands over his rib cage and around his waist. "I like the way you think, sugar."

But she'd hate what he was going to do.

He raised his head because he needed to breathe air that didn't smell like her skin grown damp with arousal. Her wide violet eyes were fairly glazed, and her hands worked madly at his belt buckle. Her juices were flowing, and he had to be crazy, but he knew he had to pull away.

When he slid from the barstool, she took his hand in both of hers and backed toward the end of the bar, obviously intent on using it as a makeshift bed. But he dug into the pockets of his pants for his car keys.

Chloe stopped, her expression incredulous. "You wouldn't dare."

"Watch me." He bounced the keys in his palm.

Her eyes narrowed to glittering slits. "If a woman pulled this stunt, she'd be called every foul name in a man's vocabulary."

"Chloe, I love you."

Her lashes fluttered, then stilled. Her mouth softened, but remained closed.

As reactions went, it blew beets, but he gamely forged ahead. "I'd kill right now to be inside you, but it's not going to happen here or tonight. I don't want a quickie on a bar counter. Next time I want a bed. And all night. And your full agreement that we're not going to have sex."

She blinked. "We're not?"

Grinning at her disappointed tone, he stalked purposefully forward, grabbed her by the wrist, ready to take her home. "No, princess. We're not. What we are going to do, when it happens, is make love. It's about time you learned the difference."

12

ERIC HAD YET TO SEE a single supermodel.

Here he was at gIRL-gEAR's Wild Winter Woman fashion show, sitting in front of the runway, sharing prime real estate in the George R. Brown Convention Center with Leo Redding, Ray Coffey, Nolan Ford, Jess Morgan, Doug Storey and Anton Neville.

And there wasn't a supermodel to be seen.

Chloe, the sneaky little thing, had obviously been willing to pull any rabbit out of her hat, since it had been the promise of the supermodels that had swayed Eric, way back when, to go along with her plan.

Well, that wasn't quite the truth, he mused, shifting in the utilitarian convention center chair. What had convinced him in the beginning to barter his services had started months ago, before he'd been paired with Chloe for Macy's scavenger hunt.

Because he played soccer with Anton, Eric had originally been introduced to Chloe by Lauren last year during the league's spring season. He'd seen Chloe off and on during the months that followed and heard tales of her reputation through the local testosterone grapevine.

Tales that left him curious and disbelieving.

Curious because he'd never been able to reconcile the stories of her ball-busting skills with her sugar-coated, marshmallow appearance. And disbelieving because he'd never met a woman who had it in for all men.

The scavenger hunt pairing had made him a convert.

But knowing the truth of her nature hadn't made a bit of difference when he'd glanced up that late Saturday afternoon to see her sitting at the bar, wearing a football jersey, cross-trainers and a look of distress.

He'd dusted off his knight-in-shining-armor duds before she'd even filled him in on the particulars of her dragon. Now that he'd gone a round with the son of a bitch, Eric could testify to the beast's bullying hide, intimidating scales and razor-sharp teeth tempered in cruelly abusive flames.

This damsel-rescuing business was hard work, though being a damsel had to be worse. Still, the lack of reward was almost reason enough to throw in the towel…or the chain mail.

Eric hadn't seen Chloe for two weeks now, not since the night he'd driven her home and walked her to her door after the party they'd hosted. Telling her what they were going to do, then not doing anything, had been as hard to pull off as a two-outs, bases-loaded, bottom-of-the-ninth save. He'd started to kiss her there beneath the covered portico leading to her front door. But, true to form, she'd told him not to bother.

And now, sitting and tugging on the collar of his tuxedo shirt, he was trying to convince himself that he was here at the fashion show because he was her escort and that he wasn't doing the kick-me, beat-me, make-me-beg routine.

It wasn't an easy case to make when not one of the gIRL-gEAR partners was to be seen.

Up until a few minutes ago, at least, he'd been able

to carry on a conversation with Ray, who sat on his right, or with Anton and Leo, to his left. But now, with the DJ mixing old disco and new house music, setting what Eric supposed was a clothes-wearing mood, he had nothing but his thoughts for company.

Compared to supermodels, it was lousy entertainment.

The lights dimmed. Colored spotlights swept the room. The music surged to a crescendo, then died down to a low background beat. "Ladies and gentlemen. Please welcome our hostess for the evening. Star of the locally produced and nationally syndicated talk show *Speak Up!*, Dr. Kate Lindsey!"

Automatically rather than enthusiastically, Eric joined the huge crowd in applause as the auburn-haired psychologist stepped from behind the curtain and made her way to the podium at the left of the stage.

"Good evening, Houston." Dr. Lindsey's greeting was met by another lively ovation. She smiled warmly out at the crowd. "It's wonderful to see this amazing turnout and so many familiar faces. But save your energy for the show. Trust me. You're going to need it. Because what I've seen backstage will blow you away."

Again the crowd roared. Again Eric offered desultory applause. He was too much of a blue jeans and T-shirt kinda guy to get excited over seeing a bunch of women's clothing. Now give him a supermodel...

"Houston? Get ready to be wooed. Get ready to be wowed. Get ready to open up your wallets and spend till it hurts! We have bragging rights to the hottest fashion ticket in the country. Now, let's show the world how we dress it up, Texas! Get ready for the girls of gIRL-gEAR!''

Eric shook his head and sat back. No wonder the girls had made themselves scarce. Supermodels. Right. And he was a major-league ball player. Still, he couldn't wait to see Chloe strut her stuff…uh, as long as her stuff was covered.

The spotlights returned to dance across the stage. The curtain parted. Ground-hugging fog rolled forward, hovering over the platform, dissipating feet in front of the runway in smoky fingers of orange, yellow, pink and green.

The music turned funky and eight lithely androgynous gymnasts, poured into leotards of like colors, tumbled through the murky haze. Eric found himself caught up in the stylish production. But then the stage lights brightened and he quickly pulled a straight face.

Dr. Lindsey adjusted the podium's reading lamp and moved to her script. ''Recently awarded a full scholarship along with the title of gIRL-gEAR gIRL, please offer your congratulations one more time to Miss Deanna Elliott.''

Eric nodded to himself. So, Chloe's favorite had won. She hadn't told him. He wondered why she hadn't. Not that he'd thought to ask…

''Most likely to go to the head of the class, Deanna is wearing a classic back-to-school look. Her red letter sweater tops a kicky private-school plaid kilt. Add a pair of red leather bad-girl boots and find *yourself* the teacher's pet.''

Deanna strutted down the runway with one hand at her hip, her chin in the air and a saucy no-one-can-stop-me-now grin on her Julia Roberts mouth. Looking at the girl, Eric could only chuckle under his breath and hope the partners knew what they were doing. They definitely had a monster on their hands.

Deanna tossed her head for the return trip, her sleek black ponytail slapped her shoulders like a whip, and Dr. Lindsey raised her voice above the thunderous response. "Thank you, Deanna. Now, please welcome the woman who gives you the best in guidance and games, editor of gIRL-gEAR's Web site, Macy Webb.

"From the lemon-yellow tennis shoes and matching cuff watch in neon plastic, Macy's ensemble is paint-spattered street punk personified. Her skin-hugging pullover in a Picasso-patterned mosaic is paired with a matching skirt covered in colorful subway-car graffiti. This is fashion at its silly unmatched best."

Eric cast a surreptitious glance to his right toward Leo Redding. Leo, who rarely showed emotion, who wore the straightest of straight faces, sat with his arms crossed, the corners of his mouth lifted in a sardonic twist that said silly wasn't the half of what Macy was wearing, and she wouldn't be wearing anything once he got her home. Eric chuckled.

"Macy Webb, ladies and gentlemen," Dr. Lindsey said, as Macy skipped off stage and Lauren started down the runway.

"Lauren Hollister has given the gIRL-gEAR Web site a wildly popular retro design, but now she reaches back further in time to give us a peek at her own inner Victorian. Wearing distressed leather boots laced to the knee and a tiered black taffeta skirt above, Lauren has embellished the antique panache with delicate extras including a fringed scarf from Grandma's attic, knotted behind the stand-up collar of a denim weskit."

Lauren made the turn at the end of the runway and Eric made his own casual turn to the right. Halfway down the row of seats, Nolan Ford sat with his head down, disregarding Lauren in favor of taking a call on his cell phone. *Interesting,* Eric thought, rolling his shoulders and looking to the left and Anton Neville.

Anton sat forward, elbows braced on his knees and hands clasped, his expression a mix of longing and regret as his gaze moved from Lauren to the floor between his feet. Chloe had been so wrong, accusing Anton of putting on a missing-Lauren act. Eric seriously felt the other man's pain.

"Our next model, Sydney Ford, holds the proverbial reins of fashion's rising empire and rides onto the scene wearing white pants with long lean lines tucked into black riding boots. Her sheer white blouse is strategically striped with ribbons of winner's circle satin. At her waist hangs a belt buckle styled to look like a silver stirrup, and a silver horseshoe bracelet adds the finishing touch of equestrian class."

Eric had to admit it—Sydney looked hot. Sophisticated, uptown hot. Which made perfect sense, being that she was a Ford. Again Eric had to check out Nolan's reaction, and this time the cell phone was totally out of sight. Sydney's father literally sat on the edge of his seat. And the smile on his face was nothing if it wasn't beaming.

And then there was Ray Coffey, directly on Eric's right and looking like invisible chains were the only thing keeping him from throwing Sydney over his shoulder and heading for the closest cave.

In his peripheral vision, Eric registered Poe walking down the runway, wearing chunky black-and-white stripes in what Dr. Lindsey described as Soho and Op Art in a mod, mod, mod world. But what had drawn

Eric's attention away from the stage was more than Ray wanting to get his hands on Sydney.

It was the caliber of looks shooting back and forth between Nolan and Ray. And Eric's curiosity would've continued to stew if he hadn't heard Chloe's name. He swung his attention back to the stage and forgot not only his burgeoning conspiracy theory, but that anyone else in the room existed.

"Chloe Zuniga's savvy finesse of cosmetics and accessories modernizes the hippie-chick with wispy gypsy layers of a cotton gauze paisley in colors of deep pink and red. A peasant blouse with shirred sleeves and a matching multiwrap skirt give a dreamy, carefree feel to the ensemble. Silver and garnet drop earrings, stacks of silver bangles and a flower choker in the same paisley print complete the look."

Eric's gaze tracked Chloe's performance as she made her way down the runway. She twirled and posed. She held out her arms, showing off the cut and the transparency of her blouse. She lifted the hem of her skirt and kicked out in a mini cancan. She waved to audience members, blowing flirtatious kisses.

The other "models" had done similar routines, firing up the crowd for the unorthodox fashion show that epitomized the firm's individualistic style. Eric just hadn't followed every step of the other acts the way he was following Chloe's.

Which was why he was watching when she looked down from the runway and into his eyes. And why, when she crooked a finger his way, caught the tip of her tongue between her teeth and smiled, Eric felt like he'd been sucker-punched in the very worst way. Because he didn't know where she was coming from.

Maybe this come-on was a payback for leaving her

at her door when she'd wanted him to take her to bed. Or maybe this was a public demonstration of their exclusive arrangement, less for his benefit than for that of the rest of the room.

Whatever. She had him. She so had him.

In a faraway corner of his mind, Eric heard Kinsey's look described as blues traveler in rock 'n' roll indigo denim. And then Melanie took the long runway walk in form-fitting, classic background black to show off pagers and wireless headsets and text messaging tools.

But he didn't get a look at either of the final two girls. His attention was divided between ignoring the ribbing from his seatmates and working his way backstage. He planned to find out what his sexy little hippie-chick had on her mind.

And what she intended to do about it.

"YOU KNOW, ERIC. This getting me into your bedroom to show me something business is hardly very original."

Climbing the stairs to the second floor of Eric's house, Chloe reached up to take off the choker she'd worn for her modeling stint in the fashion show. She was unaccountably edgy, wondering what Eric had on his mind, and the choker was, well, choking her. "All you had to say was that you'd changed your mind about sleeping with me again."

"I haven't changed my mind about sleeping with you again." He reached past her head and planted his palm on the bedroom door. "And don't take that off."

Her clutch purse tucked beneath an arm, Chloe's hands stilled on the choker's fastener. She looked up and into Eric's eyes, where he hovered in her space. She waited for him to push the door open, uncertain, if pressed, whether she'd be able to remember what it was he'd just said.

He was so close she could see the tiny flare of his nostrils as he breathed. He had one brow lifted, yet the whole of his expression remained unreadable. He smelled like comforting warmth and lightly spiced male skin, and her anticipation heightened.

When he shoved open the door, she moved forward, aware of how close he still stood. Aware that they hadn't yet touched.

She'd missed their intimacy. She hated to admit it, especially after the way he'd so audaciously turned her down the night of the party at Haydon's, but she had. And it wasn't only the sex she missed, even if it had been three weeks since he'd taken her apart in her kitchen.

She'd missed Eric, the teasing and taunting, the playful put-downs, the serious heart-to-hearts and being able to talk to him about anything. She'd missed the way he insisted on opening her car door, the way he called her even if he had nothing to say because that's what friends were for.

He was the first person to come to mind when she had news to share or a story to relate about the happenings of her day. Yes, what they shared was much more than lust. It was even more than friendship. But she was still afraid to call it love. She wasn't sure she was ready to give up that much of herself.

Eric closed the bedroom door and leaned back against it, his hands shoved into the pockets of his pants, his pleated tuxedo shirt unbuttoned at the throat, his tie dangling loose around his neck.

Chloe wanted to gobble him up. She wanted to slowly feast. She no longer knew what she wanted where Eric was concerned. He had her so confused…and so terribly, terribly frightened that she'd never be able to meet his expectations.

What would she do if she tried? And then failed?

And if he hadn't changed his mind about sleeping with her, why had he swept her up and away after the fashion show even before she'd had time to change back into her own clothes?

What could he possibly want?

She stopped in the center of his room and turned to wait. "You mean there really is something in here you want me to see?"

He nodded, so she walked through his room, admiring the color scheme of navy and rust and deep pine green, admiring, too, the highboy dresser. His sleigh bed was queen-size, his comforter smoothed beneath a stack of pillows in cotton cases of navy and light blue plaid.

But she didn't notice anything extraordinary. Nothing strange or obvious that he'd want her to see. The curtains covering the room's one window were a marbled pattern of rust and blues. The door to the bathroom stood open. The color scheme continued into the smaller room.

A stack of folded T-shirts sat on top of an overturned laundry basket. A pair of inline skates and three pairs of athletic shoes had been tossed into the corner beside the closet door. The haphazard mess made Chloe feel better. She'd been deluding herself into thinking that Eric was perfect. Perfect as a man. Perfect for her.

She'd circled through the entire room and now returned to perch on the side of the bed, looking up at Eric, who still leaned against the door. She wasn't sure she'd ever seen him looking more relaxed. Or more sure of himself, sure of what he wanted, sure of his success.

A shiver ran the length of her spine and settled in to tickle the small of her back. Keeping her voice level required no small effort. "I guess you're going to have to point it out to me, sugar. I'm obviously too dense to get it on my own."

Eric pushed away from the door and straightened. Hands still in his pockets, he made his slow and lazy way toward the bed. Toward *her*. The room didn't seem big enough for both of them, suddenly. One minute Chloe's excitement simmered, the next it seethed. Even the tips of her fingers tingled, wrapped around the clasp of her purse.

He didn't stop when they bumped shins. He continued forward, giving Chloe no choice but to scoot back into the center of the bed. He climbed on top, bracketed her thighs with his knees and bore her down to lie flat on her back, his hands holding his weight on either side of her head. And still she clutched her purse with anxious fingers.

"You're lying to one of us, sugar. Because if this isn't about sex, the only thing I can think that you might want me to see is your ceiling." She couldn't believe that was her voice sounding so breathless, her stomach launching a flight of butterflies.

"I don't want to show you my ceiling. And I'm not lying to either of us." He lowered his body, bracing his weight on his forearms and elbows, stretching out his legs along either side of hers.

She felt the bulge between his thighs against the cleft between her own, a bulge still soft and only beginning to stir with interest. But it was the look on his face, the gentle intensity brightening his eyes, that stirred both Chloe's interest and her uncertainty.

Eric dipped his head, rubbed his nose over and beneath her earlobe, nipping lightly, then kissing the spot he'd teethed, finally blowing warm breath against the skin between her jaw and her temple before he whispered, "I'm going to show you what it's like to make love."

She could barely swallow past the lump of emotion balled tight in her throat. She was shuddering from the inside out. Her bones, her muscles, her skin. No part of her failed to respond to his words.

"Then I was right," she managed to answer finally in a strained voice. "You do want to sleep with me."

"What I want is to love you." He moved his lips to the corner of her eyelid and lightly kissed her brow and her lashes. "I'm going to use my mouth to show you what you won't let me use my mouth to say."

"Sure thing, sugar." And maybe he hadn't heard the crack in her voice. "Whatever floats your boat."

"You just won't give an inch, will you," Eric said with a chuckle, his lips moving along her jaw to her chin. He raised up to look into her eyes. "Busting my chops from here to Tuesday every single time."

What was she supposed to say? Admit the defense mechanism kept her from getting too close? Kept her heart safe? Kept him from controlling any part of her life? "C'mon, sugar. You know you wouldn't have me any other way."

He toyed with the choker, his finger teasing beneath the fabric band. "I'll have you any way I can get you."

"Hmm. Is that a touch of desperation I hear?" Even

if it was, she couldn't deny the small thrill she felt at his words.

He sat back on his heels, braced his hands on his thighs for a thoughtful moment before yanking his tie from his collar. He next went to work on the studs of his shirt.

Chloe couldn't tell what he was thinking. She hated that she couldn't. He had a smile on his face, but still his expression seemed pensive. Shouldn't she be able by now to better tell what was on his mind?

"Let me tell you something, Chloe." He shrugged out of the tuxedo coat and pitched it to the floor. And now that his shirt hung open, exposing the muscles of his abdomen, lightly dusted with golden hair, he moved to undo his cuffs.

Chloe swallowed hard at the pure masculine beauty above her. She felt tiny and feminine and on the verge of losing an internal battle. "What do you want to tell me, sugar?"

"Two things, really." He held up two fingers, then went back to working his cuffs. "First of all, I gave up being desperate the year I turned thirteen. Up until then, I'd held on to the hope that my mother would show up from wherever it was she'd disappeared to ten years before.

"But hitting my teen years was like hitting a brick wall. I had a great foster family. And desperately wishing for the blood family I was never going to have was making me a miserable little dork."

He tossed his shirt to the floor and loomed above her, his widespread legs straddling her hips, his hands moving to the fastenings of his pants. Chloe was torn between watching his economical movements, his agile fingers, his belly being bared, and wanting him to

stop and put what he'd just told her into an under-
standable context.

She had no grasp on this conversation.

"Secondly," Eric continued, "you've called me
sugar at least ten times in the last ten minutes. You
do that a lot when you're nervous. I don't want you
to be nervous. And I want you to call me Eric."

He was going too fast. Chloe couldn't catch up
when he was moving this fast. She was still back on
his blithely made comment about a foster home and
desperation, and he was complaining about her habit
of calling him sugar.

"Eric, wait." She raised a hand, then scooted from
between his legs and up toward the headboard. "Why
are you telling me this now, here, in your bed? Why
didn't you tell me when I told you about Aidan's visit?
Or when we went to the movies and I popped off about
showing your mother respect?"

He showed less interest in her confusion or in answering her questions than he showed in her feet, having moved both to his lap, where his fingers were now
busy stripping away her shoes. "You accused me of
being desperate. But what you call desperation, I call
impatience. Desperation is an entirely different animal.
That's all."

That's all? "And the foster home bit? Where did
that come from?"

And where had he learned to do that to her feet?
Rolling the knuckles of one fist into her arch like that,
wrapping his other hand around her ankle, propping
her opposite foot against the bulge behind his fly.

She couldn't help it. She flexed her toes. And Eric
smiled.

"It came from the same place as the issues you have

with your father. The past. But that's not where either
one of us lives. We're living now.'' He turned his
attention to her other foot, massaging it in turn.
''You're wary of men. I understand why and don't
particularly blame you. That doesn't mean I'm going
to let you lump me in with the masses.

''That's not who I am, Chloe.'' His hands slowed
in their manipulation of her very tired feet. ''The family who raised me for most of my life taught me better
than that. They taught me acceptance, not judgment. I
realize that I have to earn your trust. That's part of
who you are. And I love who you are.''

Hope and fear wrestled for dominance, constricting
Chloe's chest. ''Who am I, Eric?'' This was the one
thing she had to ask. The one thing she most wanted
to know. ''Why would you want to love me?''

He placed the soles of her feet flat on his thighs and
worked his hands beneath her skirt to her garters. ''I
guess I should leave out the obvious guy-type things,
like that fact that you have the most incredible set of
knoc—''

''That's not what I'm talking about. Though at least
that I can understand,'' she said, as he rolled down
her stockings and bared both of her legs. His hands
were warm, his touch incredibly distracting. But this
time, the ache in her heart was too powerful for the
one between her legs to overcome.

''Ah, Chloe. Guys aren't all about tits and ass.'' He
lifted a foot, kissed her instep. ''There are a few of us
who like a woman with a brain.''

He kissed her ankle, bit at her Achilles tendon. ''We
like it when she stands up for what she believes in,
what she wants, and doesn't cower when the bad guys
try to mow her down. And personally? I especially like

it when she doesn't mind working up a good sweat on the volleyball court.''

He nibbled his way up her calf to the pit of her knee, his fingers slipping beneath her skirt and up her inner thigh. Then he lifted his head to stare into her eyes.

"Chloe, you sweet, beautiful idiot. I love the way you can make me laugh even when I want to strangle you. I love the way you'd go to the mat with anyone who threatened one of your friends. I love your ambition. I love your energy. I love the way you snore.''

He smiled at her widening eyes, then sobered. "I love that you don't treat me like a dumb jock and, because you don't, I'm forced to think and act like a smarter man. A *better* man. Don't you see, sugar?''

What she saw in his beautiful blue eyes shattered the last of the shell surrounding her heart.

"I love everything that makes you who you are, Chloe Zuniga. Now.'' He lowered her leg to the bed. His hands went to the tie holding her wrap skirt closed at the waist. "I don't want to talk anymore.''

He pulled the ends of the tie closures through their fabric slits, separating the skirt's layers of gauzy material until she lay beneath him, bared to the waist but for her garter and thong. And then he stopped, his gaze sweeping over the treasures he'd uncovered.

Chloe felt the urge to suck in her belly, but she didn't. If Eric loved her for who she was, then she had to give him her honesty. She couldn't hide any part of herself, including the vulnerability seeping in as he scrutinized her barely clothed body.

"You're making me nervous…Eric.''

"Aw, honey.'' He blew out a choppy breath.

"That's nothing compared to the way you're making me shake."

His near tremulous smile was almost her undoing, and she closed her eyes for sanity's sake. What she saw was so real, so full of Cary Grant promises. She wanted to be bold, aggressive, to demand he show her body the way to heaven again, as only he, among all men, could do.

But none of those hard-hitting attitudes that had long served her well were within her emotional reach. At this moment she felt nothing but tenderness, gentleness and a softly loving response to Eric's attention.

And when he shifted on the bed, when he leaned forward and sweetly kissed the skin of her belly above her navel, Chloe had to squeeze her eyes even tighter to hold back the tears.

Eric nuzzled his way up her breastbone, pushing her blouse up over her breasts and running his tongue along the lacy edge of her bra before taking one nipple into his mouth through the fabric.

Chloe arched upward, pressing her head back into the pillow and lifting her chin as Eric sucked hard, pulling with his lips and circling her areola with his tongue. She wanted to tug down the cups of her bra, to free her breasts and guide his head to her naked skin.

But she kept her hands where they were, on either side of her head, one still holding her purse. She couldn't believe she still held her purse. She tossed it in the direction Eric had tossed her shoes, then slipped her hands beneath the pillows so she wouldn't slip them behind his head.

He wanted to teach her about making love. Which meant she had to let him take control. She had to surrender her mind as well as her body, and give him access to parts of herself she'd shared with no other man.

But now that Eric was urging her up and pulling her blouse over her head, she couldn't think anymore, because she was nearly naked in his bed and he was so close and the look on his face was way beyond her comfort zone. She was seconds away from falling apart.

Eric tossed her blouse to the floor and, before he lowered her back to the bed, rid her, too, of her choker and her bra. The bra went the way of the rest of her clothes. The choker he held on to. And when he returned his affections again to her breast, he used the fabric flower to tease the other.

Her nipple, already peaked with arousal, tightened further as he drew the soft gathered edges over the tip. But he didn't stop there. In fact, he replaced the gauzy flower with his mouth, rolling her nipple with the tip of his tongue and drawing the flesh of her breast between his lips to nip and suck and kiss at her skin.

The fabric petals he skimmed down the center of her body. Chloe shuddered as Eric tickled and teased her belly, exposed between garter and thong. He moved his mouth to her breastbone then kissed his way down the flower's path. Coils of expectation burned feverishly in the wake of his lips.

By the time his mouth reached the elastic band of her panties, Eric had opened her legs with his hand. He teased the lips and mouth of her sex with the flower, brushing the choker over her plumped flesh covered with the thinnest layer of pink silk and mesh.

His attention was mind-numbingly gentle, infuriatingly tender, when what Chloe wanted to feel was the pressure of his body stroking hers. She'd never known the arousal of waiting, of hovering at the edge of completion, of being pulled back and dangled, unmercifully, above orgasm's precipice. She was used to going for broke.

This was what Eric was showing her, even as he moved the flower down the skin of her inner thighs, from one leg to the other, until he reached her knees. He was showing her pleasure's torture, how much sweet suffering her body could take. All the sweeter because it was Eric doing the torturing.

When he'd moved the flower from her crotch to her legs, he'd sat back on his heels, so his mouth had never made it beyond the barrier of her panties. But still, he had to know how wet she was already. The damp, musky, sugary scent was strong enough to have reached her own nostrils.

Suddenly, he tossed the choker to the floor, then stood to shuck off his tuxedo pants, leaving them both in nothing but their underwear. Leaving them both open and exposed beneath material meant to cover.

The crotch of her thong was barely wide enough to hide her sex. And Eric's erection strained at the fly of his long-legged boxers. The material showed a ring of dampness from his early release. Dampness of the same sort soaked into her panties.

He moved forward then, one knee on the bed, then the second, slowly sliding up the comforter and between her legs. He placed his broad palms on either side of her sex, framing her between his index fingers and thumbs.

And then he leaned down and tasted her through the material of her thong. He flicked the tip of his tongue over her entrance, pushed against her hard center of nerves with his tongue's flat surface. Chloe clenched her fingers into the comforter, clenched her inner muscles to keep from coming in his mouth.

He slipped one index finger beneath the crotch of her panties on one side and out the other, twisting the material into a rope and exposing her feminine flesh to the air and his eyes. The air was cool, but his breath was hot when he opened his mouth and warmed her with a stream of blown heat. Then he spread open her sex with two of his fingers and inserted his tongue.

Chloe panted, pointed her toes, flexed her thigh muscles and froze. Because Eric wasn't finished. While he made love to her with his tongue, stroking deep, withdrawing, licking between the folds of her flesh so wildly aroused, he rubbed the twisted rope of her panties back and forth until she thought she would burst.

"Oh, Eric," she whimpered. "Please."

"Please what, Chloe?" He lapped at her again, chuckled softly when she shuddered. "You want me to make you come? Is that what you want?"

Her head thrashed on the pillows. "I want you. I want you to fu— I want you to make love to me."

"Chloe, honey. I am making love to you." He replaced his tongue with a finger, two fingers, three. He kissed her clitoris, sucked it into his mouth, then made his way up the length of her body to bury his face in the curve where her shoulder met her neck.

She turned her face toward him, kissed his forehead, shivered and seized his hand. "I want to feel you. I want you inside of me."

Raising one knee, she leaned in toward him, hugging his body with her leg, since she was trapped beneath his weight. Her one free hand she moved down between their bodies, reaching as far as she could until she touched the waistband of his shorts and the swollen head of his penis stretching the elastic away from his waist.

"This is what I want," she said, slipping her hand down the length of his shaft, so sleek, so smooth, so incredibly solidly strong. "I want you, Eric. Only you."

He pulled in a strangled breath and rolled away and off the bed, padding barefoot to the bathroom for a condom. On his way back across the room, he pulled off his boxers. Chloe couldn't take her eyes from his body, the long length of him, the hard muscles in his thighs, his lightly sculpted chest and the breadth of his shoulders.

Most off all she couldn't look away from his flatly ribbed abs, his straining penis jutting upward and the sac of his balls drawn tight beneath. Her body wept with wanting him. And then he was there and he was crawling over her between her legs.

When he kissed her, she tasted herself, her salty sweet flavor mingling with his. He reached down and aligned their bodies and, in one smoothly controlled thrust, he filled her.

He filled her and continued to kiss her, moving his tongue in sex play with hers while his lower body pressed forward, pulled back, setting a rhythm that she matched with a measured lift of her hips.

It was the sweetest of matings, the gentlest loving Chloe had ever known. Eric took his time, patiently holding himself in check as Chloe's fever rose. She dug her fingers into his tight buttocks, pulling him into hard contact when he insisted on a soft touch, urging him to press forward when he was content with an easy rolling pace.

So when the first jolt spiked through her, she wasn't prepared. She was used to wildly reaching, not having completion unexpectedly steal her breath. It was the barest of tickles and it had no end. Spasms rolled like waves, one after another, drowning her in liquid sensation until she was gasping and spent.

Eric buried his face in the curve of her shoulder, buried his hands beneath her backside. His thrusts increased in strength and in speed, and Chloe followed him as he climbed toward release. He cried out, the sound muffled by her shoulder. But nothing muffled her sob when she came so suddenly again.

Together their bodies rested, comfortably joined for long, quiet minutes, until Eric rolled away, then drew her close again, working them beneath the bedcovers. Chloe heard his whispered, "I love you," before she heard his even breathing and his satisfied snore.

She waited for his sleep to deepen before slipping out of his bed. He would be hurt when he woke up alone, and the thought of causing him pain after he'd given her such joy squeezed a tiny moan from her throat.

She froze, but he slept on undisturbed. More than anything in the world she wished she could stay, wished she could show Eric her love in return. But before she could allow herself that luxury, she had to make a break with her past.

If she didn't, she and Eric had no future.

13

ERIC PULLED INTO the parking lot of Taco Milagro, having driven by on Westheimer and seen Chloe, Deanna and Annabel Lee walking out of the Tex-Mex restaurant.

He wasn't going to question the coincidence, but he was going to take full advantage.

Since the night he'd made love to her, the night she'd walked out on him, ten days ago now, he'd called Chloe at home and at the office. He'd called more than once. And he'd left messages on her machine, her voice-mail and with her assistant.

He was tired of being blown off when he had something he wanted to say.

He'd told her he wasn't desperate and, by damn, he was tired of looking like a liar. But her refusal to return his calls didn't make it easy to look like anything else.

He knew he was out of wishes, but he still had one to make. If she turned him down this time then, yeah, okay. He'd accept that nothing was going to happen between them.

But he had to give it one last shot, had to make one last effort to convince her that he didn't want to own her. That he didn't want to run her life. That he didn't want to mold her into some sick and twisted ideal.

He only wanted to love her and, no matter that she

expected differently, he wasn't going to say, "Here's the catch."

Pulling his Mustang into the parking space three down from Chloe's VW Beetle, he braked hard and jumped out, needing to get to her before she got to her car. All three women were headed his way. Deanna and Poe probably wouldn't appreciate the holdup but, hey, they'd get over it.

He walked toward the laughing trio, his long strides eating up the pavement. At Chloe's carefree smile, at her throaty trill of delight, Eric's gut knotted. Must be nice to be able to relax, enjoy lunch with friends. Eric had felt ready to snap now for ten days.

Poe caught sight of him before Chloe did; her head was turned to the side as she chatted up Deanna. Poe gestured, looking his way, though she spoke to Chloe from the side of her mouth.

Chloe's head swung around. Deanna's followed. The women stopped talking and their steps slowed as he continued to approach at full speed. All four of them wore sunglasses, so he was as blind to Chloe's expression as she was to his. He was, however, able to see her mouth and her smile freeze in place.

Eric shrugged off the cold. He didn't care if he was putting her on the spot. He didn't even care if he did look desperate. Last-ditch efforts often did.

The group came to a stop and Chloe was the first to speak. "Eric. Hey. You remember Poe."

Eric nodded. "Miss Lee."

"And this is Deanna Elliott," Chloe said, inclining her head toward the younger woman. "Our gIRL-gEAR gIRL."

"Miss Elliott." Again, Eric nodded. But that was it

for the small talk. He pulled off his Ray Bans. "Chloe, can I speak to you privately?"

"I don't know, Eric." Chloe gave a quick glance toward the other two women. "We really do need to get back to the office before Sydn—"

"This won't take but a minute." He gave both Deanna and Poe a dismissive look, one he hoped conveyed the apology absent from his tone of voice, then turned back to Chloe. "I can give you a ride back if that will help."

"Chloe, you stay. I'll get Deanna to drop me at the office. In fact, I think I'll put her to work." Poe linked her arm through the younger woman's and teasingly tugged her in the other direction. "Now that she's the proud owner of a high-school diploma, we have to keep her busy. We can't have her getting any wild slacker ideas."

Chloe frowned. "Are you sure?"

Deanna giggled, tossing her long dark braid over her shoulder. "Are you kidding? Like your office is so totally the coolest."

Eric could've given the teen a brotherly hug and kissed the dragon lady. Though Chloe now appeared to be the one breathing fire.

She watched the other two women walk off, then turned her flames his way. "You sure know how to put a bad mood on a good time, don'tcha, sugar?"

Eric hung the Ray Ban's earpiece over his T-shirt's ribbed neckline. "At least I know how to return phone calls."

"Oh, now that is a big fat lie." Chloe stomped off toward her car, digging in her macramé bag for her keys. "I called you fifteen times if I called you once before I ever came to see you at Haydon's. If you'd had the courtesy to call me back, we might not be standing here now arguing in a parking lot.''

"I'm not doing any arguing.'' Eric crowded in between Chloe's car and the one beside it, blocking her only easy escape route.

"No? Then what are you doing? Why are you here?'' She opened her car door, tossed her bag on the passenger seat, slammed her hands on her hips.

Eric couldn't believe it. They were right back where they'd started. She was doing her best to break him. And she sure had the ammunition. "I'm here because you wouldn't call me back. You could've saved me the trip and saved yourself the embarrassment of being stalked in a parking lot.''

She stared at him for a minute, though she still wore her sunglasses so he couldn't see her eyes. Then she turned her head to the side, her gaze sliding away, her lips pressed together in a flat, grim line.

Eric shoved a hand back over his hair. "Chloe, I'm not here to stalk you. Or embarrass you. And I'm sorry if I have.''

She waved him off with one hand. "I'm not embarrassed. And I should have called you back. I know the frustration of waiting on a return call that never comes,'' she said, her mouth twisting wryly.

That look gave Eric hope that she wasn't hell-bent on never speaking to him again. "I thought you were blowing me off. Call me masochistic, but if that's what you have on your mind, I'd rather be blown in person.''

Her lips quirked and she chuckled at that. "I'm sure you would, sugar. And you deserve better than me leaving you to stew in your own juices. But my not returning your calls is about me. Not about you.''

And if that wasn't the oldest kiss-off in the book, he didn't know what was. *Oh, well,* he thought, and shook his head.

"Eric," she began, reaching out and placing a hand on his forearm. "I know how that sounds. 'It's not you. It's me.' That's a crappy thing to do to someone."

"Glad we agree on that, at least." Not that he felt any better. What he felt, in fact, was dumped. Stupid for being here. And like a whipped sucker.

Her fingers tightened a minute before she let him go and moved her hand to the car's open door. She held her jaw tight, as if holding back a mouthful of the wrong words.

Eric put his hands to his hips and watched the late lunch-hour traffic crawl by. "Look, Chloe. If you can't tell me what you're thinking, then I don't need to be here. I thought we were beyond being tongue-tied with each other."

He started to turn away. She stopped him with a whispered, "Wait." So he arched a brow and waited.

She took a deep breath. "I'm not giving up. Or throwing away what we have…this thing we have. But I'm not ready to be part of an *us.* Too much of *me* has been stirred up lately, what with Aidan's visit. And with…you."

"What about me?"

"You scare me to death, Eric." Her voice quivered. The car door squeaked as she leaned her weight into it. "You talk about love and make it sound so simple. But I've never known it to be anything but complicated. It's complicated and it's hard. Your mother abandoned you. My father's an abusive ass. Even Lauren and Anton can't get it right."

She paused, slowly closing the car door and resting her forehead against the curve of the roof. "I'm not even sure I know what love is."

He could counter every one of her lousy arguments. He had his foster family. She had four brothers. He had a feeling Anton and Lauren weren't totally kaput. But even if they were, look at Leo and Macy.

And then there were Eric's own feelings for Chloe. Which he thought he'd made clear. And, yeah. It hurt that she still didn't get it. So he'd say what he'd come here to say and leave his heart in her hands.

"Chloe, I know our arrangement is a done deal. And I know I used up all three of my wishes. But I have one more to make." He was going way out on a limb here, but at this point did he really have anything to lose?

Her head still resting on the car, she rolled to the side to see him. "I supposed I can descend from my ivory tower long enough to hear your petition."

Seeing the smile that touched her face, Eric felt his gut clench. He didn't think he'd ever loved her more than he did right then. "Haydon's Hammers have a tournament on Memorial Day. I want you to come."

She was already shaking her head. "I can't. Ray's having a barbecue. I've already committed."

"That's okay. You don't have to play. Just show up."

She frowned and stood up straight. "I thought you liked the way I played."

Eric laughed even though his mood was anything but lighthearted. "I do like the way you play."

"So, what? You're looking for your own personal cheerleader?"

"No. I'm looking for someone who plays for

keeps.'' She pulled off her sunglasses then, and Eric continued, spitting out what he'd come here to say before those big violet eyes did him in.

"I want to renew our exclusive arrangement. I want this relationship to be a real commitment, Chloe. And this time I want it with all strings attached. If you don't want the same thing, then don't show. I'll take that as your final answer.''

Heart pounding in his chest, Eric turned and walked away, wondering how he was going to make it through the next two days before finding out if he was a winner.

Or the biggest loser since Cary Grant waited on top of the Empire State Building for a woman who never showed.

TTHE SUN GLARED DOWN on Stratton Park and on Eric's bare shoulders and bad mood. Haydon's Hammers were sucking wind, and he was going to end up shelling out for a helluva lot of brew by the end of the day.

He wouldn't have minded so much losing the tournament or that much beer if he hadn't felt like he was losing a big part of his future happiness the closer it got to the end of the day.

Chloe hadn't showed.

A hundred scenarios had run through Eric's mind. Her Beetle had been squashed on the drive over in the holiday traffic, and she was being scraped off the pavement while he played ball.

She'd gotten stuck flipping burgers or had to make an emergency beer run for Ray...and her Beetle had been squashed in the traffic and she was being scraped off the pavement while Eric played ball.

He knew none of his conjured imaginings were anywhere close to the truth. She'd just decided she liked
things better with no strings attached.

He guzzled a paper cup of bright orange sports drink
and scrubbed the ball of his drenched T-shirt down the
center of his chest. The Memorial Day heat was taking
no prisoners.

The park was packed with picnickers—families,
couples, teens and kids. Kites soared and baseballs
zipped and Frisbees winged across the fields. The
smells of burning charcoal and smoked sausage and
grilled chicken and burgers would've had his stomach
growling if he'd had an appetite.

Instead he was growling at anyone who made eye
contact. All these shiny, happy people were getting on
his nerves. What did they think they were celebrating,
anyway, besides a day off from work? He doubted half
of them knew what the holiday was about. They didn't
deserve to have fun.

And who made you king of the world, Haydon? A
king needed a queen, and he couldn't even convince
a princess to come to a volleyball game. And, hell.
Who needed a princess, anyway?

All that ivory tower wall scaling cost a man too
much time and effort, made him old before his time.
And put a big damper on his fun with the damsels.

Good thing his princess had showed her true colors
before his armor got too rusty. Now he was free to
rescue at will. Since he would obviously never learn
his lesson...

"Damn it, Chloe. You're not a quitter. I can't believe you're giving this up." He muttered the words
under his breath. And, yeah. He had to admit it. Hear-

ing them spoken aloud, even in his own rough and raspy voice, made them real.

Real enough to accept. Hands planted at his hips, T-shirt caught in one, he hung his head and faced facts. He'd had an affair to remember, but it was over. Finished. Kaput.

He'd do better with an overgrown mixed-breed, big-footed mutt. Unconditional love would go a long way toward healing the wreck of his heart.

"Yo, Haydon. Let's go."

"Gimme a sec." He jogged to his car, tossed his T-shirt onto the floorboard and dug in his gym bag for another. Then he went to play the game.

Not quite as satisfying as playing for keeps, but he'd live. Yeah. He'd live.

"RESIGN? What are you talking about, resign?"

"You can't resign! You're a partner."

"You *are* gRAFFITI gIRL. No one else can take your place."

"This is insane, Chloe. You're one of the original girls."

"It might not be insane, but it's certainly not cosmically sound. Chloe, have you really thought this through?"

Wearing a skinny black skirt, plus a shell and cardigan of pale pink cashmere, Chloe sat at the conference table, legs crossed, foot swinging, hands laced in her lap, waiting for the shock to wear off, the objections to die down.

She'd delayed making her announcement until the end of the partners' brainstorming session, thinking it the perfect time to present her proposal, knowing the five female brains in the room would be in rare form.

And now that the uproar had settled and stunned silence had descended, she glanced around the table at the faces looking at her as if she'd lost her mind. Which, truth be told, was not out of the question.

Macy, the wild child. Lauren, the ethereal willow. Kinsey, the bohemian mystic. Melanie, the technical wizard. Sydney, the classic beauty.

All Chloe could do was smile and count her blessings. Joyful tears pricked her eyes and, with a tremulous sigh, she said, "Do you know how much I love all of you? How much I owe all of you?"

Sydney frowned, blinking rapidly, and tapped the pointed end of her pencil against her legal pad of notes. "You don't owe us anything, Chloe. I don't know why you would think you would."

Now that she was being honest—with herself, with her friends—Chloe saw no need to sugarcoat the truth. She took a deep, cleansing breath. "Because all this time you've been putting up with a fraud."

"Fraud?" Melanie screeched, nearly coming out of her seat and overturning her chair in the process. She righted her seat, adjusted her headset and glared. "Get real. You're the most open, honest, tell-it-like-it-is person I know. Fraud my butt."

Chloe closed her eyes briefly, realizing this was going to be a lot harder than she'd thought. Even painfully squeezing her fingers hadn't kept them from going numb. "Well, okay. I'll give you that. Personally? I am who I am. But this fashion business?"

She let the question settle and got to her feet, lifting the leather satchel from the floor by her chair as she did so. She pulled out the five binders she'd put together on her own, using feedback gained over several lunches and dinners with both Deanna and Poe.

Picking the brains of gIRL-gEAR's gIRL and the firm's number-one buyer had given Chloe the confidence to go forward with her plans. She was doing the right thing. And, for the first time in her life, she was going to be true to herself.

Which also meant she was going to be true to Eric. The two statements were synonymous, and it was time she accepted that fact gratefully. But first things first…

"Brace yourselves, because this is going to be a shock."

And, hugging the binders close to her chest, Chloe told her best friends the story of her life.

She told them of being given no choice but to major in fashion design when she'd wanted nothing more than to study phys ed. She shared the news of Aidan's unexpected visit and, with permission, of her conversation with Poe.

Leaving out the details of Poe's modeling career, Chloe used the other woman's pursuit of her dream as a paradigm for her own decision to change her career focus, to take what she'd learned in life and put it to use.

After all, cosmetics and accessories, for all the fun she'd had managing her product lines, would hardly make a difference in any girl's life. Chloe wanted to make a difference. She wanted to share the riches found in following one's heart.

"I know this is not the most conventional way to approach a change in gIRL-gEAR's structure," she said in closing, circling the table to distribute the binders. "But I had to see if I could come up with a halfway feasible plan before I brought it to the table. What I've put together is only a draft, but it should answer most of your questions."

Sydney quickly scanned the opening page and spoke first, lifting her eyes and meeting Chloe's gaze. "gUIDANCE gIRL? You want to set up a mentoring program?"

Having passed out the proposals, Chloe returned to stand behind her chair. Her hands anxiously gripping the chair back, she nodded. "The name is open to debate. I'm more interested in discussing the fundamentals. We have such reach, such influence. I want to do more with our celebrity than we've done so far."

"Am I right in understanding that this is more than simply offering advice? Like Macy does in her column?" Lauren asked, her eyes already sparkling with enthusiasm.

That sparkle was the only affirmation Chloe needed. "Yes, exactly. Advice would be a part of it. But it's more encompassing. I want to include career counseling and peer groups and even organized lock-ins."

"Slumber parties?" Macy asked.

"Sure. Why not? A girl's got to have some fun." That said, Chloe cast a glance around the table, taking in the expression on each partner's face as they intently read through her ideas.

Feeling the need to spread her enthusiasm, she started pacing again, circling the table and feeling five separate gazes following. "I don't expect this to be decided today. And it's not like I'm giving two weeks' notice here. The entire concept will require a lot of preparation, study and development.

"But I am determined to do this. If not here at gIRL-gEAR, then wherever." She came to a stop behind her chair once more and took a deep breath. "Which is why I'm going back to school in Septem-

ber. I don't think a degree in fashion design qualifies
me for any sort of social services work.''

"What about gRAFFITI gIRL and gADGET
gIRL?'' Melanie asked. "You can't mean to walk out
on your babies?''

"Actually, no. I've covered that base as well.'' She
could hardly keep the grin from her face.

If they thought she was out of her mind now, wait
until she told them about Poe.

CHLOE ZUNIGA STEPPED inside the doorway to Haydon's Half Time and paid no attention to the unholy
blast of noise. She was a woman on a mission, and
she would not be deterred by chumps with bad man-
ners, lame come-ons or beer breath.

It was the end of June and baseball season was in
full swing. Knowing now what the sport meant to Eric,
she found that the crack of the bat rang like sweet
music from the big-screen TV across the room.

In light of her recent journey of self-discovery, she
found it hard to believe she had ever thought it
sounded otherwise, especially when she considered
what a powerful driving force volleyball had been during her first seventeen years.

That she and Eric shared a love of sports, one that
had started at such an early age, had to be fate. An
omen that they were meant to be, that they had only
been waiting for Kinsey's cosmic forces to collide and
open discovery's doors.

During the wee hours of the night they'd made love,
he'd told her about baseball. About the group of kids
he'd lived with going together to games. About the
family who'd raised him cheering his talent, and his

affinity for the sport consuming his life. About his dreams dashed by an injury that was nobody's fault.

He'd told her, too, that she made him a better man. She didn't believe it. Nothing she'd shown him or offered him could have made him a better man. She just hoped he hadn't given up on her while she'd been working to find her own better self.

Who was she kidding? Of course he hadn't. And she'd kick his butt to Cleveland if he had—or so she had to keep telling herself. She needed all the confidence-shoring she could get to make it through the next few minutes. Her palms had started sweating against the package she held.

She'd chosen today's outfit as carefully as she'd chosen the one she'd worn to Haydon's two months ago. Her goal was similar: to convince Eric he was the only man for the particular job she had in mind. Then, she'd needed him to help save her reputation. Now she needed him to accept her gratitude…and her love.

Her skirt was calf length and pencil thin; her matching cowl-neck top was sleeveless. The soft pink cashmere blend hugged her hips, snugged her waist and molded her breasts without being provocatively tight.

Her sling-back sandals left her feet bare and provided sexy peepholes for her toenails, painted in bright Pixie Passion. She'd taken special care with both hair and makeup, and even she had to admit she looked hot.

A few of Eric's customers agreed. But she ignored the wolf whistles, the catcalls and the cries of "Oh, baby, I've got what you need!" Her quarry was straight ahead of her, pulling a draft beer from a tap behind the bar, wearing butt-hugging blue jeans, a white Nike T-shirt and a red Haydon's towel tucked into the back of his waistband. It draped so sweetly over his rear end that she ached to walk up behind him and squeeze. Oh, he was cute!

He turned and slid the mug to his customer just as she reached the bar. His eyes widened, then brightened, before a wary veil came down. She clung to the lifeline of his first reaction. Wariness was a protective response, and the least she deserved. She slipped between two stools rather than taking a seat, and clasped the package tight to her chest.

Holding himself aloof, Eric managed a neutral bartender greeting. "What'll it be? A diet soda? A cosmopolitan?"

He wasn't fooling her a bit and she smiled. "It's nice to see you remember."

He reached for the towel at his back, wiped his hands free of nothing. His expression remained overtly cautious. "I remember a lot of things."

She could read so many of the things he remembered in his eyes. He remembered more than her walking away. But it was the pain she'd put there that gave her the courage to try and take it away. To put her pride…and her love…on the line.

"Eric, could I see you in your office? Just for a minute? I, uh, have something I'd like to give you."

He had yet to look away from her face, but when she offered the package as proof of her claim, he glanced at it and frowned. For a minute she thought he was going to turn her down. She saw the possibility flicker in his eyes. Then he called over his shoulder, "Jason! Cover the bar. I'll be back in a few."

Chloe took a deep breath and stepped back from between the stools. *So far, so good.* Her knees wobbled like rubber, but somehow she managed to follow Eric down the hallway to his office. He pushed open the door and motioned her inside.

She brushed by, purposefully touching her shoulder to his chest, feeling his heart pound as she did. He was so warm and he smelled so wonderfully familiar, and if she screwed this up she'd never forgive herself. And she'd never forgive Eric, either, for making her fall in love. She'd never known anything so scary as the possibility that she'd waited too long.

He closed the door, crossed the room to his desk, putting the huge piece of furniture between them. She wanted to jump across the wide expanse and into his arms and break down all of his barriers. She wanted to demand he give her another chance. Instead, she handed him the magazine-size package she'd wrapped in nondescript brown paper.

Reluctantly, he accepted her gift. "What is this?"

"It's a thank-you." She twisted her fingers together, held her hands in front of her waist. "A belated token of my appreciation for your help with my redemption."

"You mean all that exchanging of favors we did worked? You've been redeemed?" A hint of amusement softened his grim features.

Her heart leaped with hope, even as she narrowed her eyes. "Very funny."

"Just making sure we're on the same page here. I don't want to take credit that belongs to one of your other escorts."

"I know I hurt you, sugar. And I'm more sorry than I can say. I wish I could go back in time and do things differently, but, since I can't..." She was so ready to grovel. "Would you please just open the package?"

For one horrible moment, she sensed his hesitation. His urge to shove back her gift unopened, a fitting revenge. Then he shrugged. ''Whatever you say, princess.''

Ripping off the paper in one home run swing, he stared down at the simple black document frame.

Her heart in her throat, her fingernails drawing blood in her palms, her lungs working like a pair of bellows, Chloe waited.

And waited.

And waited, while Eric's inscrutable gaze roved over the autographed eight-by-ten glossy photo, similar to the ones already hanging in his office gallery. Only this one wasn't of any hometown or nationally known sports figure.

It was a portrait of Chloe herself, standing in the sand pit at Stratton Park, her back to the net, a volleyball in her hands. She wore her cross-trainers, her long denim shorts and a Haydon's Hammers T-shirt.

And scrawled in black marker across the bottom of the photo was her autograph: ''To Eric, who holds all the strings of my heart. I'm ready to play for keeps. Love, Chloe.''

It wasn't enough, she thought. It was too little, too late. She wanted to speak, to ask, but she had no voice and her lips were quivering and Eric wasn't saying anything. He wasn't even moving.

She shouldn't have come. He'd told her weeks ago that their business arrangement was a done deal. She'd blown her chance of continuing their relationship on a personal level by not showing up for the volleyball game. He couldn't forgive or forget—

He looked up. And she stopped breathing.

His eyes bright and liquid and swimming with some

powerful emotion, he moved from behind the desk and walked…away from her and toward…the couch? No, not toward the couch, but the trashcan on the floor at the end! Chloe wanted to close her eyes. She wanted to run screaming into the night.

Instead, she forced herself to watch…as Eric reached over the can to the wall behind, where his beloved photo gallery stretched.

When he removed his most prized photo of all, and tossed Anna Kournikova into the trash, Chloe choked back a strangled sound. When he reverently hung her gift in the center of the shrine, she pressed her hands against a heart too full to be contained. When he opened his arms, she ran, launching herself into them with a sob of joy and relief.

Eric caught her up and swung her around until she thought she would pass out. Dizzy, laughing giddily, she punched his shoulder. "Eric, put me down before I puke all over you."

He slowed and let her slide down the length of his body, and since she was wearing cashmere, top and bottom, her skirt stayed bunched around her waist. She reached back to tug the material down over her rear, which was now feeling a rush of cool air. But Eric got in one good smack before she finished.

"Hey. That's no way to treat a princess." With Eric's arms still wrapped around her waist, she had to push against his chest and lean back to see his face. "Especially a princess who loves you."

He blinked hard and he smiled, and then he cupped the back of her head and pulled her close, pressing his lips to her hairline for several long seconds. Her hands, trapped between their bodies, absorbed his every heartbeat. Her hair fluttered with his every raspy breath. She watched the rhythm of his pulse in the hollow of his throat, and she flexed her fingers into his chest.

He'd understood what her gift had meant and considered it—and her—precious. She was the luckiest woman alive. Her own eyes burned with the emotion she couldn't wait to share with this most amazing man who loved her. This man whom she loved. She sighed in contentment as Eric set her away.

"You know I was about to give up on you," he said thickly, wrapping his arm around her neck and guiding her toward the door.

She knew he needed to get back to work. And they had plenty of time. They had forever. "What can I say, sugar? Good things come to those who wait."

"Now that's about the most romantic thing I've heard today."

"Even better than hearing that I love you?"

"I must've missed that part. Maybe you should tell me again."

Chloe reached up to lay a palm against his cheek, stood on tiptoe to replace her hand with a kiss. "I love you, Eric Haydon."

"Aw, Chloe. You're breaking my heart."

"C'mon, sugar. I'll buy you a drink. And you can tell Dr. Chloe all about it." She took his hand and headed for the bar.

"Wait one sec," he said, pulling away. He stepped back through the door, dug the Anna Kournikova photo from the trash and shoved it in the bottom drawer of his desk.

And then he cut off the office light, winked at Chloe when she arched a brow, and said, "Just in case."

The instant before darkness hit, Chloe cast a steely glance at the desk across the room. *Don't hold your breath, sister. The Red Sox will win a pennant before you kick me off his team.*

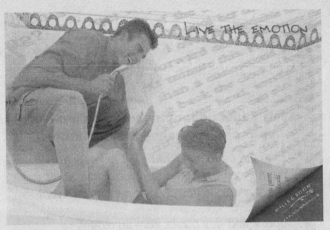

Modern Romance™
...seduction and
passion guaranteed

Tender Romance™
...love affairs that
last a lifetime

Medical Romance™
...medical drama
on the pulse

Historical Romance™
...rich, vivid and
passionate

Sensual Romance™
...sassy, sexy and
seductive

Blaze Romance™
...the temperature's
rising

30 new titles every month.

Live the emotion

MILLS & BOON®

MB3 RS

FREE!

2 Books
and a surprise gift!

We would like to take this opportunity to thank you for reading this Mills & Boon® book by offering you the chance to take TWO more specially selected titles, one from the Blaze Romance™ series and one from the Sensual Romance™ series absolutely FREE! We're also making this offer to introduce you to the benefits of the Reader Service™ —

- ★ FREE home delivery
- ★ FREE gifts and competitions
- ★ FREE monthly Newsletter
- ★ Books available before they're in the shops
- ★ Exclusive Reader Service discount

Accepting these FREE books and gift places you under no obligation to buy; you may cancel at any time, even after receiving your free shipment. Simply complete your details below and return the entire page to the address below. *You don't even need a stamp!*

YES! Please send me 2 free Romance books and a surprise gift. I understand that unless you hear from me, I will receive 4 superb new titles every month for just £11.18 (2 Blaze and 2 Sensual), postage and packing free. I am under no obligation to purchase any books and may cancel my subscription at any time. The free books and gift will be mine to keep in any case.

K3ZEB

Ms/Mrs/Miss/Mr ....Initials ....
BLOCK CAPITALS PLEASE

Surname ....

Address ....

....

....Postcode ....

Send this whole page to:
UK: The Reader Service, FREEPOST CN81, Croydon, CR9 3WZ
EIRE: The Reader Service, PO Box 4546, Kilcock, County Kildare (stamp required)

Offer not valid to current Reader Service subscribers to this series. We reserve the right to refuse an application and applicants must be aged 18 years or over. Only one application per household. Terms and prices subject to change without notice. Offer expires 27th February 2004. As a result of this application, you may receive offers from Harlequin Mills & Boon and other carefully selected companies. If you would prefer not to share in this opportunity please write to The Data Manager at the address above.

Mills & Boon® is a registered trademark owned by Harlequin Mills & Boon Limited.
Sensual Romance™ & Blaze Romance™ are being used as a trademarks.